SAXON SHORE

**Other Collections Of Short Stories
By Writers Of Whitstable**
Beyond The Beach Huts (2016)
A Different Kind Of Kent (2017)
A Pinch of Salt (2020)

**Other Books
By Writers Of Whitstable Authors:**
Sherlock Holmes and the Great War *Richard Barton*
The Realignment Case *RJ Dearden*
Domekidz *PJ Ferst*
The Ginger Flic Casebook *Duarte Figueira*
Molluscs and Me *Helen Howard*
From This Day Forward *Kerry Mayo*
Catch, Pull, Push *Kerry Mayo*
Whitstable Through Time *Kerry Mayo*
Archie Comes Home *Peter Quince*
The Flesh and the Cross *Peter Quince*
Grace Under Pressure *Peter Quince*
Pearls in the Web and Other Reflections: Thoughts on Nature and Spirituality *Peter Quince*
The Eagle and the Dove *Oliver Whitefield*
The Lovers of Today *David Williamson*

Saxon Shore

Writers of Whitstable

© This edition Writers of Whitstable, 2024

The copyright for individual stories remains with the named authors.

ISBN 978-0-9935492-4-3

All rights reserved. No part of this publication may be reproduced, copied, stored in a retrieval system, or transmitted, by any form or in any means, without the prior written consent of the copyright holder, nor be otherwise circulated in any form of binding or cover other than that in which it is published and without a similar condition being imposed on the subsequent purchaser.

The authors have asserted their moral right under the Copyrights, Designs and Patents Act 1988, to be identified as the authors of their own works

A CIP catalogue record for this title is available from the British Library.

Published in the UK in 2024 by Coinlea Publishing

www.coinlea.co.uk

Interior: Coinlea Services

Cover design: David Williamson

Printed in the UK by Clays Ltd

Illustrations:

p30 Duarte Figueira

p56 Maggie Johnson

p63 Gemma Ferst

p148 Lin White

p152 Jo Bartley

p157 Jo Bartley

p161 Jo Bartley

p164 Duarte Figueira

p179 Tim Rolfe

p217 Sofie Quine

*This book is dedicated to
John Wilkins, Nick Hayes
and Harry Harrison*

Contents

Foreword *by Nick Sweeney*	1
The Ill Tempered Clavier *by John Shackell*	3
The Town That Disappeared *by Kerry Mayo*	6
Return To Whithaca *by Duarte Figueira*	18
The Reunion *by Eileen Wellings*	31
Wonderful Things *by David Williamson*	35
Standing's Algorithms *by R J Harrison*	41
The Circle of Life *by Lin White*	51
A Matter Of Convenience *by John Shackell*	57
Come into my Parlour *by P.J. Ferst*	61
A Living Presence *by Peter Quince*	68
Foreseen in Whitstable *by Richard White*	73
ChristmaZ *by Nic Blackshaw*	82
A Brief Tale *by Gillian Rolfe*	93
A Drink Before Work *by Richard Barton*	101
Of Human Tithe *by Guy Deakins*	105
One Flew Over a Seagull Nest *by Oliver Whitefield*	113
Strangers *by Richard White*	122
The Lady in the Lane *by Aliy Fowler*	133
Stranded *by Lin White*	140
The Golden Owl Flies to Whitstable *by Joanne Bartley*	151
How To Neuter A Tomcat *by Duarte Figueira*	162
A Whole New World *by Richard Barton*	169
Gridlocked in Whitstable *by Gillian Rolfe*	178
A Fluttering of Doves *by Peter Quince*	181
If You Go into the Woods Tonight *by Aliy Fowler*	189
Magic Touch *by P.J.Ferst*	197
The Last *by Guy Deakins*	204
Doctor Dieterle's Patented, Practical & Complete Cure for Sorrow & Sadness *by Nic Blackshaw*	208
Taken For A Ride *by Harry Harrison*	224
About Writers of Whitstable *by Joanne Bartley*	231
About the Authors	

Foreword

by Nick Sweeney

Most people remember both the good and bad times, the past, and even the present, somewhat imperfectly. Was it really a romantic night when you fell in love on the Saxon Shore – did the stars really align just for you? Perhaps the night just hid the daytrippers' traffic smog and the cat scavenging among the discarded oyster shells. And the night you got arrested for something trivial, was it really so terrible? Maybe you needed a lesson as you read the peeling posters in the charge room, all sadly out of date, and the old jokes cracked by the desk sergeant brought at least a little smile. This also applies to the world around us. Writers or not, of the Saxon Shore or not, we all have our own ideas about the places in which we live, and where we visit. We all want to own a piece of them that doesn't belong to others, and it's of little importance whether that piece is 'true' or not; it's ours, and that's what matters.

The Saxon Shore, though it is home for many of us, can, with a trick of pen or pixels, be made to disappear, or to host ghostly women in foggy lanes, and can reveal the sharks' teeth among the pebbles. In these pages you might find yourself in a job for eternity by accident or chance, but there may be worse jobs than being an incidental loo attendant in Thanet. Whitstable and the towns into which it is steadily merging, is presented in these stories, both as it is and how we might want it to be remembered. Does that mysterious house on the shore on the way to Tankerton have twenty steps up to it, or an easier ten, to facilitate the quicker entry or exit of a curious-minded protagonist? It doesn't matter. Can you really see the towers of Reculver from the moon? Well, you'd need to go there to really be convinced.

Do we see the writing in the sand? A bit difficult at times on the stony Saxon shore, pelted by rain and wind. The stories are all around us, and only some of them are collected here, so, for now, look no further, and read on.

Nick Sweeney

Nick Sweeney's writing reflects his interest in Byzantium, bike racing and Eastern Europe and its people, places, languages and cultures. His books include a hapless lover's jaunt around Poland in Laikonik Express (Unthank Books, 2011), an opportunist's wander into the wrong part of Silesia in The Exploding Elephant (Bards and Sages, 2018), and a look at genocide-surviving gamblers of 1960s Nice in A Blue Coast Mystery, Almost Solved (Histria Books, 2020). The Émigré Engineer (Ploughshares, 2021) shadows a man fleeing the bullets of the Russian Revolution only to find more in Prohibition America. Cleopatra's Script (Golden Storyline Books, 2022) examines the repercussions following the murder of a Roma child in 1990s Rome. The Fortune Teller's Factotum came out with Hear Our Voice Books in 2023, and looks at a friendship between two young women and the horror stories in their family backgrounds. His forthcoming book The Dali Squiggle is due out with Veneficia Publications in 2024: a story of unrequited love so painful it verges on an eye-watering comedy. He is a freelance writer and musician, and only a relatively recent blow-in to the Saxon Shore.

The Ill Tempered Clavier

by John Shackell

I was walking along a shore recently and noticed that one small inlet had collected all the plastic cups and bottles, while another, only a short step away, was blessedly unsullied. In a similar fashion our village in the Canterbury area collects failed musicians, artists and writers. Of course, we didn't realise this when we decided to live here. In fact, it had seemed rather trendy, to use an old-fashioned word. We fitted in well.

As our furniture was being unloaded into our new house on arrival day, we noticed a small, battered home organ of uncertain antiquity. It had to pre-date the use of electricity, since its power was provided by pushing pedals up and down in the style of a flat-footed French onion seller.

The air that had to be pumped in to operate the reeds sometimes escaped into the mechanism, where it could linger for quite some time and then escape unexpectedly. According to the estate agent the previous residents hadn't wanted to take it with them when they moved out. We got to understand why.

I don't know whether others see their musical instruments as having personalities, but this organ certainly had one. It was mischievous, sly and at times downright malevolent. We named him the Ill Tempered Clavier. This was quite a mouthful to keep pronouncing, so we eschewed the modern mania for acronyms and shortened his name to Clav.

Clav gave a hint of his character when we asked the

furniture men to put the organ onto the dais and the wretched instrument got a foot stuck down a large knothole. Getting it out took much heaving and straining, and a fair tour through the Anglo-Saxon roots of the language.

Shirley and I had often talked about making our home a local centre for the arts. Now it seemed we were in the right place to do this. Shirley wasn't a bad parlour pianist and I felt my oil painting was much improved.

Clav had his own ideas about the project.

We announced our opening to the village and offered tea and biscuits as an inducement. Of course, quite a few only came for those. At the set hour a small gathering trooped in. We commenced with a short recital by Shirley and for once Clav cooperated. Perhaps giving him a polish had sufficiently flattered his vanity.

Mrs P. was well known for giving herself airs. As soon as the polite applause had died down she heaved her considerable bulk onto the dais. Her voice was dripping with culture.

'I hope you don't mind, dear, but I can show you an interesting little variation for the end of your last piece. Perhaps you could give those pedals a little push.'

She didn't deign to sit on Clav's seat, which would surely have been catastrophic, but leaned over and gave a flourish on the keys. Clav gave out the first two or three notes to order and then produced a long expiration of wind, uncannily reminiscent of one of the lower bodily functions.

Two adolescent recitals, one on flute, the other on viola were played accurately but lacked expression. Tea was then served. As the small crowd mingled round the table to grab the biscuits, I tried to interest some of the more artistic-looking individuals in the paintings of mine on the wall. I was well into a spiel about the way the Impressionists handled light when Clav gave a clearly audible sigh. I took the hint.

The afternoon's piece de resistance was provided by Hon Ron Don. When we first met, I introduced myself with 'Hi I'm Dick.'

'The Honourable Ronald Don,' was the reply. I eventually found out that he represented a constituency in another part of the country.

Hon Ron Don's approach to music was that it was to be fought and overcome. He sat on the organ seat, pumped the pedals furiously and crashed out some chords with all his might. Clav did not take kindly to this effrontery and proceeded to shed various bits of wood, ending with the support for the seat. I apologized of course and Hon Ron Don tried to make light of it. But anyone could see he was seething inside.

A bit of amateur carpentry soon had Clav patched up, but I suspected that Honourable dignity would take longer to heal.

We didn't repeat the experiment of our afternoon soirée. A couple of years later we decided that the house was too large to manage and found a smaller one closer to the city. As we were packing up, I looked at Shirley and nodded my head towards Clav.

'Are we going to take him?' I said.

'Nah. Let the next lot suffer.'

The Town That Disappeared

by Kerry Mayo

Old Monty Duff was the first to go. He was last seen watering his marrows the size of grotters as a glorious sun set out over the island but the next morning he didn't turn up at the bowls club for his weekly roll-up at the castle. Ray Carpenter, captain of the team and unofficial warden for those members who lived alone, felt he ought to go round and check he was okay.

Monty lived just off Borstal Hill, on a road that sloped down towards the sea, in a bungalow with some of the best views in Whitstable; the wind farm, the forts, the Isle of Sheppey, even the tallest whitest buildings in Southend were visible on a clear day.

There was a brisk breeze on Monty's front step, cooling the warm day the lower reaches of the town were enjoying. Ray rang the bell and heard the faint chimes of The Yellow Rose of Texas. He smiled; Monty always seemed a little formal with his extra-starchy whites and groomed moustache, holding forth about his days as a lab rat at Pfizer in the years before the backside fell out of Sandwich when most of the researchers left. That had been way after Monty's time but to hear him talk, with a post-match cup of tea and a slice of Ray's wife Sheila's Battenberg in his hand, it was a slight he took more personally than those who'd received their P45.

How many rings should I do? thought Ray. Was one enough? He didn't really want to get caught chatting for hours. Sheila was putting the Welsh Rarebit under the grill at ten past and he wanted to be back for when it came out; Sheila's cooking waited for no man, least of all him. He gave another ring out of obligation, pressed his forehead to the stained-glass double-glazing on the door, but could see no sign of movement, nor a pair of feet sticking out into the hallway from the living room door.

He wasn't worried enough to miss lunch. Besides, he'd be passing this way again tomorrow when he dropped Sheila at the Knitty Natty Crafters morning at the happy clappy church in Seasalter. He'd pop by again then.

*

Sheila opened her pinking shears with two hands; they were getting stiff again and the mild arthritis in her right hand meant it was too painful to do one-handed. She opened the blades, passed them over to her right, cut one strip off the old curtain she'd found at the RSPCA shop, before disengaging and repeating the whole process. The fabric was soft with age, green and black swirls on a silver background. She was attempting to cut a waistcoat for the bear she'd made for one of the grandkids. She wasn't sure which one yet. Looking at the sad figure, with its turned-in eyes, wonky nose and one leg lifting as though to pee, she supposed it had better be the one least likely to have nightmares. That was undoubtedly Griffin, an eight-year-old ball of terror that she was going to suggest her son, Dean, got DNA tested in the hope of distancing her gene pool from the little tyke as much as possible.

Her hand cramping, she gave up on the material and went over to the serving hatch where magnolia-coloured cups of tea were being served with some of Aldi's cheapest biscuits.

'Hi, Sheila, how's your Ray?' smiled Vera, thrice-widowed siren of the Knitty Natty Crafters, taking the bottle of water Sheila handed over. Sheila was notorious for being unable to drink 'tap' which she told people was because of her fluoride intolerance but was really because she thought it was common.

'He's in the doghouse, that's how he is,' said Sheila, as Vera emptied the kettle and poured in the bottled. 'Dropped me off three minutes late this morning.'

'Trouble in Paradise?' Vera dropped two sugar cubes in a cup with half an inch of milk in the bottom.

'Not at all,' said Sheila, thinking she'd burn in hell before telling Vera she'd started a diet that morning and was only going to have one lump.

Once she had her tea, she turned back towards the bear, wondering what she could salvage in the last half hour.

*

The answer was not much. She stood at the front of the church while the other crafters streamed past her, clutching her bear that looked like a magician's evil prop, getting angrier with each minute that passed. Where was Ray? He'd be sleeping on the conservatory futon for a week if he didn't get there soon.

Marilyn, who ran the group, was last out and offered to run Sheila home. Sheila tried Ray's mobile once more but there was no answer.

There was no sign of him at home so she turned on BBC Radio Kent while she made up the futon, but as she pulled the flat sheet tight around the lumpy mattress the main news story made her stop quite still.

A spate of disappearances had happened in the last day or so in Whitstable, all in the same road. It was the name of the road that made her go cold; it was where Monty lived, where Ray had gone that morning.

She rang Dean but he hadn't seen or heard from his dad. He promised to go round Monty's on his way back from a job in Faversham. Should she ring the police?

She rang Maggie instead, her useless daughter-in-law, who found Griffin as much of a challenge as Sheila but which fact created no bond between them. Maggie looked it up on her computer but there was no new information, only rumours and exaggerations on social media. Some people were saying everyone in the street had disappeared. She didn't have time to do more as her boss was breathing down her neck for shipping 5000 oysters to a house in Margate last week which Maggie was denying was her fault but Sheila thought likely it was.

Sheila decided to wait until after Countdown before calling anyone else.

*

The next morning the radio said there'd been more disappearances overnight and, come two days later, a huge chunk of the town had gone – everyone who lived west of Borstal Hill, including Mariners View and all the posh jobbies in Joy Lane down to the beach.

Dean and the rest of his family were next along with all their neighbours and everyone who lived off Millstrood Road. Everyone except Griffin who was away at camp with the Beavers.

People were leaving in droves, a State of Emergency was declared by the government and plans to evacuate the whole town at 6 a.m. the next day were hurriedly put in place.

Sheila, in Cornwallis Circle, watched as army tanks pulled onto the green and made camp, offloading tents, catering supplies and huge containers of water alongside guns, a reel of barbed wire and a searchlight.

Harry and Margaret, on her left, loaded up their Jazz and set off before it got dark. They offered to take her along but, without Ray, Sheila found herself surprisingly lost. The futon was still made up, as though she'd make him sleep on it should he return, but in fact she was dying to talk to him about what was happening and for him to tell her what they should do.

She wouldn't do it, of course, but at least she'd know what he thought.

*

The next morning she peered out just after sunrise, her bag packed next to a smaller one for Ray, just in case.

9

The soldiers were still there, packing up their camp and, at the sound of a klaxon at 6 a.m. sharp, Sheila put a penny on top of the phone so she'd know if anyone rang whilst she was away, picked up the two bags, her handbag, and with a last spritz of Glade, left the house.

Outside, she approached the nearest soldier, who directed her to a green canvas-covered truck with long bench seats down each side. Another lad, who didn't look much more than twenty, took a more hands-on approach to pushing her up onto the truck than she'd have preferred but once she was in she settled near the front, leaving room for everyone else. Her bags were loaded onto a separate truck and a docket handed over to her.

The soldiers sounded the klaxon again but no one else emerged from their houses. They banged on doors and peered through windows but found no one.

Finally, at 8 a.m. the order to leave was received. Sheila, her two bags and about 250 of Her Majesty's finest, rolled out of town and down towards Manston.

Every other truck was empty apart from soldiers. Sheila rang Dean one more time, and even Maggie's mobile, but got no answer, just like when she rang Ray.

The reception centre in an old aircraft hangar processed Sheila with unsurprising ease and she was taken to a holding area with red plastic chairs and tea strong enough to go to war on. A television was playing the news. Reporters were massed outside the cordon that had been set up, struggling for the best background view. They looked like they were on Clapham Hill, the marshes and Sheppey visible in the distance; the town itself, not so much.

Reports were that every single person in the town had disappeared from the Seaview Holiday Park in the east to the Alberta in the west and out as far as the line of the old Thanet Way.

All except Sheila.

*

In the weeks and months that followed, Sheila was medically examined more times than a cadaver at a pathology rave but no reason could be found for her exemption.

The town was measured, assessed and analysed by the best scientists in the world, without conclusion, and the temporary cordon erected by the army was made permanent. Metal fences ten feet high were erected and an exclusion zone established. No one who had left was allowed back in and eventually the media interest moved onto a whale that was living in the Thames by Tower Bridge.

Sheila was allocated a flat in Herne Bay and reunited with Griffin, who ran her ragged while he grew into a surly teenager with a wispy moustache and a penchant for the stronger forms of marijuana.

He dropped out of school at sixteen, college at seventeen and got his first criminal record at eighteen. Sheila, worn down by the boy's selfish refusal to bend to her will, and the everlasting question of why she was left behind, gave up, spending her days yelling wrong answers to the Conundrum and berating the ASDA delivery man for being late.

One day, when she hadn't spoken to him for over a month, Griffin came into the kitchen where she was pouring a SmartPrice bottle of water into the kettle, a rucksack over his shoulder.

'I'm going,' he said. 'Don't try and stop me.'

She looked him up and down, from his tousle-haired head to his tapered jeans and DM boots and said, 'I won't.' If she felt sorry for the boy who'd lost his mum and dad and grown up without love or tenderness, she didn't show it. She turned back to her tea and spooned in two sugars.

'I'm going back.'

She didn't turn round. 'Back where?'

'Back home.'

That got her attention. 'You can't. You won't get in.'

He kicked the pedal on the pedal bin, the metallic clunk loud in the small space. 'I'll find a way.' After a final hesitation, he left.

*

He slapped the concrete walls on the way down four floors of grime and graffiti. Had he really expected her to stop him? Outside, it was getting dark. It was spring but the nights were still cold and few people were about.

He hitched a lift to Greenhill but from there he'd have to walk. No one liked going anywhere near the cordon, even after all this time.

An hour later he was at the fence and it was fully dark. No light shone above Whitstable, no ambient glow blocked out the stars. The fence had downlighters and a security camera on each post but he doubted whether the cameras were monitored all the time. Warnings of electrical current hung from the wire but was the threat real or fake?

Half an hour later, when no one had passed by on patrol, he decided to chance it. He stepped out from the cover of an overgrown bush and approached the fence.

The camera on the nearest post swivelled in his direction. Movement sensors. Bugger.

He walked towards Swalecliffe and tried a couple more times but the same thing happened.

At midnight he was at the Seaview Holiday Park where the cordon met the sea. The fence ran down the small cliff and protruded into the water for at least 100 metres.

He sat on the grass and considered his options. He knew the sea could be unpredictable that far out and he wasn't a strong swimmer by any means, but what choice did he have?

By the time he dragged himself onto Swalecliffe beach, inside the cordon, he'd swallowed more water than he thought possible, lost his backpack along with his phone and both his boots.

The water was as briny on the way back up as it had been

when he swallowed it but he was too exhausted to move away from the patch of soiled stones.

Eventually the cold made him get up. He broke into one of the caravans by smashing a window with a large stone and found quilts and pillows, clean clothes and a pair of trainers only one size too small. He got changed and passed out on one of the beds.

*

The next day, Griffin woke late, the silence encouraging him to sleep on. He made his way into the town centre. There didn't appear to be any cameras and he stayed away from the beachfront in case he was spotted by a passing boat.

The further he walked into town the more he glanced around nervously at every junction or imagined footsteps behind him, spooked by the deathly quiet, the total lack of signs of human life and the call-to-arms screech of a herring gull overhead. What disturbed him more than all of these, after he passed east of the harbour, was how well kept the streets were, how neat the gardens looked, how few weeds and overgrown bushes there were. The whole place looked... tended?

At Cornwallis Circle he ran his eyes around the curve until they rested on number 42, a sensible black door with silver numbers and a pot plant outside.

He sidled up to the gate, glanced around, and ran in and up to the bell, stabbing at it before retreating.

No one came. What had he been expecting?

He was hungry but doubted even ten-year-old tins in a shop would be any good. Still, he made his way to the old Windy Stores shop front and peered in the clean glassed window.

There were packets of food on the shelves, brown packets with spidery black writing like a poncy greengrocers, saying things like 'Samphire Flour' and 'Dried Oyster Powder'.

He was just about to break in and chance finding something edible when a loud noise rang out from further up the street. It sounded like a door slamming but it was a windless day and there was no way a door could have banged on its own. Besides, it happened only once.

He looked up Nelson Road, empty of cars, their owners presumably having packed up and left before the official evacuation. The blank windows all stared him out, as unyielding as a game of Guess Who.

He panicked and ran. Up Island Wall and out past the golf course before he stopped. Too far and he'd be at the barrier the other end.

As his breathing slowed he knew there was only one place he needed to go and only one place that terrified him more than anything.

Home.

He'd been putting it off all day, scared of what he might find, but he had to go before he left and it would be dark again soon. The thought of another night inside the cordon did not appeal.

He threaded his way across the golf course and through the backstreets to Grimshill Road. His heart started beating like hummingbird wings the nearer he got, bile rising as he recognised his friend Nathan's house, and that of his old nemesis, Luke Hatton.

He recognised the van on the drive first, the name in big red letters popping into his mind before it appeared in his line of sight. *Carpenter's Plumbing*; he got the joke now. Memories of his dad on the phone laughing and joking with every new enquiry. 'Yes, I'm a plumber. No, I don't do cupboards, ha ha.' His mum had explained it to him a hundred times and he'd pretended to get it but eight had been too young for the complexities of oxymorons.

The sight of the stuffed figure hanging from the rearview mirror was like a kick in the gut. It was a Gills figure his dad had bought him when he'd taken him to his first football match at Gillingham FC, complete with tiny kit and a football sewn to his right foot. Griffin insisted it hang from the mirror on the way home and there it had stayed. That was only a few weeks before the town had disappeared.

A flicker of movement in the house caught his eye. He looked at the front window – the one into the lounge – but saw nothing. Maybe it was the excess moisture in his eyes making things fluid.

Slowly, he walked towards the window, noticing how clean the glass looked. Glancing down, he saw the grass was neatly mown. He looked up and down the street. The windows of the houses opposite reflected the setting sun off their gleaming surfaces. The hedges up and down the road were clipped and flowers coloured the borders between houses. Griffin was no gardener, didn't know what this meant exactly, he only knew something about this whole place was off.

He turned back, looked straight through the lounge window, towards the open-plan diner and the garden at the back.

The sofa was the same but in a different position to the way he remembered it. The TV cabinet his dad had made was gone but in its place was some kind of games table with a chessboard inlaid on top with board games stacked in neat shelving underneath.

He placed a hand on the cold glass, as though reaching out to the past. The warmth of his hand seeped into the glass and multiplied, as though reflected back out to him.

The sun was getting weaker, would soon set. The shadows in the lounge were deepening. He should go.

He tried to remove his hand from the glass but couldn't, held by memory and ancestry and a feeling he belonged like none he'd had in the last ten years. Had his gran even thought about him since he'd left?

Something flickered inside the window, a ghostly apparition of times past that flared and died. It happened again. The shape stronger this time, staying for longer before fading. He was sobbing, full-on ragged breaths and gasping tears, long before his mum appeared behind the window, hand outstretched, palm to palm with him through the glass. His dad, older, sadder, stood behind her, his grandad Ray's hand on his son's shoulder, fingers digging in as though he, Ray, might fall.

The front door opened. A very old man he didn't recognise, with a faded waistcoat and a groomed moustache, gestured to him.

'Hello, Griffin,' he said. 'You'd better come in.'

*

Three weeks later, Griffin pulled the door to the house closed behind him and set off to The Ship. He was going to have a game of pool and a pint with his dad, all grown-up like. He knew his mum would be waving him off from the window but he couldn't see her, wouldn't see her and his brothers and sisters, until later. After sunset.

He still wasn't over the shock of what Monty Duff had told him that first night: how he'd developed a chemical compound that could be ingested without side effects which made people vanish when the sun rose; how he'd used the town's water supply to affect an ever growing area until the whole town – those that had stayed – had disappeared; how, when they reappeared at night, he, and a growing army of supporters, talked to those newly affected and gave them two choices.

The first was to stay, wait until the outside world faded away and live a gloriously free life, using self-sufficiency and self-regulation as ways to live.

The second was to go back to the 'real' world with the politics and poverty and division and stress.

Every single person chose the first option.

And now he had joined them. No more dole queue, no more assessments, no more Sheila. That his family had seemingly left him behind without so much as a backward glance was something he dwelled on at night after everyone had gone to bed. How could they have left him with her? But when the alternatives were staying and pretending it didn't hurt or going back to his gran, he knew he would stay and suck up the pain just to have his family back.

When Monty had told Ray what was happening right at the beginning, Ray told him Sheila never drank tap water, only bottled. Monty had told him to swap some water in her kettle for tap so she could stay but, all things considered, Ray had decided to let things be and Granny Sheila had left with the army. Grandad Ray had Vera now and they seemed happy, even if Vera did keep Ray on a tight rein and he wasn't allowed to join Griffin and his dad for a game or two.

Tomorrow, Griffin's dad was going to start teaching him how to be a plumber.

Tonight was about new beginnings and having his dad back.

Return To Whithaca

by Duarte Figueira

I first noticed him one Wednesday evening in mid-July. He was being shown around the place by Tel, the club coach, while we in the youth team practised serves and volleys. School had finished and most of the rich kids had already been packed off to holiday homes in France or Italy, so there were only half a dozen of us hitting in the heat and western breeze of a Whithaca summer.

Tel was doing most of the talking, pointing out the new resurfacing and boasting about the success of the youth programme. He meant Rob Eagleton of course, who had battered the local competition and was now being entered for national events. And Tel didn't even train Rob anymore, having been replaced by a sponsored LTA coach.

The stranger was quite a sight. He wore discoloured tennis whites and battered trainers that still shone against his deeply tanned skin. His face was surrounded by wavy, collar-length reddish hair held in place by a faded golden tennis headband and a scruffy brown and grey beard that made him look rather like an old lost mongrel. He moved slowly on pigeon-toes, his shoulders hunched up as if the ground was red-hot. I noticed a deep scar running down from his left knee to the top of his sock. And he looked sixty if he was a day.

Practice ended early and I had a few minutes of rest before leaving. He sat down next to me on the bench outside the clubhouse. I looked at him as I put my bottle of water in my bag.

'Joining up?' I said.

'Just taking a few lessons, see what I think. Is it a well-run club?'

'Tel *is* the club really. He leases the courts from the council. Collects the court fees and gives lessons. We just have two youth teams.'

'I see. Well, I wasn't told there was a club as such. Now I see it.'

'No, there isn't one. We have some older guys who play. Rich guys. They can invite you to play with them – if you are good enough.'

'Cozy.'

'My dad told me there was a club once, apparently. Lots of teams, tournaments, socials,' I said.

I stood up. So did the old man. Christ, I could hear his joints creaking.

'Well, thanks, young man,' he said, 'my name is Oddie.'

'You mean like Bill Oddie?'

'No, Oddie is my first name.' He shrugged. 'My grandad's joke. What's yours?'

'Homer.'

'Thanks, Homer. Keep using that backhand of yours.'

When I looked back from the sea wall he was being introduced to the four guys who 'own' the courts – those who give Tel his lease money and tell him how to run the place.

*

I didn't expect to see him around for long. I guessed he wouldn't be good enough to keep the guys interested. A couple of weeks later I caught him having a lesson with Tel, who was feeding balls to his backhand. He was a leftie. His footwork was light and the swing smooth, but without much pop. The balls were dropping in though, all within a foot of the baseline.

He waved at me and mimed like he was having a stroke or something. I waved back.

I asked Tel later how he was getting on. He said he'd played a few of the guys and run them close a couple of times but he couldn't close out and he didn't have enough power to beat them, plus over three sets he faded. Well, they were all twenty or more years younger.

'But hey, they like having him around and use him as a hitting partner, like for practice.'

'Like a sort of pet,' I said.

'Like an old dog,' said Tel. 'They are like, here Oddie, Oddie.'

Over the next few months, I saw him around the courts more and more often, making up a doubles with the guys, always losing to one or other of them, collapsing on the courtside bench between games. He irritated me a little. His game had not improved at all, still landing the balls inches from the baselines, but with no power. It was like he was begging to be beaten. He never made the guys run by dropping them short or volleying away at the net. He stayed in games with his serve, which was definitely a weapon. He served well, looping out wide on the deuce as well as the ad court, and flat down the middle or into the body.

It was getting to September when I found out Oddie was playing in the invitational tournament, the only one the whole year that Tel runs for men. He is allowed to invite the top guys from the Fankerton and Taversham public courts clubs to make up a 16 player singles, secure in the knowledge that the Whithaca guys will cream the opposition and get their pictures in the local paper.

'We had trouble getting Fankerton and Taversham to put up players this year,' said Tel.

I wasn't surprised. Taversham was a nice little club, but was basically a retirement place, with players to match. Fankerton was organising itself, and had a part-time pro coach now, but most of its players were women who were either repelled or discouraged by the Whithaca set-up.

I could see Tel was edgy. His 5-year council lease was due for renewal around the invitational and he needed to make a success of the event.

Oddie dropped by the courts that afternoon and watched me playing Rob Eagleton. I'd been upped to the 1st youth team and today Rob was letting me know who was boss. He was two years older and six inches taller. Anything marginally short was being slammed past me. He was missing some shots long but not enough of them. Half-way through the set Oddie signalled to me at the changeover. I was 4–1 down.

'Mix it up – topspin and slice. Drop some short.'

'You're telling me to vary *my* game?' I said quietly.

He backed away from the fence as if my words had scorched him.

'Is Bjorn Free giving you advice now?' said Rob. He was arranging all his various bottles in order on the bench.

I glanced over. Why hadn't I seen it? The headband, the pigeon-toed walk. Rob laughed.

'It's what my dad calls him. The tennis equivalent of a punch-bag. You know he lives in some battered cruiser in the harbour?'

I didn't take the advice until Rob had set-points on me. 40–15 at 5–1. Then I thought, why not? He dumped three straight points into the net and threw his racket into the fence. It hit a stanchion and cracked.

He was still furious with himself when we resumed.

'My dad is going to kill me,' he said. 'That racquet was £250 from Wigmore's last week.'

He started taking it out on his spare, hitting long all over the court. He graduated to swearing loudly after that. Tel stopped training the 2nd team and walked over. Oddie was sitting on a bench looking at his battered tennis shoes.

'Hey, Rob. Cool the bad language a *little*?'

'You cool it, dude. Just letting off steam like everyone else on these courts.'

He was right there. The guys were foul-mouthed when they

played, intimidating their opponents and passers-by alike. Tel would wince but let it ride.

I beat Rob 7–5 despite him making a series of insane cheating 'out' calls on my winning serve game. It didn't matter by then. He was over-hitting everything. On set point, I dropped a dolly serve in and he hit it so hard it was still rising when it stuck to the back fence. I glanced over at Oddie but he was walking off. Something did not compute. Rob's LTA coach was standing outside the court shaking his head.

Rob didn't do anything as classy as shake my hand before heading off to have his next lesson. He just pointed at me.

'You just got lucky. Next time, sprat.'

*

The first day of the invitational was approaching fast. Oddie was in demand, practising with one or more of the four guys on an almost daily basis. Still he didn't drop short, slice, volley. But all his ground strokes were perfect, landing softly inches from the back line or angled exquisitely across the court. He often sat with Tel in deep conversation but I didn't see much evidence of any coaching taking place. In the end I asked Oddie about it.

'Can't take the strain of going for it,' he said, pointing at his scar.

'But you can move side to side OK,' I said.

'Yes, that's OK.'

We fell into silence. He looked around the five courts sunk down behind the sea wall that made the club a natural amphitheatre.

'God, I love this old place,' he said.

*

I picked up the invitational draw the day before the tournament started. I saw that Oddie would have to play perhaps three of the four guys to win. The rankings had the guys meeting up in the semis, as usual. Oddie was probably the oldest man in the draw by ten years.

I agreed to ball-boy along with some of the lads from the second team. So I went down early on Saturday to the wooden snack-bar that passed for a clubhouse to help Tel set up. He was there with Oddie, who sat at the stringing machine. He'd already strung half a dozen racquets and was now doing his own.

Tel made me a tea and we watched Oddie stringing, his hard fingers quick and precise in their motions. I wanted to ask where he'd learnt to do it when Tel spoke.

'I was telling Oddie the good news. The Council have approved my application for another five-year lease a week early. It means developing the club a lot, getting more teams, more ladies, more kids involved.'

'Sweet,' I said.

'Yes,' he said, 'some won't like it. Got to win them round.'

Good luck with that, I thought. I glanced at the 'Eagleton Car Parts' sponsor banners on the back courts.

As if by magic Yuri Eagleton, Rob's older brother, and his mate Ant appeared at the bar.

'Two flat whites, Tel. Oddie, what the fuck are you doing?' said Yuri.

'Tel gave me some tips on this, so I'm doing my own,' said Oddie without looking up.

'Shit, Oddie, you haven't strung mine, have you?' said Ant.

'Tel's done yours,' said Oddie, 'they're just here.'

Tel lifted the rackets over. The guys made a great show of testing their strings against their palms.

'Just fifty, right?' said Ant.

Tel nodded.

The guys smiled.

'Powerrr!!' they growled in unison.

Yuri turned to me.

'Hear you caused Rob to total his racquet,' he said.

'He did seem a little upset,' I said.

Yuri gave me a hard stare, then looked over at Oddie.

'What are you tensioning yours to?'

Oddie looked up. He had a cold expression I'd not seen before.

'Sixty-two.'

The two guys looked at each other and burst out laughing.

'Christ, Oddie, they'll be coming over in slow motion.'

They moved off still laughing. Oddie loosened the mechanism and raised the stringed racquet. One tap and a sharp hard sound came out. Oddie smiled and laid it aside. He picked up his second racquet and placed it on the stringer. Tel looked at me.

'Best get ready,' he said.

The matches started at 10am, best of three sets. Final was on Sunday on what we called the show court. That meant fitting in fourteen matches by mid-afternoon.

Oddie played the weakest of the four guys first and from the first I noticed a change in his play. He served first and followed up his serve down the tee with a volley at the net, cracked short to the side. The other guy was so spooked he sprayed his next three returns all over the place, two wide, one into the net, even though Oddie hadn't moved from the baseline. On his service returns and ground strokes Oddie pinned him back to the baseline. Most of the shots were still soft, but every third or fourth stroke he'd hit a little more sauce and send the guy scrambling. It was over in an hour. 6-2, 6-1, but I got the sense there was an awful lot more in Oddie's tank. He followed the guy off the court after receiving a short graceless handshake at the net.

In his next match Oddie played Taversham's best player. A very tall bloke in his thirties, with a big serve and a solid forehand. Oddie lost a couple of games and started hitting to the backhand, a mix of slice and topspin, mixed with a succession of drop shots. He won the first set 6-3 and was 3-0 up in the second when Yuri and Ant came over to watch. They'd both won easily and immediately lowered the tone.

'Hey old man, show him you've still got it,' shouted Yuri.

'Oddie, I've a tenner on the other guy,' added Ant.

Hysterical.

They then chanted 'Oddie, Oddie, Oddie' for a bit. If the catcalls had any effect on the players, neither showed it, but Oddie reverted to his traditional play and lost the next four games. Once the guys were called to their next matches, he picked up where he'd left off and won the second set 7–5. I heard him apologising for the disruption to his opponent at the net. As they walked off I congratulated him.

'You've got to ignore those tossers,' I said.

'I was.'

'But you stank while they were there heckling.'

'Did I? Just tired, I think. Needed a breather mid-set. You know, winning isn't everything at my age.'

I watched him shamble off for his lunch break. Semi-finals would be after lunch and he'd be playing Ant who I'd watched beat one of the Fankerton guys in the last of the quarter-finals. His game had some finesse but was still predominantly about power off both wings. He'd finished a 6–3, 6–2 win with a smash put-away. He'd raised his arms with a whoop of victory. In his head he was Djoko at Flushing Meadows. I was too embarrassed to look around at the spectators.

I had lunch with Tel in the 'Queen's Gambit' pub overlooking the beach. Oddie was nowhere to be seen, but the guys were holding court in the lounge, loudly celebrating their victories and taking the piss out of the Taversham player Oddie had beaten.

'Don't worry, bruv,' Ant boasted to him, 'I'll give him a tennis lesson this afternoon.'

Tel and I picked up our drinks and went to sit outside.

By the time the guys returned to the courts they'd all had a few. In the bright sunshine, Oddie sat on the bench looking exhausted. He raised himself wearily and smiled as he shook hands with Ant. The coin was tossed – Ant won and opted to serve.

'I'll go easy on you,' said Oddie.

Ant was so gobsmacked he couldn't answer before Oddie turned to trot to the back of the court. Ant had a good serve but now he decided he was going to blow Oddie away. He hit the first two serves hard but long. 0–15. Oddie won the next point with a sharp cross-court return on a second serve. Ant double-faulted again at 0–30. Oddie had three break points and took the second one.

After that, Ant grew progressively tighter. You could see his growing sense of impending shame at being beaten by an old man. Everything was over-hit and over-thought. Oddie didn't have to do much except knock the ball back with just a smidgeon more pace than any of the guys were used to. He dropped balls short with slice, set up passing shots and wrong-footed Ant over and over. Ant's reaction was to hit the ball ever harder, combined with ever worsening decisions. For every cannonball forehand that went in, three flew long. It was over in a flash – 6–3, 6–2. Oddie flighted a drop shot at match point and Ant turned to look at his mates. He looked as if he was going to blub. There was a smattering of applause from watching locals.

I stood behind Tel and Yuri Eagleton at the fence. Eagleton didn't take his eyes off Oddie, watching him slump into his seat.

'Good match play from the old man,' said Tel.

'What I wonder, Tel, is whether your friend is a ringer,' said Yuri.

Tel kept staring at Oddie.

'Then he's the oldest ringer in town,' he said.

Eagleton disposed of the other guy 6–0, 6–2 in the second semi. He moved around much better than anyone else. He had a consistency the other guys lacked despite hitting the ball flat. He ran a lot along the baseline to hit cross-court running forehands and backhands. He came off court with a serious expression but barely a bead of sweat on him.

'You know the guy runs marathons,' said Tel to me.

As the spectators dispersed I saw Eagleton conferring with

his guys at the bar, casting a few looks over to Oddie. His final opponent was sitting with a smiling woman on one of the benches outside the show court. She was scribbling into her notebook. After a while Eagleton and the guys walked over. Tel closed the bar, nodded to me and we followed.

The guys were standing around Oddie and the woman in a tight semi-circle. I could smell the testosterone as we approached.

Tel held up the court keys.

'Just closing up the courts, folks,' he said.

The guys barely glanced at him. They were too busy listening to Oddie in conversation with the woman, answering questions.

'Well Penny, I doubt it's the feature story you think it is, but I hope it will encourage a diverse mix of people to join and make this a real club. Tel here is a great coach, and he's the man with the plan for the community to get more involved. He was telling me all about it. And young Homer here is a real talent.'

'So are you saying that the club does not presently represent the community?'

'Well, it would be good to have a women's tournament, some doubles, vets games as well as more girls playing. It's such a great opportunity for it to be the club it was in my day.'

'So if you win tomorrow, will that herald a new dawn?'

'Penny, if I win tomorrow it will be more like a blue moon, and you can print that.'

She laughed, showing her teeth.

'I definitely will, Oddie. You're such a character.'

'Well I hope it takes things forward, whatever. Tel here will tell you all about the club's plans. And I assume you know my nemesis Yuri right here.'

She squinted up.

'I know Yuri very well. You going to go easy on this lovely man tomorrow, Yuri?'

'Oddie doesn't need any charity. And of course the club

can't be one either, given our limited resources. But we will of course do our best within those constraints,' said Eagleton.

Penny pursed her lips and stood up. She suddenly looked middle-aged and sadder.

'Thanks so much, Oddie. Tel, do you have a moment? Let's grab a drink in the pub and you can tell me all about your plans for the club.'

'Sure.'

I walked back with Oddie to his car, an ancient racing green MX-5. He offered me a lift home. On the way I asked the question.

'In my day?'

'Pardon?'

'Come on – you said, in my day. When was that?'

'Oh, a while ago. Before I went looking for adventure. Many years back.'

'Did you find it?'

'Yes, actually. I did the right thing – but left a lot behind.'

'Did you make your fortune?

He laughed.

'I did find treasure, but it was more the splendid journey.'

I wish I'd asked him more questions about his past. But we fell into a companiable silence and before I knew it he'd dropped me off and was pootling away towards the harbour.

*

The following morning I turned up at the courts twenty minutes before the final started. There was quite a crowd gathering around the court. It took me a few moments to clock that the Eagleton's advertising banners on the courts had been taken down and replaced with plain green backdrops.

Tel was reading the paper and drinking a coffee in the club house.

'What happened? Eagleton drop the sponsorship?' I said.

'God no. I dropped him. I've got a new sponsor. Funded the lease on condition of anonymity, and that we took down the old hoardings. Yuri's furious – you've just missed a beauty of a row.'

'God! Who's the sponsor?'

'Can't say, it's confidential. And what's more we've got some publicity.'

He passed me a printed-out online edition of the local paper. The headline was 'Veteran returns to reclaim his crown' under two pictures of Oddie holding his racquet. The older picture of him dated from 22 years earlier, when he'd won the last of his five club championships before going off to sea. The article emphasised Oddie's quotes about opening up the club and making it part of the community and closed with Eagleton's drab comment about the club not being a charity. Ouch.

There was a cheer outside. We stepped out and beheld a younger version of Oddie, hair neatly cut and beard trimmed and shaped to a fine moustache and musketeer goatee. His battered trainers and faded kit had gone, replaced by sparkling whites. Even his arm and leg muscles looked more defined. The only thing that remained from the original was the gold headband. He caught sight of us and pointed at Tel and then the courts.

'Got the club back then?' he said.

'Thanks to my anonymous benefactor,' said Tel.

'Well then, you've won whatever happens.'

I won't describe every turn of the match that ensued. Eagleton tried everything to discomfit Oddie, without success. Oddie just played his match, every ball straight down the middle almost on the backline, mixing topspin, sliced and flat. Eagleton was unable to use his movement to get the wide angles he wanted. He had to generate pace off Oddie's softer shots, hitting them flat long or hard into the top of the net. Occasionally he would charge in behind a better ball. Oddie would pass him or lob him most of the time and won the first set 6–4.

In the second set, Eagleton got increasingly frustrated. He tried to drop balls short but Oddie got to most of them with ease, hitting them away or playing exquisite drop shots of his own, which drew gasps from the spectators. He had the power, but he showed complete control. At the net, the exchanges were one-sided, Oddie showing the reflexes of a cat. Eagleton had the inevitable meltdown, smashing his racquet at the changeover when down 4–1 and swearing loudly on every lost point thereafter. In the end, he gave up, bereft of ideas and broken at the baseline, jammed in by Oddie's shots landing like arrows at his feet. The crowd roared.

They shook hands briefly at the net. Oddie drew Eagleton close and whispered into his ear. Eagleton left the courts immediately, disgracefully not even staying for the presentation. It was the last time he played at Whithaca courts. Tel told me that he and the other guys took up golf at a course in Canterstable, the nearest large town. Rob Eagleton was dropped by the LTA and I was offered a place on its National Age Group programme.

So Tel got his club, Penny got her big story, the town got better. About a week later I saw someone else driving the racing green MX-5 in Whithaca. Oddie's boat had long since disappeared from the harbour. I guess he's still sailing for treasure.

The Reunion

by Eileen Wellings

I am glad they put this bench here. There is a view of the sea and the children's playground and I can watch the children play. There are a lot of benches nearby; I think this is a popular spot. I heard someone complaining the other day that the council had refused permission for any more benches because it was getting overcrowded. Some people only come to sit on them occasionally, not every day – perhaps anniversaries or birthdays. Some of us come every day to sit and watch the world go by.

I always hope to see my daughter Clare. We parted with such angry words three years ago and have never had the chance to make up. I know I can interfere and poke my nose in sometimes when I'm not wanted, but I worry about her. She didn't seem in control of her life and all we ever want is for our children to be happy.

Fred has just arrived on the next bench. He is a regular like I am. We don't speak of course but I can sense he is unhappy and he seems to be looking for someone. We could speak to each other but no one does; we all have our reasons for coming here to sit. A young man sits on the bench on the corner. He wears a leather biker jacket and boots and there are always flowers on that bench.

Every spring there is a fun run along the beach for charity and the benches are full then, everyone cheering their family and friends along as they raise money for the various charities. Tom, my son, ran in the last one and raised money for research into heart failure and I heard my grandsons saying they were going to do the 5k next year.

We have had a couple of reunions over the last three years which are always nice to see. After they reunite, people don't come back. There was a touching reunion at the oldest bench under the tree just after I arrived. That bench has fallen apart now and been taken away by the council. Perhaps they will let someone put a new one there.

The benches are full today. It is always busy over the Christmas period, so many people visit their relatives then come for a stroll along the seafront. It can be almost as busy as the summer. The children are running along, all wrapped up in winter coats and scarves. Some of them are learning to ride a new bike, obviously a present from Father Christmas.

I watch the people and listen to the children's laughter. A couple come and put a Christmas decoration on the bench closest to the playground. No one ever sits on that bench and it is painted bright pink. Sometimes I hear the council workmen muttering about its colour but no one really minds and the family keeps the paint very fresh, repainting it every spring. It cheers the place up and with its bright colour amongst all the rest of the dark brown benches. The children always play around it and use it as a base when playing tag.

I turn my head when I hear a child cry. A small girl aged about two has fallen and her mother picks her up and I hear the mother say, 'Let Mommy kiss it better'.

I look across, unable to believe my ears. It sounds so much like Clare.

The mother and child walk towards my bench and I can see the little girl is carrying a bunch of flowers.

'Here you are,' the mother says. 'Here is Granny's bench.'

My heart swells with joy, and then I realise Tom is there as well.

'I am sorry,' Clare says and I am not sure if it is to me or to her brother.

'I was so cross with her and then she died so suddenly I didn't have a chance to say I was sorry.'

'I'm sure she knows you are sorry,' Tom says. 'I'm sure she was sorry for the things she said as well.'

Clare nods. 'It was only after I had Mary I realised that you never stop loving your children.'

'Mum always said you would understand when you have children of your own. I know I did when Andrew and Philip were born.'

I look up and see his two sons leaning against the harbour wall. I often see them around when I am sitting on my bench. They're always getting into mischief.

I look back to my daughter Clare as she fastens the flowers to the arm of the bench.

'I am sorry, Mum. I know it's too late but I am sorry,' she says.

I want to tell her it's never too late, and to thank her for naming her daughter after me.

The wind ruffles my daughter's hair and she looks round.

'I'm glad you put the bench here,' she says to Tom. 'I can almost imagine her sitting on it.'

'Yes, it was a favourite spot and we were lucky that there was a space,' Tom says.

'I was still too angry to come back when you did this. I was angry about so many things.' Clare is silent for a moment. 'I was even more angry that she had died before I had a chance to say I was sorry.'

She sits down for a moment on the bench next to me and Tom sits next to her; little Mary climbs up on her mother's lap and we sit in silence with the three of us as a family again for a few minutes.

'Let's go and get some lunch,' Tom says, standing up. He reaches out for Mary and swings her up on his shoulders.

'I'm glad to have you back.' he says to Clare as they walk away. 'I have missed you, especially since Mum died.'

I watch them walk towards the cafe. My son, my beautiful daughter and all of my grandchildren together again at last; and I feel myself begin to fade. I won't be coming back to my bench every day now because I won't need to. I might visit at Christmas and anniversaries though just to watch little Mary grow up.

Wonderful Things

by David Williamson

Kent can proudly boast that it has more escaped parrots than any other county in the Southeast of England with the exception of Sussex. The fierce storms of 1987, lifting the roof off many aviaries, were partly to blame. Some simply grew bored of sitting on their perches watching endless repeats of Midsomer Murders and flew out the window, never to return. Sitting on a long, gnarled branch of a fine Kent oak, two large turquoise and gold macaws gazed down on a dozen khaki-coloured tents pitched in the undulating valley between Selling and Badlesmere on the Kent Downs. Close by was Holly Grove Mound which had been identified as a Bronze Age round barrow. The team had also identified other sites that looked highly promising, at least two cremation pits, sites No 3 and No 4 and, judging by some early finds, the likelihood of a Neolithic tomb at Domgasse No 5. It was turning out to be a great season.

Professor Eine Kleine Friedrich stood outside his tent, shaving razor in hand, smiling at his reflection in a small, cracked mirror hanging from his tent door flap by a thin piece of twine. The blade slid effortlessly though the shaving foam. It was already 26 degrees; it was going to be a hot day at the dig. He hummed to himself as the macaws talked to each other in the nearby oak.

'What's on the telly?' said one.

'Dinner's ready!' said the other.

'Breakfast!'

'Jesus Christ!' yelled the Professor, as a surge of blood suddenly appeared in the white shaving foam. 'Look what you've made me do, you shouldn't go creeping up on people like that, Constanze.'

'I'm sorry, Professor Friedrich, I saw you were up, thought you might be hungry. They didn't leave much before they set off.'

*

Constanze was one of his PhD students working for the summer on the dig, very enthusiastic, up at the crack of dawn each day, always ready to get her hands dirty. She was an expert in Bronze Age burials.

'And what delights has the cook prepared for us today, I wonder?' sighed the professor as he wiped his bloodied chin on a towel.

Constanze held out a battered aluminium plate between her dirty hands. 'Fried bacon and a sausage, fried egg, tomato, fried bread...'

'Stop; stop. I've heard enough. Why does everything have to be fried? We'll all keel over with heart attacks by the end of the season at this rate. Leave it on my camp table, will you. I'll be over to the rest of you soon and we can plan for the day.'

'Professor, maybe you didn't hear me, the others have already left and gone over to Domgasse No 5, they thought they'd make an early start.'

'What! Without me? What the hell!'

'You were snoring heavily, Professor, and they thought they would let you rest and ...'

'Never mind the snoring, someone should have woken me, I need to get over there and join them.'

'Your fried breakfast...?'

'Forget it, no time to waste, I don't want No 5 touched until I've discussed the schedule for the day with everyone.'

Constanze drew up close to him. Uncomfortably close; 'Professor...' he stepped back '...as there's only the two of us here...' she stepped even closer, placing the tips of her dirty fingernails against his chest '...I was wondering if you would like to come over to my tent and look at my...'

'Got to go, Constanze, the dig, got to go!'

'...bones.'

Grabbing his hat and rucksack, he bounded off across the field and down the valley.

Jumping over the stream, the Professor climbed the hill up to the flat ridge, sweat pouring off him. He mumbled to himself as he looked down on the group below, scraping away at the dry earth. 'Starting without me, what's the idea? Not wearing hats either, they'll fry under this sun, madness!' Elvira was calling up to him.

'Professor Friedrich! Get down here quickly, we've found something!'

Elvira had worked several seasons with Friedrich as his Senior Finds Manager. She was an expert in early Bronze Age Chalcolithic weaponry. He marched down to meet them all.

'Morning everyone. What have you found?'

Tony Salieri, the Site Manager and a leading expert in Bronze Age uncha kernelscrews, pointed to a hole in the side of the pit. 'We think it might open into something bigger, a tomb maybe, should we dig at it? Have you cut yourself? Your chin?'

'It's nothing; someone get me a torch, I'll take a look.'

'What's on the telly?'

*

There was excitement among the group, if this really was a tomb it would be a major find. Even the macaws had flown in to watch and perched on the pitchfork handles. Friedrich threw off his rucksack and knelt by the hole.

'What's on the telly?'

'Are we sure it's untouched? There's evidence of disturbed soil here.'

Dorabella, the Ethnoarchaeologist of the team and an expert in Bronze Age bronze, knelt beside him and handed him a torch.

'Are you okay? There's blood on your shirt?'

Friedrich ignored her and peered inside the hole. As his eyes grew accustomed to the light, details of the inside of the hole emerged slowly. It seemed like an eternity to the others standing by. Friedrich was struck dumb with amazement, and when the others were unable to stand the suspense any longer, Dorabella inquired anxiously, 'Can you see anything?'

'Yes, wonderful things. Wonderful things.'

'What things, Professor?'

'Broken pots, embalming bandages strewn here and there but no body; no bones...'

'Any uncha kernelscrews? inquired Tony.

'Not from what I can tell, but wait, oh my dear Lord, there's a ...'

'What is it, Professor, what do you see?'

'A giant fried egg. Someone's been here, taken the bones and left a giant fried egg, a greasy giant of a fried egg, two metres across, easily.'

'At last! At last!' cried Tony, hugging everyone and kissing some of the women without asking for their consent. 'Let those sceptics try to laugh at my ova magna theories now! I knew it! The fools! I knew it! A fried sensation!'

'Is it? I'm rather weary of fried food,' sighed the Professor, passing the torch back to Elvira, 'shame it wasn't poached.'

'Shall we inform the media, Professor?' asked Dorabella excitedly. 'This is going to be the biggest gamechanger in 100 years, it'll rock archaeological science to its very core! Have you cut yourself?'

'Yes, shaving.'

'Dinner's ready!'

'Look, Dorabella, my instinct tells me to keep this under

wraps until we've had a chance to comprehend what we've unearthed, but I suppose they'll get to find out eventually. So go ahead, contact the press. I'll leave you all to poke around here, but leave that egg untouched, you hear?

*

A short while later he arrived back at the camp. He went over to Constanze's tent and stood there a while before speaking.

'Are you in there, Constanze?'

'Yes, Professor.'

'It's me, Professor Friedrich.'

'Yes, I know.'

'Dinner's ready!'

'Did you take those bones?'

'Yes.'

'And did you leave that enormous fried egg there?' There was no reply. 'Constanze, I'll ask again, was it you?'

'How's your chin?'

'Never mind that. Are you the egg culprit?'

'What's on the telly?'

'Constanze?'

'Yes, it was me. I thought you liked eggs.'

He smiled to himself. It was true, he did have a penchant for eggs. How kind of her to think of him. 'Well yes, Constanze, I am rather partial, but...'

'Dinner's ready! Dinner's ready!"

'....you wouldn't happen to have a catapult or a pea shooter in your tent perchance, would you, Constanze?'

The tent door flap unzipped and a familiar, slender hand with dirty fingernails, poked through the gap holding a very handsome looking AK47.

'Excuse me a moment, Constanze.'

The Professor was an excellent shot and the two macaws dropped into the bracken with a soft thud. Constanze gave a little clap. Such beguiling eyes. If only he was 30 years younger, or she 10 years older. Or, even better, if he wasn't married. He handed the gun back to her.

'Well, you've put me in a very awkward position, you know. I'd rather not have this yoke hanging around my neck. The media will descend on this place in a matter of hours, and they'll be asking me about the significance of fried eggs in Bronze Age burial rituals. Do I lie to them? Tell them they worshipped monster-sized fried eggs or something like that, or save myself a whole heap of trouble and expose you? What should I do, Constanze?

'I think... I think I'm in love with you, Professor.'

'Oh, Constanze, Constanze.'

Standing's Algorithms

by R J Harrison

'Brindall,' said the PM. 'You are my Parliamentary Private Secretary, aren't you?'

The civil servant nodded.

'Then,' continued the PM, 'between you and me, is it Co-bra, or Cob-rah?'

Brindall tried to save his heart from sinking but it sank anyway. Three Prime Ministers in one year produced the oddest of situations. Having decided upon travelling by train to demonstrate green credentials, the PM had commandeered an entire carriage with morose bodyguards at each end and uniformed police officers at two sets of doors.

'I don't think it matters,' said Brindall. 'It's a cabinet office briefing, but it's not in Downing Street so you can call it what you like. I think "summit" will do the job.'

The PM smiled, although his eyes were unaware of his mouth curling at each end. A glimpse of expensive dentistry vanished, followed by another question.

'And our destination, Brindall?'

'Whitstable. Oakwood, sir. Early eighteenth century. Overlooks the bay and the Swale Estuary. Churchill loved the view and painted it often.'

'I mean. How do you say it, Brindall? I must get these things right.'

'Sir?'

'You say it's Whit-stable?'

'Exactly sir, although many just call it the Bubble. The home of native oysters.'

'I see,' mused the PM as the train slowed into that very same station. Three limousines sent from London pulled up outside as the Government party disembarked. There were no crowds, just a few schoolchildren and two elderly shoppers looking for a bookshop located on the other platform. This did not deter the PM who, in the short space between Pullman car and Rolls Royce, stopped to wave at the unassembled citizens.

'I am glad to visit the Bubble,' he announced, 'and shall be sure to enjoy some of your wonderful winkles.'

'He should try some oysters,' said the woman of the bookish couple. 'They're poisoned with sewage.'

The PM and his team swept out of the carpark, and through the town.

When he glimpsed Oakwood from the brow of a hill, the PM relaxed into his pillow-soft leather seat. Eighteenth Century it might be, but not half as imposing as his own Georgian pile in Kirkby Sigly. His constituency retreat had not only the heated swimming pool he had installed, but its own lake and boathouse. Oakwood simply could not have that sort of Grade Two listed class.

Through the gates of the walled estate, a serpentine track laid with gravel wound between trees. At each bend, Brindall noted, a uniformed figure could be seen, with either Sauer rifles or Heckler and Koch sub machine guns.

'A lot of men with guns,' he said.

'You must never be too lax about security,' said the PM, with irritation. His parliamentary private secretary was becoming tiresome and needed replacing. Brindall stared out of the window, regretting his comment. Four black figures could be seen standing on the parapets circling the roof.

Despite serving four prime ministers, Brindall had never visited Oakwood. The name had suggested a cosy country residence, but it was, as he now saw, a rather grand house built in Palladian style with Italianate gardens to match. He sensed the PM become tense, his spindly legs twitching with another unknowable annoyance. Next week, Brindall thought, he must put in that application for a post at the U.N.

The staff at Oakwood, much depleted after another round of departmental cuts, stood at the top of a long series of steps. The PM dashed up to meet them with the energy of a schoolboy at the gates of an amusement park, shook hands with the men, smiled at the women and rushed inside. Brindall followed, giving thanks, and smoothing ruffled feathers. The PM was a busy man. It's hard, governing a country. He was sure the PM would meet with them properly at some point.

Distant, muffled thudding announced the helicopter arrival of the Home Office Secretary of State, or SB as she preferred to be called. The military Chinook hovered over the box hedges and roses before swooping round to the discreet tradesman's helicopter pad in the stables yard at the rear of the Oaks. Her car was dispatched from the front to fetch her.

*

Brindall did a quick calculation. SB's Chinook journey at three and a half thousand pounds an hour would cost the country seven thousand pounds. Chickenfeed, she had argued when her own private secretary had queried her requirement. He had shared the exchange with Brindall.

'I am not making a request for helicopter transport,' she had told her PPS. 'I am *requiring* you to organise one, and not one of those fecking little toy ones. I want a fecking Chinook,' leaving the elderly civil servant wondering if it was sexist of him to recoil at her language, as a minister, when male MPs swore all the time.

Whilst other cabinet ministers began to arrive by car at the head of the drive, SB had evidently brought a companion, another lawyer, who had once worked on behalf of the Foreign Office, was later Foreign Secretary, Deputy Prime Minister, then crashed and burned on charges of bullying and indecent ego exposure.

Dan, as he was known to his many enemies, had mastered karate at Cambridge before going on to bully anyone at hand. Brindall remembered how he had skewered his early political career by referring to feminists as *obnoxious bigots*. Once, a justice minister as well as Deputy PM, Dan had every chance of persuading SB to bring in the powers he had failed to secure himself; to deport non-British prisoners serving a year or more.

*

The great hall at Oakwood promoted relaxation. Cool jazz whispered softly from expensive speakers to the throng of cabinet colleagues and their staff scattered around the tub and bucket chairs that made public-schooled servants of the Crown as comfortable as they would be in their own clubs of Mayfair and Knightsbridge. Waiters circulated with champagne and canapes, then the crash of a mallet on a table drew everyone's attention.

The PM took his place on a small dais, and assuming a crouch, as if suffering vertigo, or falling off his plinth, started to address his team.

'My people,' he announced. 'It is time for us to gather, and the staff of this great house will guide you to the stairs and a lift to take you downstairs to the principal briefing room.'

'Stairs and lift?' whispered Dan to SB. She too was perplexed. 'I thought this entire centre floor goes down, hydraulically.'

'You,' said Dan, to a white jacketed man ushering people to the four corners of the room. 'I understood this room descended to the briefing centre. Why must we use the stairs?'

'You can use the lift, sir,' said the attendant. 'That *descends*, sir.'

SB tugged at Dan's forearm, but it didn't deter him.

'It's the 21st century,' Dan reminded the man, beginning to raise his voice already. 'Why don't we have proper services and systems here?' He looked around for approval of his forthright and commanding attitude.

'You mean James Bond gadgets?' said Brown, a staff member for forty years. Dan glowered.

'I think all that sort of thing stopped after the Paternoster incident,' said Brown.

'That's it,' said SB. 'Religion always holds back progress.'

'The Paternoster was a kind of lift put in here in the sixties, Miss,' said Brown. 'It kept going all the time and had no doors on it. Just step in, and step out.'

'That's the kind of thing we need,' said Dan. 'We should install more, only up to date of course. I think I know a company we could work with. They offered me a job when I did my MA at Oxford.'

'Well, sir,' said Brown. 'We had to take it out, sir, in 1974 after the under-secretary at the Department of Employment and Productivity had a problem with it.'

'Surely,' said SB, 'one man's objections,' but stopped short. 'What happened?'

'Madam,' said Brown. 'The Under-Secretary, I think it was a Mr Stringer, was divided by the Paternoster, if I can put it that way.'

'Divided?' said Dan.

'You have to be confident in a Paternoster,' continued Brown, relishing his story. 'You steps in, or you steps out, but you mustn't hesitate, which is what Mr Stringer did. He was half in, and half out, and then half left behind. A hell of a mess, sir.'

Dan went white and mute whilst SB marched furiously away, correctly deducing that Brown had enjoyed himself far more than any staff were entitled to.

*

The windowless briefing room pleased the PM, Dan and SB. The walls were carpeted in navy blue with discreet red and white trimmings. The carpet before the stage featured a giant Union Flag design and LED lights twinkled everywhere.

The PM spoke first, reading his script from a glass auto-cue.

Brindall, sitting at the back, levelled his sceptical gaze at the small group of men behind the PM. Two, he knew, were close protection staff unlikely to take a bullet for their master. The third he also recognised, as Edward 'Teddy' Standing of the Standings estate and family seat in Somerset. As if things couldn't get any worse.

Teddy, Brindall thought, was that half-wit rejected from Sandhurst and the civil service. Where did he work now? The PM answered his thoughts by introducing 'My dear friend Teddy Standing who I first met at Winchester College and then later at Stanford. As the intelligence lead for the Command Circle Group, he works closely with our own MI5.'

This was news to Brindall. MI5 had long ceased to be Military Intelligence and was now the Security Service, incorporated into SB's Home Office. MI6, as the Secret Intelligence Service, had gone to the Foreign Office. SB looked around her, nodding sagely, acknowledging the smiles of other, lesser ministers.

Teddy moved to centre stage as the smart logo of CCG drifted into view on-screen behind him. It bounced lightly, twirled, and landed with a shower of sparkles to make any Disney fairy proud. Teddy admired the animation, smiled with the affable confidence that only a public school bestows, and faced his audience, half hidden in the gloomy, cinematic atmosphere.

'CCG,' he began, 'is the future of our home security.'

Brindall wished he were allowed to put his head into his hands.

'CCG has been contracted, and is working alongside our gallant domestic security professionals in the Home Office,' Teddy continued. 'But we can offer what until now was impossible for our wonderful spooks.' He obviously liked the word 'spooks'. The way it made you pout. The association of glamour it promised.

'What CCG brings to you today, what I bring to you today, is the answer to a new and terrifying threat that has lain unseen for many years. Our weapon? Our gift to you? Big data! That's what my colleagues and I have been using to analyse this new threat to every honest British working family in this country. Our complicated and patented algorithms have detected a domestic terror program that has, until now, evaded our systems and filters.'

'Why, I hear you ask,' he demanded rhetorically, 'have we not been told about this mortal danger before? The answer is simple. The terrorist group has made no demands, called no attention to themselves, and work alone or in very small unconnected groups. Our data analysts can now reveal that a hundred and ninety-eight women alone in the UK were fatal victims of this secretive cult since the end of the COVID pandemic last year. We will be working with our friends in MI6 in the coming year because we now think this is a global campaign of terror by a fanatical group of hate-filled extremists. The deaths are rising, and no-one has done anything about it.'

Teddy let the figures speak for themselves. That was CCG's methodology. Combine numbers, rhetoric, and ranting, thought Brindall. What on earth was this shadowy terrorist organisation? Why were they murdering women? Teddy anticipated his question.

'We think their tactics are simple. Of course, some of our brave men are killed too, but it is our wives and our daughters that are being targeted to strike at the heart of our British family life. To bring down our democratic institutions step by step.'

From an initial, shocked silence, anxious murmuring could be heard throughout the briefing room as Teddy introduced more graphics, tables, and data. The spread of terrorist incidents, the frequent use of knives, led Teddy to advise the room that initial analyses pointed to extreme right-wing, controlling patterns, potentially linked to Islamic fundamentalism given what he described as frequent patterns of 'over-killing.'

'Over-killing,' he continued, 'is the evident use of violence beyond that needed simply to murder a person. These people are savages.'

As COBRA split into working groups to discuss strategies against this new threat, a worried-looking PM approached Brindall tapping away at questions for Google.

'You're my eyes and ears, Brindall,' said the PM. 'Why don't I know about this?'

'I had no idea,' said Brindall. 'None at all. First I've heard of it. How could they keep this quiet for so long?'

'You tell me,' seethed the PM. 'Go tell them I want a plan by tonight. I want to know what resources, what money SB and CCG need. We need to identify these murderers and stop this terror campaign in its tracks.'

'Yes Prime Minister,' said Brindall, slipping his phone into his pocket. 'I'll meet you in the reception hall.'

Having pressed the rest of the cabinet, experts, and staffers to write their ideas into a plan by 9pm, Brindall hurried up the stairs and found the PM alone except for his guards.

'What are we going to do, Brindall?' he said. 'How can we explain this to the voters? Teddy says it's been going for years. Two hundred deaths in the last year alone. Thank God we brought him on board. Brought CCG's powers to bear on the problem. We've been blind, Brindall. Do you think we're safe? Our wives? Our families?'

Brindall nodded reassuringly.

'I think we're safe,' he said. 'Let's take the car back to London and see what they come up with tonight. No point in hanging around.'

SB and Dan must have had the same idea as their Chinook rose menacingly above Oakwood and flew west. The PM watched them go, then squinted myopically at the gardens in dazzling spring sunshine.

'Bloody great lake they have here,' he said, almost muttering. He seemed no longer confident. No longer king of the pack. Bewildered.

'It's the North Sea,' said Brindall gently, as if to a child. The

PM looked at him with a genuine smile.

'You're a good man, Brindall,' he said. 'A good man.'

*

Enveloped by the luxury of the ministerial car, both men were quiet, and Brindall resumed his internet searches, took out his notebook, and scribbled some thoughts for that night.

The PM, still crestfallen, had forsaken the train back to London in favour of the privacy of his car. There were so many rough people on the trains nowadays, even if you had the carriage to yourself. Their car purred along the M2.

'Prime Minister,' began Brindall hesitantly. 'I think we should interrogate the data with more care before tonight's meeting. Before we announce the discovery of a new terrorist campaign. Especially one that will frighten families everywhere.'

'You think so?'

'I do. I realise Standing is a friend of yours, Prime minister, but I've come across him many times over the past years, and frankly, I believe him to be an idiot.'

'What did you say?'

'An idiot, Prime Minister. I can find no trace of a registered company called Control Circle Group. I think Teddy made it all up. The company, that is. And that dreadful amateurish logo.'

He hurried on before the PM could silence him.

'I talked to my contacts in the Security Service. They've never heard of CCG and if Standing has been given a contract by SB, it's the first they've heard of it.'

'You are sailing close to insolence,' said the PM but Brindall pressed on.

'The data he's talking about is partly true,' he said.

'There you go.'

'Yes, but it's our own national statistics. There has been a surge in femicides. The murder of women by men. It was nearly two hundred victims last year, but the perpetrators were not political terrorists. They were husbands, boyfriends, ex-partners, and stalkers. It was men, Prime Minister. British men.'

'This can't be true, Brindall. It can't. What do we do with them? These horrific murderers?'

'On the whole, most of them went to court and were convicted of manslaughter with diminished responsibility. They tend not to spend a long time behind bars. I'm sure Teddy Standing knows all that. He's not that much of a fool. I expect SB gave his fantasy CCG group a fat contract and a million pound advance.'

'Two million,' said the PM, disconsolately.

'And he probably knew that we can't touch him for it because if knowledge of this whole charade came out, it would bring your government into disrepute.'

'Can we have him shot, Brindall?'

'No Prime minister. I think you know we cannot.'

The PM stared out of the window as they soared over the new interchange at Sittingbourne.

'Brindall,' said the PM. 'You're fired.'

'Thank you Prime Minister. Although, before I go, and the next PPS joins you, do you want me to make arrangements with the Home Secretary, the Deputy PM and the rest of the cabinet, that this unfortunate business does not reach your voters?

'I do, Brindall. I do.'

'Then, one more thing. I'd be grateful for your endorsement, of me, for a certain position at the UN.'

The PM nodded, his face that of a man tasting raw lemon squeezed over a fat oyster.

The Circle of Life

by Lin White

Becky had always wanted a family. She had Jack, sure, but wanted more. Money was tight; she took on more and more work as a home help, aiming to save up enough money to eventually have a child. And in the meantime, she gained many honorary grandparents.

One in particular proved a challenge. While Becky got on well with Edie, who lived in a magnificent house with views over Tankerton slopes, the other workers in the agency found her impossible to work for. Edie was a little picky, to be sure, and she frequently called her helpers 'stupid girls', but underneath that exterior was a sweet old lady, and Becky became especially fond of her.

And she had to admit it felt good to be the only one who could handle her. Carer after carer would return miserably to the office, amid complaints about their work – they hadn't cleaned properly, the tea they had made tasted funny, they talked too much instead of working, the food was undercooked or burnt, they were too busy scrubbing at unnecessary tasks instead of being willing to chat…

In the end Becky became Edie's only carer, visiting her every morning to help her dress and preparing her breakfast, running errands for her during the day and then helping her to bed at night. Sometimes she would help her across the road to the shelter on the slopes, where Edie would look out to sea and tell Becky stories of her childhood.

Edie's only family, a distant cousin, lived a long way away, so Becky was listed as Edie's emergency contact with the agency she used for her emergency button, and it felt like Becky had gained a grandmother. A grumpy one at times, one who needed to be cajoled, persuaded and handled carefully, but one who appreciated her work and paid her generously.

Then the trouble began.

Edie became grumpy and demanding even with Becky. One day she threw a plate at the wall, the carefully cooked food sliding down the flowery wallpaper. 'Stupid girl, it's burnt.'

She would phone at all hours. 'Someone has been in my house, and they've taken all my money.' The first couple of times it happened, Becky abandoned her half-eaten dinner to hurry down the road and sit with Edie, carefully questioning her to find out that in fact Edie had forgotten that she had insisted Becky hide her roll of banknotes inside the old teapot, and had panicked when the biscuit tin was empty. Then she began to understand and tried to deal with the matter over the phone, but the phone calls became more and more frequent until there was no other option but to visit, even though she was scheduled to visit within a few hours anyway.

A few months on, it was more likely to be the police on the phone. 'We understand you're the emergency contact for an old lady we found wandering along Tankerton Road at 3am in her nightdress.'

'You can't keep doing this,' Jack would grumble at Becky as she yet again left the warm bed to pull clothes on and hurry down the road to check on Edie and persuade her back to her home and bed.

Becky was exhausted. She was spending most of the day and often part of the night running around after Edie. At one point she suggested moving in with the old lady, so she could care for her better, but Jack reminded her that she worked for her, that was all.

'Maybe we could move her in here with us,' Becky suggested hopefully.

The expression on Jack's face gave the answer away. 'No way am I having that tyrant moving in with us. We get barely any peace as it is. How are we going to start a family with her around? How are you going to care for her as well as a baby?'

Becky knew he was right. Their savings had built up over the past couple of years, and Jack was starting to drop hints about it being time to try for that baby, but she was beginning to wonder whether they would ever cope.

Becky stopped taking the pill and tried to devote more time to her own household and to Jack, but she was so distracted by worry about Edie that every month brought another round of sadness.

Then, after a year of trying in vain to cut down on her hours with Edie, and of trying in vain to get pregnant, Becky was just cuddling up to Jack and trying to summon up energy for another attempt when the phone rang. It was the agency, saying that Edie's alarm had gone off.

'She's just causing trouble again,' Jack moaned, nuzzling her stomach. 'Ignore it.'

Becky tried her hardest, but as fraught as her relationship with Edie was becoming, she knew she was an old lady, and had become very unsteady on her feet recently. Unable to bear the thought of the lady being in distress, she reluctantly pushed Jack away and pulled on the clothes that she always kept ready by the bed.

A few minutes later, she let herself into Edie's house with the key she held for the back door. The kitchen was empty, a dirty cup sitting on the table and a used plate lying in the sink awaiting her attention in the morning. She checked the rest of the house, anxious about what she might find.

She found Edie lying trapped between her bed and the wall, groaning in pain, and called an ambulance. She sat with her while they waited, holding the old lady's hand and ignoring her ranting about how Becky was a stupid girl and all she needed to do was help her back to her feet.

Edie was admitted to the hospital in Margate with a broken arm and hip, and it was soon obvious that her days of independent living were over.

It broke Becky's heart to see the old lady so helpless, and she sympathised with the nurses who were berated as they went about their daily tasks, but the sense of relief that she was no longer responsible for her was incredible. The first couple of days she felt completely lost, but after that she slept soundly for the first time in years and wondered how she had ever coped for so long.

Edie's cousin was summoned. She was shocked to hear of Edie's problems and found Edie a care home that would be able to cope with her. The staff were used to dealing with cantankerous old ladies and would share the burden between them, handing over to someone else at the end of the shift. Becky visited her a couple of times, and Edie was delighted to see her, but on her next visit she started complaining to her about the staff. 'They're useless and lazy. The stupid girls always burn my dinner.'

She fixed her beady eyes on Becky. 'You could look after me. Take me home. You're useless, but you're far better than these idiots. You'll take care of me properly.'

Becky felt sick at the thought. 'You're far better off in here, Edie,' she reassured her. 'These people are very good at their job. Why don't you try to join in with some of the activities? You'd like it here if you gave it half a chance.'

'I don't want to play bingo. I want to be in my own home, with you to care for me. These stupid girls are useless.'

Becky shook her head and tried to change the subject, but the old lady had had enough and refused to say any more, closing her eyes and laying her head back to doze off.

When Becky returned to Jack and burst into tears, he held her close. 'She can't help it, but she's not your problem anymore. You need to step away, let others care for her now.'

Becky knew he was right, and she threw herself into her new

job in a clothes shop, pushing away all thoughts of her time caring for Edie. A couple of months later, she finally became pregnant, and as the pregnancy was a difficult one she was thankful every day that she was no longer running around worrying about Edie as well.

Her baby was born on 5th March 2019, at the end of a two-week stay in hospital, and Becky loved her at once. They named her Mary. Her face scrunched when she cried, and she was all wrinkled, with beady eyes. She was very demanding, keeping Becky up most nights as she struggled to feed her, and sometimes she thought back to her days caring for Edie and smiled to herself. Yes, it was just as tough in many ways, but with one big difference; it was her own child, and she would soon grow and change.

But Mary remained difficult to soothe, and only Becky could calm her down when she started to scream. She was a fussy eater, and Becky struggled to find food that she would eat. She dreaded the move towards the terrible twos, the age when children notoriously became hard to manage. Jack would disappear happily to work, often returning late, leaving her to manage by herself.

One day when Becky put a plate of food in front of Mary she stared at it with her face screwed up in anger, before grabbing the plate and throwing it at the wall. 'Stupid girl,' she said. 'Stupid burnt food.'

Becky stared at her in shock. 'What did you say?'

The toddler's face creased in a scream, giving her the appearance of a little old lady. Becky felt a chill down her spine. She fought to ignore it, but when she had finally settled the girl to playing with her bricks, she picked up her phone and consulted her old diary. She found the phone number for Edie's cousin and sent a text. She'd rather know for certain, she decided.

Sorry I haven't been in touch for a long while. I've been so busy with the baby. But I was wondering how everything is going with you. Is Edie still with us?

A short while later, a reply came.

Sorry, we tried to get in touch with you at the time. We lost Edie on 5th March 2019, after a short illness.

5th March 2019. The same day the baby was born. Becky put the phone down and looked apprehensively at the child playing at her feet.

Mary picked up a brick and threw it at her. 'Stupid girl. You'll look after me.'

A Matter Of Convenience

by John Shackell

Over the years I have been stuck in quite a few traffic jams on the M25, but this was something else. It didn't move, not even a bit, for absolutely ages. I turned on the car radio and got a lot of pop music I wasn't keen on, plus traffic info which I already knew.

When I'm driving I like to dress casually, to be honest in old gear. In a strange way this turned out to be a blessing. I was on my way to a rather promising first date, and I had allowed plenty of time to change in my office, which was near the restaurant. Even so there would now be no chance of arriving in time. I tried her mobile but got no reply. She had probably given me up as a dead loss by this stage. I'd try calling her again when I got to the venue, but I didn't hold out a lot of hope. That was all I could do. The traffic moved not an inch.

What was becoming a pressing problem was that I needed a pee. Having that second cup of coffee hadn't seemed a problem at the time. Now it did. I was in the outside lane and the central reservation was out of the question.

Then I realised that the lorry in front of me was carrying four mobile toilets. They were roped in place, but such was the arrangement that it might be possible to open one of the doors. Moreover, it looked as if it was slightly ajar.

I couldn't really, could I? But I was getting desperate; I wouldn't be able to hold on much longer. Hell, I was going to take the chance that I could squeeze through that door.

I got out of my car and ran over to the lorry. A couple of quick heaves got me onboard and I went immediately to the door. I needed to hurry for more than one reason. Good luck! The door was manageable and in I went. There was a lot of stuff stored inside and it would be awkward to piddle while standing up. So I lifted the cover and sat down. The cubicle smelt strongly of disinfectant and faintly of something more unpleasant.

I'd only just got started when the lorry gave a lurch and moved forward. Just as well I wasn't standing up. The hold-up had been so long that this movement had hardly seemed possible. It would probably stop in a few yards anyway.

Alas, it accelerated smoothly away. I could hear a screeching of horns behind me; my car was blocking the carriageway.

It was quite a long time before the lorry stopped at all. The first time it did I peered out, but we appeared to be waiting at traffic lights and it seemed best to stay where I was. The same thing happened a couple more times, but eventually we moved more slowly and onto rough ground before coming to a halt.

Presumably my car had been towed away by now, and it was going to be expensive to retrieve it, to say nothing of the inevitable fine. Thinking about money prompted the realisation that my money and mobile as well as my car keys were in the car. I was in a fix. I squirmed out of the cubicle and jumped down, to be confronted by two men. The first wanted to know what I had been doing on his lorry, and the second accused me of trying to get in without paying.

'Get into what?' I asked.

Apparently I was at the site of some pop festival; not at all my sort of music. I tried to explain what had happened and eventually they accepted what I said. The second man laughed and called his mate over. I had to tell the story again.

The first man was not amused, however. He wanted £35 for the journey and £2 for the use of the toilet. I said I was willing to pay but all my money was in the car. He thought for a bit and softened slightly.

'I need someone to help take the money for the bogs and to make sure they stay clean. If you'll do the work through until 10 o'clock, which is when we finish, and help with the clearing up, I'll waive the £37 and you might earn enough to get you home. Where do you live, anyway?'

When I told him I lived in Whitstable, he said, 'That's on my way. I can give you a lift.'

It seemed the best, and indeed the only realistic, option. So I spent many hours listening to frightful music, taking the money and scrubbing the toilets. Finally it was finished and the two of us loaded the cubicles onto the lorry.

The driver, whose name was Bert, roped up and I climbed into the passenger seat. The comfort was a long way short of my top-end Merc but it was a lot better than the toilet cubicle.

'Tell you what,' said Bert, before he started to drive out of the field. 'You worked well, and I had to do the driving anyway. So there's no charge for any of that. Nor for using the bog, which you cleaned yourself. I'd have given my usual assistant £100 for the day and that much is yours.' He dug in his pocket and handed over five grubby twenties.

I knew this wouldn't be anywhere near enough to get the car out of the police pound, but even a small bit helped. It had certainly been hard earned. I thanked him and away we went.

It turned out I was not so very far from home. Soon we were slipping off the Thanet Way and passing Estuary View. The view coming down Borstal Hill was as fine as ever, even in the dark.

He dropped me by the mini roundabout at the foot of Cromwell Road. He would have taken me all the way, but I didn't want the embarrassment of arriving back in a toilet lorry, nor of him seeing how expensive a neighbourhood I lived in.

When he had pulled up, he handed me a card.

'If you ever want any more of this work give me a call. You know the rate, and it's all casual.' He touched his nose. As I shut the lorry door he said, 'Cor! Wait till I tell the lads down the pub about this.'

*

It was far too late to call Sally on the landline when I got in. Next day I did so in some trepidation, but she was very understanding.

'I saw on the news that there was a huge traffic jam on the M25. Apparently it was made worse by somebody abandoning their car. It must have been really awful to have got on the news.'

'I'll tell you about it sometime,' I said.

She'd actually thought to cancel our reservation at the restaurant. Even better, she still wanted to see me. When, on our third date, I told her what had happened, she howled and cried with laughter.

'You certainly start your dates in style,' she said. 'I know it didn't happen, but I can't get out of my head the thought of you arriving at that snooty restaurant in a toilet van.'

We are still together two years down the line.

Come into my Parlour

by P.J. Ferst

Audrey was lying in bed listening to the wind howling round her house on Tankerton Slopes. Who the devil was ringing her doorbell at seven o'clock on a March Monday morning? Audrey reflected that her voice was the only part of her which had retained its original power and it now seemed a suitable moment to exercise its considerable operatic repertoire. 'COMING,' she bellowed, but first she had to perform her morning manoeuvres: spectacles, slippers, robe, stick, lavatory, stairs. Then, as she peered through the peep hole in her front door, she spotted an unfamiliar, grotesquely magnified face peering back at her. An avid reader of noir detective novels, Audrey did not release the door chain until she saw the distinctive logo of her home care agency. *Manus in Manu,* (aka Hand in Hand to those who lacked Latin), an agency that was both high class and high priced.

Audrey reluctantly opened the door to a biting March wind and sing-song intonation, something which she had observed characterised conversations between the non-elderly and the elderly.

'*Good* morning, Miss Godfrey. May I call you Audrey? I'm so very sorry to disturb you. Let me introduce myself. I am Mrs Cassandra Davidson, the new Deputy Manager of *Manus in Manu*. Please do call me Cassy. I'm here to inform you that there has been a change in your home care service.'

Audrey raised her eyebrows. 'Change?'

'Yes, dear. Unfortunately, Jasmine, the carer who, I have been informed, has tended to you for the last four years, has been obliged to return to the Philippines due to her mother's terminal illness. She phoned me to say she had to dash to Heathrow. She has gone for good, I'm afraid, but she told me to send you her best wishes.'

Audrey bit her lip and feigned a smile. 'I see.'

'But there is absolutely no need to worry yourself, Audrey, dear. Naturally, I have another carer lined up for you – Stacey.'

Audrey frowned. 'Stacey?'

'Yes, Stacey joined us recently but let me just say that she's a jolly fast worker.'

'Right.' Audrey hunched her shoulders.

'The good news, Audrey, is that your home care days will stay the same: Tuesdays, Thursdays and Saturdays, only Stacey will be starting Thursday this week. She will let herself in. Is that acceptable, dear?'

Audrey winced. 'Perfectly, Mrs Davidson.'

'Well then, Miss Godfrey. Keep nice and warm and if you should need anything ...'

Audrey cut in with a brief, social smile. 'Thank you for calling, Mrs Davidson. Now will you please excuse me?'

Mrs Davidson departed and as Audrey walked slowly back down the hall towards the stairs, she passed Jasmine's small plastic sandals. Sandals waiting for feet which would never return. Audrey lowered herself onto the fourth stair, put her head in her hands and wept uncontrollably.

Monday afternoon came and went. When early dusk descended, Audrey found herself standing in her bathroom, staring at the razor in her tooth mug, the razor she used to shave her chin hairs. But what if she were to use it to slit her wrists? Would anyone care? Jasmine had gone and four joyous years had gone with her. The delicious Filipino dishes she'd cooked, the jokes they'd shared at tea time on the balcony. She felt like a fly trapped in a spider's web. There remained only

Lyle, her nephew in Edinburgh, who phoned once in a while.

Audrey stroked her bony wrists experimentally with the blade. She put the plug in the bath, placed the razor on the soap dish and turned on the mixer tap. It was then that her eye caught something living – and moving. A large black spider with an unusual green front was frantically trying to climb up the side of the bath to avoid the rising water. Audrey had never paid particular attention to the creatures but now she was curious.

Whatever was this unusual creature doing in a place like Tankerton? And why had the spider chosen this particular moment to appear? Did it have a lesson for her, like the spider in the cave where Robert the Bruce hid many centuries ago, teaching him the importance of tenacity?

A twist of the tap, a jerk of the plug and a loan of a towel helped the spider to climb onto the rim of the bath. Audrey watched him climb up the window frame and glance at her with bulbous eyes, before disappearing into a crevice. 'You're safe now, Spidey!' she reassured him, reflecting that she and the spider had colluded. 'I have saved your life and you have saved mine.'

That evening Audrey finally located the Encyclopaedia in her chaotic bookcase. Apparently, her spider was a *Segestria Florentina,* also known as the *Dracula Spider*. How thrilling! Furthermore, it had a bite like a stab wound and ate its mother after hatching. It occurred to Audrey that if she had possessed the latter characteristic, her beloved puppy, Bessie, which her father had bought her would not have been destroyed by her mother on the grounds that schoolwork took priority over pets. Then Audrey's thoughts were interrupted by the telephone.

'Hey, good evening, Aunt Audrey. How *are* you?'

'Oh Lyle, what a surprise!' But Audrey's tone belied her words.

'Is everything OK? You sound upset.'

Audrey couldn't hold back the tears. 'That's because I *am* upset, Lyle. Where's my handkerchief? Oh here it is! Sorry, darling boy. Have you got time to cheer up a silly old biddy?'

'I always have time for my Aunt Audrey. Anyway, right now. I'm on Spring Break. No students for a week and we academics know how refreshing that is, so spit it out.'

And Audrey did – in detail, although she omitted the razor and spider episode.

'Basically, Audrey, now that Jasmine's gone, you sound as if you feel trapped.'

Audrey blew her nose loudly. 'Yes, I do feel like that way. Like a fly in a spider's web.'

'I realise that, Audrey. What I meant is why not come to Edinburgh then? Stuart and I would love to have you. Leave that Miss Havisham house and its memories.'

'It's too far, Lyle and too late,' Audrey muttered, 'but thank you for your kindness. I must go now.'

'Keep your chin up, Audrey dear or should I say your chins?'

'Oh, you always were a cheeky boy.' Audrey laughed and it

felt good. Suddenly she felt hungry and realised that she was humming as she buttered a couple of currant buns. Then she was looking forward to saying goodnight to Spidey on her way to bed.

Spidey wasn't on the window frame but to Audrey's delight, she saw that outside his crevice home, he had constructed a tube-shaped web. His supper was waiting – two small trapped flies who had foolishly entered 'his parlour', as in the poem by Mary Howitt.

On Tuesday, Audrey decided to give the spider a new name – Draccy. When she said his name he simply showed her his green fangs, but on Wednesday, when Audrey addressed him, he responded by waving his little front legs at her.

But Thursday morning brought Stacey, and Audrey was woken by Vesuvius-like tremors from the sitting room below. The sound of loud laughing and vacuuming. Forgetting to perform her morning manoeuvres, Audrey tottered downstairs to investigate.

'Oh, Hello. Miss Godfrey, innit?' Stacey's strident tones made Audrey blench. 'You've woke up, have you? All right for some!'

Stacey's voice was evidence enough, Audrey was thinking. The Northern accent, the vulgarity and the bluntness. An old-fashioned word flashed into Audrey's mind. Common. Then a modern phrase instantly replaced it. Politically incorrect.

'Flippin 'eck. What a ruddy mess, Miss Godfrey. Good job I've only got the upstairs left to do. After that, it's Bob's your uncle.'

Fuming, Audrey decided on the diplomacy option – to return to the privacy of her bedroom – when she heard Stacey's voice again. Speaking, or rather shouting, her sentences interspersed with bursts of cackling. She inferred that Stacey was either performing a soliloquy or phoning a friend. Audrey favoured the latter explanation.

'Yes – flaming cobwebs all over the place. She's a right

mucky cow.'

The context proved Audrey's choice correct. She paused on the top stair, to listen. The voice went from fortissimo to pianissimo but Audrey heard its message.

'Listen, chuck, she's got loads of brass to pay this snotty agency. You should see her bank statements.'

Audrey gasped with horror. She clutched the bannister tightly, simultaneously noticing that the top stair rod was loose, then she staggered back to her bed.

A piercing scream woke Audrey from her doze when her door was thrust open and Stacey barged in. 'What on earth is going on?' exclaimed Audrey.

'A spider bit me. A ruddy big spider. Look at my finger. Where's your medicine stuff?'

'What?' With difficulty, Audrey scrambled to her feet. She stared at the two deep puncture wounds on Stacey's bleeding finger. 'Downstairs in the kitchen cupboard. Where's the spider?'

'Where d'you think it ruddy well is? In the loo.'

'Oh, no!' Audrey pushed past her to get to the bathroom.

'Look out, you clumsy cow,' Stacey snarled as she turned to go down to the kitchen. But as she did so, she tripped over the loose stair rod and bounced down the stairs with a series of syncopated bangs.

Was Stacey dead? Audrey stared at the figure lying on the doormat.

'Are you barmy or what? Call a flaming ambulance!'

No, Stacey wasn't dead. Audrey picked up the phone in her bedroom. She slowly dialled 999 then she hurried into the bathroom. Draccy's squashed little body was floating upside down in the toilet bowl. Audrey lifted him out, laid him on her palm and wrapped his body tenderly in a tissue. She must not give way to the grief which brought back the agonising memory of Bessie. Burial could come later.

Before the ambulance arrived, she had another call to make. The number was engaged and so she left a message. 'Lyle,

Darling, this is a message from your Aunt Audrey. I've come to the conclusion that you are right. I am just like a fly trapped in a spider's web – a fly that plans to escape. I am your wealthy and well-educated Aunt and I accept your very kind offer to join you and Stuart in Edinburgh.'

Audrey smiled. She then carefully descended the stairs and waited for the ambulance to arrive.

A Living Presence

by Peter Quince

She fingers the tiny shell, reads its ridges like braille. She has no need to see it, not at this moment. What she sees is beyond sight, beyond this sepulchral building in which she settles in a fragile peace. Her fingertips run softly over the pitted surface, then explore the smooth concavity. He comes back to her. She *feels* rather than sees, resurrects him in all his salty glory. She can't help idealising him, despite the faults she remembers without rancour.

The Seaman's Chapel is located on Island Wall, a stone's throw from West Beach. On warm days, with the sea-facing doors open, you can hear the rhythmic swell of the breakers, the gentle susurrations. You can smell the saline air. You can catch the chuntering of gulls. You can visualise ships balancing on the horizon on their way west to London's dockland, or out into the North Sea, forever on their way somewhere.

Flora has come here at dusk, her favourite time of day, when the light is settling. At this hour in mid-March the Seaman's Chapel is usually empty. But sometimes tourists wander in, gaze cursorily at the little stained-glass windows which line each flanking wall of the building, or muse on the monochromatic photographs of long-dead fishermen.

Sometimes they stand and stare at the Crucifix which sits between two model fishing boats. Alongside the fishing boats are two fat, white candles sitting in dried candlewax. And then the tourists leave, perhaps none the wiser, perhaps unmoved by the history here. Eager to see more of the town, its boutiques and backstreets.

No one bothers Flora as she sits in staid reminiscence, willing the connection with Tom to perpetuate for as long as she can think and feel. His voice returns to her, not every time but often after her crepuscular stroll along Sea Wall, beyond the yacht club to the tall, black buildings which fringe the harbour. Buildings her husband knew well, in which he worked prising open shells and filling bins with crustaceans until it was time to meet her outside. Often at dusk. She was always there. That daily walk still primes her, gets into the blood, cures her after a fashion. She imagines him walking beside her, joking about monster waves, the one that got away. And there were many.

She sits with the tiny shell turning over and over between the fingers of both hands, as though it were some charm, a worry egg, a catalyst. And it is. Tom gave her many shells and other objects he'd dredged up on the boat. She kept them on window sills until the entire house seemed so full of the sea's detritus that it resembled a maritime museum.

So Tom constructed a model chapel for her out of thousands of shells and shards of driftwood and fragments of netting. An exact replica of the Seaman's Chapel, except that he'd crowned it with a fossilised sea horse he'd fashioned. She possesses his handiwork to this day. If storms prevent her from getting to the chapel itself, she makes do with the model, imagines strolling in with him.

Flora sees things that no longer exist. She sits on the front pew, just to the right of centre, always precisely in the same place. Tom was like that with his fishing gear: meticulous. But he was always casual about weather forecasts. *It's in the lap of the gods, love.* She can't forget such casual statements. She always thought he was playing with fire as well as water.

She looks up at the Crucifix as though it might speak to her, might answer questions she's harboured these five years since the sea took Tom and his companions. Unanswerable questions. *In the lap of the gods.* In gathering darkness she cannot see the wound in Christ's side, nor the crown of thorns, nor the agonised features of his averted face. Everything is shadow, a chiaroscuro of faintly realised shapes.

She hears him once again. *If ever the sea takes me, Flora, don't condemn it. It's still a beautiful thing.* 'Yes,' she says aloud. But there is no one to hear. There is no one beside the still waters or the raging torrents. Only the dumb figure of Christ without his fisherman disciple, alone in eternal suffering as Flora is. She imagines Tom's face as the vessel goes down, sees it every day as if she were there. The rictus, the spar wound in his side, his head twisted, averted from disaster. His own pointless crucifixion. Fish bones are all that remain.

Light gradually leaches out of the Seaman's Chapel. There is no sound of the sea, nor gulls' cries, nor reassuring voices. Flora sits in the midst of solid darkness. She knows where the matches are. She places the tiny shell beside her and feels her way to a wall-mounted cupboard in a corner of the chapel. Yes, the matchbox is there, as always, but not the glass vases. She returns to the altar and strikes a match and puts the flame to each of the two candles. They haven't been lit in ages.

Tom used to do this years ago. It was a ritual he knew delighted her. *Where there is darkness, there shall be light.* She never quite knew if he was being ironic. The words of a humble fisherman conscious of being a miniscule part of the greater mystery. The boat went down in squally darkness, so she was told. She never did discover the details – except the splintered spar which pierced his side. They told her after they'd dredged him up.

Flora hears a sound behind her. A shuffling. A cough. Perhaps a late tourist stumbling in. In March they begin to visit. She turns and, in flickers of candlelight, sees a woman approaching her. The woman is holding a bunch of daffodils which seem to glow preternaturally. Flora is enchanted by catching sight of the blooms. As the woman reaches the front pew she sees Flora and halts.

'Oh, I'm sorry.... I didn't mean to disturb you.'

'You're not disturbing me. This place is for everyone. Sea-going and land-locked.'

'Yes, I know.' The woman smiles tenderly.

Made to feel at ease, she comes close to Flora. They stand beneath the overarching presence of the Crucifix. The two model fishing vessels seem to shudder on a swell as the candleflames, agitated by the remnants of an onshore breeze, move this way and that. Both women are transfixed by the scene upon the altar, which is akin to new life, strange to them, but compelling, magical.

'I love the daffodils,' Flora says.

'They're for my son.'

'Oh....?'

'Last year it happened. He was swimming way out there....' She turns and gestures towards the sea-facing doors, Island Wall beyond and, further away, West Beach and the unfathomable expanse of the sea. '"Wild swimming" they call it. I told him many times. "Rory, it's too dangerous. You can't trust the tides. One day they will turn and swallow you." And they did. Last March, exactly a year ago. Got into difficulties in a sudden squall. Couldn't make it back. So his friends said. Drowned. Just like that.' The woman raises the luminous yellow flowers. 'I bought these on the flower stall at the harbour. Yellow is his favourite colour. He'll appreciate the gesture.'

All this while Flora stares hard at the stranger, straining to remember where she'd seen her before. Perhaps down at the harbour. Perhaps here in the Seaman's Chapel. Somewhere. A face.

A map of pain and tenderness. A fellow traveller.

The woman places the daffodils flat on the altar, spreading them a little with a touching delicacy. 'No vases in here,' she says. 'There were some, but they've gone.'

'Yes. Gone. All gone. We need to get some more.'

'I'll be back – with a vase and fresh water.'

The woman walks out of the Seaman's Chapel. Water, Flora

thinks. *So much water everywhere.* She turns back to the altar and gazes up at the Crucifix. What she sees is not the long, pale, bearded visage of Christ but the face of Tom: husband, fisherman, model-maker. Dead these five years and yet a living presence for her.

Flora returns to her seat on the front pew and picks up the tiny shell and closes her eyes and once more runs her fingers across its ridges. This is not brailling but the clarity of a vision that goes beyond; that takes in sea and sky and all that moves and grows and dies and eventually comes to rebirth.

Foreseen in Whitstable

by Richard White

I was sitting in one of those fat armchairs, and the other one was empty because my date, Jasmine, had not arrived. Short of anything else to do, I was gazing out of the window of Amedea, a café in Oxford Street. And there he was, ambling slowly by. At first I didn't recognise him, even when he turned towards my window and stared at me. No, he didn't know me either. It was when he stopped that I was sure, and he looked down towards the harbour and began twiddling the hairs at the back of his head.

That's what I do. A nervous habit I have always had.

Then he did something odd, not odd to me, perhaps not even to him, but have you ever seen someone looking one way and walking the other? It's a unique accommodation to indecision, to which I am prone at any time, and I thought only I would do it, because it tends towards human collisions and often stops the traffic. A slight altercation occurred between him and an electric mobility scooter, resulting in indignant outcries. *That could have been me*, I thought, and as he turned my way again, I saw that he was wearing a purple sweater with herringbone design, and I thought, *he's wearing my sweater*. Then I realised.

It was me.

Let me explain. I don't have that sweater now. I haven't had it for years. Nor do I have those maroon corduroy trousers. You can't buy them anymore. Even his shoes were mine, and

I have never seen anybody else with anything like them—round-toed and in deep oxblood, and laced all the way down to the toes, they are awkward to put on and annoying to walk in because they creak, and I gave mine to a beggar a long time ago. *Was this the same one?* No, not a beggar. His whole style was like mine, but perhaps mine thirty to forty years ago. His hair was parted exactly as mine still is. The only difference was that mine is grey and his was brown, as brown as mine was when I came down here in my thirties as a surveyor. I am still a surveyor but what little work I get is now in London. Finally I noticed his jacket, deep purple velvet, with flaps at the back. Now I was alarmed. I was looking at the real me, deep in my own past when I first came to Whitstable, a shoddy place where you could buy a unique weatherboarded house for fifty thousand. I had done so. It was where I met my second wife, Tollie-Ann, who has been dead more than fifteen years.

By now this odd interloper had turned on his heels and was crossing the road, dancing between the traffic, amid blaring horns and shouting.

I shouted too, 'Stop! Wait!' And I rushed out, blundered over the road without grace but with a glancing blow from a wing mirror to my right elbow, and I searched the opposite side of the street.

He just wasn't there, nor was there any shadow of him in either direction. Several people stopped in Oxford Street to stare at me in alarm. Then I heard the cries from outside Amedea, 'Hey you! You haven't paid. Calling police.' I waited for a gap in the cars, and wandered back, laughing. It was so silly that it was funny. The waiter was still gesticulating on the pavement, and I waved a calming gesture as I headed for the door. Then I saw the other fat armchair in the window. There was Jasmine, sitting there looking at her phone.

But wait, no, it was not her. The reflection of the sun off the glass obscured her, but for a moment I saw the pale face with the wisps of black hair and the sparkling sharp eyes. It was…*no, it couldn't be*. But I should know if anybody. It *was* Tollie-Ann.

I hesitated, there was movement inside and people were going in and out of the café. As I entered and made peace with the waiter, I turned to see that both armchairs were empty.

*

I've seen a flat in Nelson Road, my sort of place and only two hundred and twenty thousand. I know Whitstable, and I know most of its current faces. I even know their dogs. They know me too. I asked Pasco, smoking on the corner amongst his garden ornaments, if he had seen someone like me go past. He gave me a funny look. 'What d'you mean, like you?'

'Well, he might be my son.'

'You said you didn't 'ave a son. You been on the sauce?'

'If someone like me comes by, try to stop him, would you?'

'I ain't stopping nobody, mate, 'less they're clutching five hundred to spend. Anyhow, sold one 1930s chicken trough today and I'm off, had enough of today.'

It would have ended my day too, except that as I went past the Ship Centurion, somebody bumped into me, and I span around to see *me*, reeling down the street after spilling out with three others, all apologising incoherently, and when I turned back to the way I was going, it looked like me rounding into Harbour Street. I called after him but my voice soaked into the traffic and he was gone.

Was I seeing things?

*

I went quiet for a while, daring not speak for fear of blurting out my problem. I needed help but how could I ask anybody? They'd stare at me and then move away. 'Did you say you'd seen *yourself* in the High Street? Oh, really? Had any weird moments recently? An accident, perhaps?' The doctor would call a colleague to his room and ask me to tell him again, then they would discuss psychiatric resources. My usual friends would suggest I go home and lie down and see how I felt tomorrow. I started to think I had imagined it all, or something had happened of which I had no memory.

I dared to discuss it with Herbert, a very old and heady friend recently arrived in Whitstable. His heavy locks of slick hair flopped over his face and he coughed pointedly. 'A senior moment?' He cracked a smile. 'No. You know that Buddhist teachings show that your sense of self is an illusion?'

I chuckled. 'So I am an illusion created in my own brain?'

'Of course. But there is also your entity with a history and an ability to do things. That entity you call *me*.'

'So where does that get me?'

'If you know that your self is an illusion, but also that you exist, you may be compelled to see the you that you know exists as a separate phenomenon, outside of yourself.'

'Oh come on. Because I know I exist does not enable me to see myself.'

'But you know you *are* and you *were* here.'

'*Are* is possible, but the past is unredeemable.'

'Unless it is an illusion. One illusion is as good as another, no?'

My next research was to discover whether only I could see my historic self. Some people I knew had seen the other me but not recognised him. First I had to reliably see myself whenever I wanted. This was the trickiest phase because this historic me obviously did not want to be seen. That was when I realised that this other me seemed to see the *I* in myself. *If the past was visiting the present, the present might know what had happened in the past, and if they found out what I had once done...* Well I didn't want to go there! History is unforgiving and the past cannot be revised.

How could I see this other me? Chase him all over Whitstable? I remembered a sensible friend had once said, 'Don't run around searching. Stay in the same place and wait. It'll come to you.' So I did, even when it started to rain again. Then I retired to the inside of Windy Corner, where I could watch through the window, with reason to believe windows might be a part of the illusion. Nothing. Tea and Times was no better, nor was the Tudor Tearoom. In the Garage Café there was nobody there but with a slight sense of a recent departure, the waitress was still clearing the table. So I thought, *Where would I go when looking for myself?* If not in a mirror the place must be full of what I liked. Harbour Books, then.

It worked. While browsing downstairs someone squirmed past me by the new fiction. He had my walk, which I only knew from an ancient home movie taken by my father which I had found when clearing his house: rather erect and rapid but loping with a tiny lift on every step. I dropped the book I was reading and hurried out after him, which caused some unease behind the cash desk. I should know by now. Out in the street he had done it again, and I was left swivelling my head left and right.

I'd swallowed a lot of tea by now and I'd need relief, so I went to the Duke of Cumberland and sat down with a glass of Pinot Grigio, knowing I could not see out to the street anywhere. Within a minute Rowan came in and asked if he could join me, and I smiled with relief to have abandoned my difficult mission. I couldn't tell Rowan of course, I'd lose a friend, but I asked him an obscure existential question, 'Do you ever think you don't really know yourself?'

'Certainly not. I know myself too well. I'd like to get out of myself.'

'Oh! And if you did…get out of yourself?'

'Then I'd be someone else. Probably someone more interesting.'

'And then, being someone else, supposing you…actually met yourself?'

He squirmed a little, looking away over my shoulder, then quizzically back at me.

'Well, I suppose…do you mean what would I say to myself?'

'Or, if you were having a conversation, what would be your first question to ask him…so what would you most want to ask yourself?'

'I'd ask him…who was the most important person to him,

alive or dead; then what was his most difficult secret to hide.'

'That's two questions.'

'So what? He can decide which one to answer first, and I expect the other would follow.'

'Not with me! The first one, yes. The second, I wouldn't answer.'

'Has anyone ever asked you those questions? Would the second follow?'

'No. There's nobody I could trust enough with my answers.'

His eyes were no longer on me; he continued almost in a whisper, 'All the way through this conversation there has been a man watching us from behind you. He's been listening.'

I swung round, but there was nobody behind. 'Where?'

'As soon as I caught his eye, he started to move. Now he's gone. Why, do you know him?'

'Don't know, I didn't see him. What did he look like.'

'Tall, blue-grey eyes, fiddles with his hair...a bit like you, but younger.'

*

Of course, I had to ask Serena, the one everybody calls Serena the Psyche, in pink dungarees and blinking eyes behind thick glasses. She did not seem surprised, so I thought she had not heard me, but no, 'I know several people who have seen themselves, some of them out in the street, like you. Now I don't mean to suggest dishonesty, but have you come clean about all the things you've done that are not quite honest?'

I was a bit shocked, but after I thought a little. 'D'you mean have I done bad things?'

'Done bad things and never told even the people you've hurt?'

That put me out. I don't know Serena that well. 'What sort of bad things?'

'You may not think of it this way, but have you done things that have damaged people you knew?'

'Definitely not...well, okay, we've all done things...'

'...that are on your conscience?'

'No! Well, perhaps just *not* done *some* things...'

'Ah-ha! You see, when you are dishonest with people you are close to, it damages you as well as them.'

I didn't like the way this was going. 'Nothing that I can remember...at least not recently.'

'I'd be surprised if you had done nothing, and if it was long ago, the pain might be very deep. I know many people who cannot face up to what they've done, in fact it's a bit of a Whitstable thing. I can think of three already...'

'Please don't tell me.'

'Secrets are safe with me. But you will feel it in yourself even if you have thoroughly covered it up. I'm not asking you to tell me. Whisper it to yourself.'

'Why? Why, do you think I am seeing myself?'

'Ah! Only you can know that. Have you tried talking to this...*other you*?'

'Can't get that close.'

'Do you dream about him?'

'No! No I don't!' But thinking about it later I wasn't so sure. 'What if I am?'

'It might be a channel...'

I was in a hurry to get away from Serena, I was not looking for a mother confessor. When I got back I was still annoyed, but something was also eating me. *Could she have meant...?*

No, that was just a silly little game.

But what about Tollie-Ann? What about the time we were going to the Far East together?

What about all that anyway? It didn't happen.

And why didn't it happen—because I didn't turn up.

I had a lot on.

Too big a commitment?

We did get married!

But it didn't last, did it? And the children—where are they?

Well, we skipped children.

Now what was I doing? Talking to myself? Or was I talking

to the other me?

Too many questions. There was a ghost of myself following me, unless I was following him; this was all getting quite personal, and I needed to escape. What was I doing in Whitstable, anyway? I had a train to catch, to London. Oh God, I had forgotten I was meeting Jasmine again in Amedea. I'd have to phone her from the train.

*

Back in town two days later, I missed a phone call. Looking on my mobile, the call seemed to come from my own number. Some technical aberration, best ignored. But remembering the last week, I stopped and wondered: what would happen if I returned the call? By then I was on the West Beach and an icy wind was creeping out of the North. I started to head back to town, until I saw Rowan a long way off heading past the last of the beach huts. I waved and shouted but he strode on oblivious, and he was not alone. A man was with him. A tall man with dark hair. A man with a lope and a bounce in his walk. Too far to see but it might be. Coming up onto the pathway between the huts, Rowan was heading away from me towards Seasalter, and he was now alone. I waited a few minutes but there was nobody else. I had forgotten about the phone call until the phone rang again.

Of course I answered it. All I heard was an echo of my own voice, annoyingly repeating every word I said. I looked at the phone a short while, then I just called back, as I had intended. A message played back, from me, in *my own voice* but rather a poor recording, with considerable static. It confused me, and I thought it was a scam or someone's prank, but it was familiar:

At the station, yes, the London platform, I've got that...

Money? Passport? Yes I've got all that...

Ten thirty-two, Friday morning...

Look, this is difficult for me. It's my job...yes of course I do, you know that...

What d'you mean? Of course I'm coming...

Foreseen in Whitstable

*

Well, the flat fell through, and I can't stay any longer in Rowan's attic room. I haven't been down there for nearly a month now. I'm not sure I want to. Whitstable is changing, and not for the better. Work's mostly in London now, this is a good one and I can't blow this chance. I'll not get many more at my age.

Martin, with his woolly white hair and sailor's tarpaulin jacket, the most insistent of my Whitstable friends, said last time, 'You've got to be down here, or they'll think of you as a DFL. They won't tell you, but if you're sensitive you'll know. You belong here or you don't.'

Me? I'm not saying I'm scared, but Whitstable has ghosts, and I suppose the locals must have strong stomachs. Living on my own I see too much of myself, and I certainly don't want any more of me. I've heard that Faversham is nice, I'm going there to see a couple of places next week. It depends how far ghosts can travel. Otherwise I've seen a very nice studio flat in Bermondsey.

ChristmaZ

by Nic Blackshaw

Tinsel in every shop, Christmas trees with blinking lights, plastic mistletoe and the Very Best Yuletide Songs on repeat: every day's Christmas since zombies took over Whitstable High Street.

Whitstable and district went into quarantine on Boxing Day the previous year. That was the start of everything and a pretty big come down after the big day. The *Christmas from Hell* people called it and fair enough, the Dead rising from their graves isn't especially festive. But catastrophes don't check the calendar to find a convenient date. The government was determined to keep the outbreak localized and within a few days the army erected a fifteen-foot fence around the area, armed soldiers with specially trained dogs patrolling the perimeter 24/7. No one was going to escape the cordon, dead or alive.

A year later survivors still lived within the danger zone. A strange kind of normality prevailed. People continued to live in their own homes, went to their old jobs or worked from home. They found a way to co-exist with the zombies. Thanks to the Human Rights Act the *killing* of any sentient being was forbidden. It didn't matter that these blood-crazed creatures had only one purpose: to consume their former friends and neighbours. So if the survivors couldn't *rub out* the zombies, they had find a way to *rub along* with them. At least until the virus burned through the last of its victims, letting them drop to the ground, inert and ready for disposal.

Absolutely no contact was permitted with the outside world but the shops, well-stocked before the outbreak, contained sufficient frozen food to cater for those still living, along with the multiplicity of products upon which modern life depends. The consumer economy was alive and kicking even if many customers weren't.

*

Kyle and Lisa, coming out of the car park and heading for the shops, had other things on their mind. It was Christmas Eve and they had presents to buy. At least, that was what Kyle thought. For him Christmas was a last-minute scramble to nab something suitable before the shops closed but Lisa had done all of her shopping weeks earlier, purchasing the final gift in the first week of December. Of course, being a couple, she also shopped for his side of the family and was only looking for what she called *the little bits*, stocking fillers and the like – the finishing touches. All Kyle had to worry about was the one present Lisa hadn't bought: his gift to her.

Kyle didn't like Christmas. Mostly because he spent Christmas Eve in a panic, rushing from shop to shop, desperately trying to find something to get for Lisa. She'd left a trail of crumbs that led to her heart's desire but he hadn't noticed. He'd missed every nudge towards this product or that in the buildup up to Christmas. And no matter how hard he racked his brain, he couldn't recall a single clue. And the music, annoyingly insistent, didn't help.

'It's all so tacky,' he said, pushing against the door to Ice World. 'The tinsel and the jingles and...' The shop's tannoy was pumping out Wham's *Last Christmas* at ear-bleeding volume. 'I mean – it's all so fake.'

Lisa rolled her eyes.

'You're such a curmudgeon, Kyle. Really – lighten up, babes.' She held his chin with her beautifully manicured fingers. 'You know you'll love it. Once you get in the spirit.'

She gave his face a squeeze and a full-on smacker on the lips. Kyle sighed heavily and smiled weakly. What he liked was eight o'clock Christmas evening, collapsed on the sofa, everyone gone home, TV on, remote in his hand, thinking – that's it, over for another year. Then he'd pull the ring on another can of beer, flick through the channels until he drifted off for a well-earned snooze. Of course, he didn't say any of that. He just grunted and picked up a basket.

'What are we here for?' he asked.

Lisa shook her head. Always with the philosophical questions. She took the basket from Kyle and whacked the zombie, arms outstretched, coming straight for her. 'Last Christmas, I gave you my heart...' went the song. She gave the girl the basket, full across the chest.

'Just a few bits,' Lisa said.

The zombie, a girl with green hair and matching eyeliner, fell to the floor but another zombie following close behind, greasy mullet and sleeveless denim jacket, grabbed Lisa's sleeve. Kyle let him have it with a rolled-up copy of Cosmopolitan. It was the bumper Christmas edition so there was a bit of weight behind it.

'What does that mean?' he asked. If only she'd give him a clear list to follow. But Lisa was a browser. *I'll know when I see it*, was her motto.

The zombie fell onto the tinned goods display, knocking over a pyramid of Campbell's Soup cans.

Lisa caught one as it tumbled: broccoli and stilton.

'Oh. You know,' she said, glancing at the can and dropping it in the basket.

They went down the first freezer aisle. Lisa peered inside the nearest cabinet. A zombie at the other end of the aisle, grey business suit and blood-red tie, formerly manager of the establishment, began shuffling towards them. Lisa held out the basket for Kyle to take.

He leant back against the cabinet.

'It's always a few bits and then we come out with half the store.'

Lisa shuffled the pizza boxes until she found one she wanted: American Hot with Extra Pepperoni.

'Pizza for Boxing Day,' she said by way of commentary.

Kyle watched the zombie continue his slow progress towards them, not really listening. Lisa handed the box to Kyle.

'Better get two,' he said, putting it in the basket.

Lisa gave him a questioning look but she knew the answer, just wanted to hear him offer it. He was so predictable she usually knew exactly what he was thinking.

'You know I like one to myself,' he said, shrugging as if it was obvious.

The zombie lifted his arms into the standard horizontal position and continued towards them. You could never find a store assistant when you wanted one but since the Zombie Apocalypse you couldn't get away from them.

Lisa fossicked around for another American Hot, leaning half inside the freezer to reach the base of the cabinet.

'Think that's the last one, babes. How about Hawaiian?'

'Pineapple has no business being on a pizza.'

The zombie was only a cabinet away, his lips moving, but all that came out was a long moan. Lisa looked over her shoulder at Kyle.

'You had one Friday night.'

Kyle snorted.

'It was all we had in the freezer,' he said. 'And I picked off the pineapple.'

Lisa turned her head.

'Also you'd had a skinful. Don't forget that.'

How could he when she kept reminding him? And who could blame him having a drink, given the circumstances, zombie-wise. He put the basket on the floor and joined her inside the freezer cabinet.

'There's a Pepperoni," he said, 'right on the top. How'd you miss that?'

The zombie went for Kyle but tripped on the basket, falling against the cabinet. Lisa yanked his red tie and shoved him into the cabinet. Kyle slammed the lid on him.

'Any shoppers want to see the manager,' she said. 'They'll know where to find him.'

It was time for Kyle to make his play.

'You don't need me getting in the way,' he said. 'When you finish here we can meet…'

'Trying to get out of carrying the basket, are you?'

'Eh? No. I need to go to the hardware shop and…'

Her eyes narrowed suspiciously.

'You haven't forgotten to get something for me, have you?'

'Nah. Got your present ages ago, babe.'

His only defense was nonchalance. It worked sometimes.

'I don't want anything special,' she said. 'And I don't want you spending too much on me.'

'It's something for my Dad, you know…'

'I got him an electric razor.'

'Great but…'

Kyle spun around, hoping something would suggest itself amongst the tins stacked on the shelves.

'I wanted to get him something… you know – to say thanks.'

There was a long pause. It was touch and go. Lisa treated almost anything he said with scepticism.

She gave a big sigh.

'OK,' she said, already turning her gaze to the next freezer cabinet.

Kyle went to go but Lisa tugged his coat lapel.

'I need your card,' she said. 'I'm maxed out.'

It takes more than a zombie apocalypse to stop the wheels of high finance and big business from turning so, while it was true that zombies now roamed Whitstable, goods and services still had to be paid for. Customers self-scanned purchases and offered their contactless card to the banking terminal. Ding. Payment accepted. Have a nice day.

Kyle opened his wallet, determined not to look triumphant.

He'd often given the game away by doing that. He knew he was ridiculously easy to read.

He gave Lisa his credit card.

'Tea and Times in an hour,' he said.

He bumbled into a zombie in tweed coat and battered gumboots milling around the counter, knocking the creature backwards into the magazine section. Noddy Holder bellowed *It's Christmas* on the in-store sound system and Kyle thought, I know, there's no need to shout about it, as he went out the door.

Freed to wander the High Street, Kyle assessed the possibilities but still without an answer to the question of the day. What could he get Lisa she didn't already possess and, equally important, actually wanted?

He ran his eyes along the shop fronts, past zombies stumbling along the pavements and other shoppers skirting them. The lights shone brightly, Christmas music percolated through half-open shop doors. All a lot of humbug, Kyle thought as he dodged two zombie teens, heads hovering over smart phones that had long gone dark. He mentally scrolled gift ideas but the magic product failed to present itself. A zombie with a *Make Britain Great Again* badge fixed to his tattered anorak swayed into his line of sight. Some wag had wrapped gold tinsel around his neck and stuck a Santa hat on his head but Kyle merely scowled as he walked past. Christmas was no laughing matter.

The black edifice of the Vogler Institute loomed over the High Street. They said a careless researcher accidentally released the zombie virus. Some also said that, even now, scientists inside were working to devise an antidote.

Kyle made his way down Harbour Street. A small crowd of zombies followed, drawn by the hot breath and steady beating heart of the living. Kyle noticed the open door of a shop and darted inside, bolting the door and switching the sign to *closed*. He realized he'd taken refuge in the old antique shop and cursed his impatience. It contained nothing of any interest. The zombies pressed against the door, blocking that exit. Hopefully the back door was zombie free.

He cast a weary eye over the cluttered interior of the shop, the accumulated plunder of centuries piled high on shelves and display cases and antique mahogany dressers: ship's lanterns, heavy brass bridge compasses, Victorian slide projectors, phrenology heads, Indonesian masks, ornate silver tea and coffee sets, Wedgewood crockery and Minton tiles. He had no idea who bought the stuff but he knew there was nothing for Lisa.

A dark shape emerged from the shadows giving Kyle a start and he picked up the first thing that came to hand, holding it out defensively. It was a carved ivory shoehorn, about four inches in length. If the zombie needed help getting his shoes on, it had met its nemesis.

The zombie came into the light, a grey-faced ghost with a long white beard and unruly white hair that had last seen a brush long before he'd stopped breathing. Kyle reached behind for a better weapon. Zombies were dangerous in close confines and he had no wish to form the man's supper.

'You won't need that,' the old zombie said.

Kyle looked sideways at him. Was his imagination playing tricks or had the dead man spoken? He stepped back and found himself pressed against the edge of a large display case full of stuffed songbirds and small mammals. This might get ugly, he thought.

The zombie picked up a silver cigarette case and flicked it open.

'No – you're not hallucinating,' he said. He glanced at the silver case, empty save for his reflection. 'I don't suppose you have a…'

Kyle shook his head.

'I shall bear this curse with equanimity,' he said, snapping the case shut and issuing a long sigh. 'Death would be easier to bear with a few of life's little pleasures.'

His cold, glassy eyes met Kyle's. There was a mournful air

about the man but that was probably to be expected; being dead but still conscious left a lot to be desired.

'You have several questions – no doubt,' the old zombie said.

'How come you can talk?' Kyle said, putting down the shoehorn.

'It's a skill I mastered as a small child. Sorry, I'm being flippant. I don't get many opportunities for polite conversation. I have moments of lucidity, when whatever is left of my brain imposes itself on this dreadful disease. I think it's my age – the virus is more vigorous in the young. Everything slows down with age, even death.'

Kyle shot a look the front of the shop. Zombies were pressed against the shop window and the bevelled-glass front door, like a swarm of wasps clustered on a Mars bar. Their mouths opened and closed in silent approximation of speech. The only sound was the shuffling of their feet and the occasional thud against the glass as another zombie joined the swarm.

'They can't get in,' the old zombie said, lowering himself onto the stool behind the counter. 'You'll be safe in here.'

He picked up the carved ebony head of a Maasai warrior and for an instant was transformed into the antiquarian he must once have been, examining an artifact and assessing its value.

'You've lost the spirit of Christmas, haven't you?' he said, lifting his eyes to meet Kyle's. 'It has become something to be endured, not a festival to be celebrated.'

Kyle snorted. 'How can you tell?'

'I see the signs,' he said. 'I was like you once. Perhaps it's hard to believe but I was both young *and* alive. Wrapped up in my work, doing deals and making money. My family never saw me. I was a stranger in my own home, passing through, never to tarry. Christmastime I'd run around like a man possessed, searching for the perfect present. Hoping, I suppose, I could exchange splendid gifts for lost family time, a penitent's payment. But, in the end, all they really wanted was time together. Not – things. And they were right. Take a look at everything here. These were presents once. Now forgotten, the only purpose they serve is collecting dust. Time is all that really matters.'

Kyle examined a set of dusty silver goblets on a silver tray and drew an S in the dust.

'That's easy for you to say. You don't know my wife.'

'That's true. But you must allow that, no longer living, I have had the chance to consider the workings of the human heart more dispassionately than I did when my own heart still beat. And from my vantage point I can tell you when people love you the time you spend with them is the most precious gift of all.'

'That's all well and good but if she doesn't have something to open on Christmas Day...'

'Of course. But it's not the gift, is it? It's the thought.'

'True. She does say that.'

'Excellent. We'll find something for her Christmas box and restore your Christmas spirit.'

The sun was going down, only ten minutes until he was supposed to meet Lisa. It was now or never and if this old codger could provide something wonderful and unexpected, how could he resist?

*

It was Christmas Day, lights twinkling on the plastic Xmas tree, Cliff Richard warbling about mistletoe and wine. The smell of roast turkey and pigs-in-blankets, spiced wine and Figgy Pudding still hung in the air, reminding everyone how much they'd eaten. Lisa and Kyle's mum were on the sofa and, their work done and several large Babychams into the evening, were laughing merrily at something they'd seen on *TikTok*. Kyle and his dad came in from the kitchen, drying their hands from the washing-up. Lisa's parents, Derek and Sheila, peered in from the patio, pressed against the sitting room window like a couple of carolers who'd imbibed way too much mulled wine. Kyle's brother, Kevin, was beside them, banging his head against the glass. They might be zombies but that didn't prevent them joining their loved ones on Christmas Day. After all, Christmas is a time for families, even if the zombie contingent wanted to make a meal of their nearest and dearest.

Lisa offered a toast.

'Dad loved Christmas,' she said, forcing a smile.

Family had been everything to her father. The meaning and purpose of his life was to keep her and her Mum safe and happy. He always said it was the three of them against the world. She'd always thought the expression *the nuclear family* was odd, not seeing what atomic bombs had to do with families. Especially as it wasn't a nuclear war destroyed her mum and dad's world, but a Zombie Apocalypse, ground zero only a few streets from where they lived.

Kyle's mum clinked glasses with her before downing the Babycham as Kyle flopped onto the settee and handed Lisa an untidily wrapped gift box with a lopsided crimson bow.

Kyle laid his hand on the knot.

'Now there's a story to this gift.'

He told them about the Ghost of Christmas Past in his antique shop and how the wise old zombie helped him find the Christmas spirit.

He took his hand off the present and smiled sweetly.

'And it's the thought, isn't it?'

Lisa shot his mum a worried look but didn't say anything. She unwrapped the gift carefully, taking her time not to rip the paper. That was her thing, removing the paper and folding it neatly. Not like Kyle, who tore it off and tossed balls of screwed-up paper at the dog.

Kyle watched her, pleased as punch, throwing a quick glance at his mum and dad.

'What do you think?' he said.

Lisa looked at Kyle and then at his mum. Cliff faded out, Lennon faded in, still hoping the war would end. Lisa shut the box and stared at Kyle. The silence, although brief, was too much for Kyle.

'You always say,' he said, smug as anything, 'I should enjoy the holiday season and...' He gave her a squeeze. 'I put a lot of thought into this.'

Lisa turned to Kyle's mum.

'All the hints, all the subtle reminders. I don't know how many times I said *I'm almost out of Eau de Cologne*. Or *a nice moisturizer/bath oil set would be lovely*, or *Adele's latest album, 42*... And I get this. I don't even know what *it* is...'

But Kyle had zoned out. He'd done his bit. He'd got Lisa a special gift and he was happy to let everything wash over him, luxuriate in the contented haze of goodwill and peace on earth: Merry Christmas, one and all. Maybe next year he'd introduce Lisa to the old zombie and, if the old codger didn't devour her, maybe she'd learn the real meaning of Christmas. That'd be something.

A Brief Tale

by Gillian Rolfe

Miss Flossie cat stood behind the glass-topped counter in the department store on Whitstable High Street. She tapped a manicured claw against the counter top, staring at the early morning memo she had read through at least three times. Pushing it aside she leant across a pile of snowy tissue paper to smooth a creaseless ribbon, but finding no solace in the action she walked to the window. Taking controlled breaths, she observed Felix the caretaker struggling to pull up the blinds in the shop window. They suddenly rattled up in a furious roll, with the toggle dangling; he swiped it a few times before catching it in his grubby claw and tucking it neatly behind the faded cambric fabric. He turned and seeing her there he grinned, pushing his flat cap back from his greasy tabby furred forehead.

Patting, in habit, at her neat cream ears with her paw she ignored him and turned to survey the brass inlaid mahogany shelves sweeping along the walls of her department. Arranged on them were silk boxes of the *Rather Ravishing* collection, Miss Flossie's flagship lingerie range.

She glanced again at the in-house memo she had picked up in her paw, the paper hot and damp, registering the words '*additional designer*' and '*a new line of merchandise*'. How ridiculous, she thought, to mix two brands of lingerie that were so different. The gossamer creations of her traditional

Ravishing collection in comparison with this new sporty lycra of the *Perfect* range was hardly worth considering. The *Perfect* range might currently be doing a roaring trade amongst young cats, but this was surely a blip. Whereas her line of *Ravishing* had a timeless quality and clients of a certain pedigree. It was much more suited to the department store by the sea.

Her musings were disturbed by the staff's arrival. There was a general flurry of greetings, divesting of outer wear and stowing of lunches that had been a soothing pattern to Miss Flossie's life for over twenty years. She had arrived as a toe-twisting youngster escaping the shadows of her depressive mother before discovering the sunlight of her own talent and capability.

This morning's routine was broken by the department store's owner arriving through the bevelled glass doors as if on oiled castors. Miss Flossie immediately straightened and smoothed her soft chignon fur. She inclined her head carefully.

'Miss Flossie,' purred Managing Director Rowley, a cloying scent expensively emanating from his thick pelt. 'Always a pleasure, always a pleasure.'

'Sir,' returned Miss Flossie, face and voice carefully neutral, displaying none of the timidity that had damaged her young egg-skin confidence.

'You've heard then, I knew you would understand. A management decision of course.' He paused, assessing the neat figure. 'I trust there will be no problem with this.'

'Sir, no problem, looking forward to a new challenge, sir.' The last bit was good, thought Miss Flossie, although it did rather stick in her small pink throat. Managing Director Rowley smirked at her discomfort.

He turned to go then swivelled. 'Poppy, the designer of *Perfect*, starts tomorrow. The fitters will be in tonight,' he said before smoothly moving out of the door.

Miss Flossie froze, her paw reaching out to steady herself on a display of boxed pastel lounging robes. Her ear suddenly swivelled towards the staff door and she quickly freed her fixed expression. She turned to greet the staff flowing onto the shop floor, who were for the moment happily ignorant of the amount of work ahead of them.

*

The trading day had been long and busy but eventually it had come to a close. As she stowed the last of the silk items from the shop floor into storage containers ready for the department's refit she mused on the day's events. The two fittings had gone well. Marcie, the youngest assistant, a coarse tabby cat with bulging eyes, was shaping up nicely. She was discreet and could find the tiny buttons and zips with the minimum of fuss. She could guess, and reasonably well at that, the size of the client even through the bulkiest outerwear. Miss Flossie would have to speak to her about poking the tip of her tongue out whilst concentrating though.

She glanced around the denuded space. After tomorrow, she wondered, would her clients still be willing to patronise the department? She flicked the switch and left for the night.

*

Overnight the underwear department, previously a cloistered area under the gentle guidance of Miss Flossie, had been forced like a reluctant kitten into a spotlight. It had been completely refitted. Underwear for felines had never been more 'out there' than this. Racks lined the walls displaying, for the first time ever out of the boxes, the latest silk and lycra creations from both collections. Life-size mannequins posed nonchalantly in items of lingerie only previously heard about in the most inner circles. Miss Flossie, on arriving in her department the next morning, stood stock-still. Goose bumps rose on her skin, causing her fur to puff unattractively.

'Fab, is it not? This is the future, no more hiding behind the fur.'

Miss Flossie turned to see a small black cat, green eyes sparkling. She advanced, holding out a life-size cardboard cut-out of a very athletic model of a grey cat. It was having cocktails on a beach, wearing its fur coat unbuttoned at the neck to reveal a *Perfect* undergarment teasingly displayed.

'It's disgusting, how can you be so... so...' Miss Flossie gasped. '...*louche*? And that underwear...' She struggled again, 'is... frankly *awful*'.

Miss Flossie clasped her paws to her chest taking controlled breaths.

The young designer, Poppy, dropped the cut-out onto the wooden floor. She eyed Miss Flossie, her mouth and shoulders dropping in unison, then rallied, ardour transforming her stature.

'We, the next generation, will no longer hide from our true makeup! Why should it be a shameful thing to be without our fur coats? Who decided that what we wore underneath was not to be spoken about? Every cat deserves to feel comfortable with or without their fur coat, especially in the hot weather, in the privacy of their own home! This "frankly awful" range has been taking the young cat world by storm!' She dangled a *Ravishing* chemise in peach satin and coffee lace from her bright red polished claw. 'So much better than your old-fashioned granny stuff!'

*

Over the months that followed, the two designers circled each other like miniature tigers. Sales were sporadic. Customers, desperate for both ranges, could barely be in the department for long without the toxic environment ejecting them back onto the street.

Miss Flossie cast around her ruined department. She fretted and snapped at Poppy but was ignored. If she had been attentive she would have noticed Poppy gently picking up a fallen piece of gauzy lace or quietly extolling the virtues of satin against the skin under fur to a young feline. She noticed nothing, which would have helped on the day the Duchess arrived for her fitting. The large white cat sailed into the department on a cloud of ancient entitlement, assistants fluttering around her like anxious butterflies. She clasped Miss Flossie's paw and gazed into her large blue eyes.

'How are you holding up, in this very modern world, my dear?'

'We move with the times, your Grace, we move with the times.'

'How brave you are, my dear, it must be so wearisome.' The Duchess spoke gently, as if to a frail, fading thing. She stayed long enough to buy a complete set of the new *Ravishing* collection and a set of the *Perfect* for both her grand-kittens.

'So modern,' she intoned, motioning for a hovering assistant to collect the boxes. 'But they will learn soon enough.' She half smiled at Miss Flossie. 'Take care my dear.'

*

After the department closed for the day, the two cats worked silently side by side into the evening. Miss Flossie snatched a petticoat from Poppy's paws.

'Mine, I think,' she snapped.

'Goes with the thermal nighties,' retorted Poppy.

There was a small pause, the sort that comes before an ear-splitting clap of thunder. The tirade of hot painful words poured out of Miss Flossie. Poppy turned away, her shaking paws clasping the low shelf edge. Her shoulders hunched into a barricade but the mist of initial shock condensed into droplets of molten anger.

'You're such a *dinosaur*,' spat Poppy twisting around. She froze. Miss Flossie's careful chignon had unfurled, her cream fur tipped with chocolate streamed out from her head. She was growling soft and low. Slowly she lifted a powderpuff paw and caught Poppy a resounding slap across her coal-black cheek. Poppy, momentarily stunned, swayed, then with speed she launched herself bearlike at Miss Flossie. For a split second they were clasped together in the air before the energy propelled them upwards and backwards into a box of satin anti-rise cami-knickers. As they hit the sensuous landing pad, the sateen material rose and enclosed them, suffocating sound, but not before they heard heavy steps on the creaking oak boards in front of the counter.

'This is going so well, my son, they are at each other's throats, just as we guessed'. Managing Director Rowley leaned on the top of the ornate till, smoothing his cuffs of fur. Miss Flossie and Poppy, caught in their frozen embrace, strained to hear.

'They will either kill each other,' he chortled, 'or flounce off to pastures new, then this...' he waved a paw randomly around the department, '...and the brands will be ours.'

'Are you sure they don't know about the brands, Father? Do they think we own them?' Leon, his son, nasal drawl sounded slurred.

'Of course they do, Miss Flossie is such a genuflecting old spinster it'll never occur to her she owns the rights to her own designs. I think she secretly fancies me anyway.' He smoothed his sleek tabby fur back with an arrogant lick to his paw. His son, snorting gently, leaned against the doorjamb.

'What about Poppy, then? Bet she doesn't fancy you. She's too busy idealistically banging her drum and wearing flowers in her fur. I think she might fancy me though,' he mused thoughtfully stroking a long whisker along his claw.

'Oh, get real,' snapped his father, his ego stung. 'She's an empty airhead, she has no idea her brand is worth thousands.' He paused meditatively. 'Do you think you could get her interested? You know, secure the brand. You could always ditch her later.'

Leon started to laugh, and his father slapped his paw around his heir's shoulders and they moved up the stairs for a lactose nightcap, their mewling laughter echoing.

The two female cats lay like mummies in a sarcophagus, rendered immobile. Eventually Poppy fought her way out of the silk entrails and extended a paw to Miss Flossie.

'Miss Flossie,' she said politely. Her paw was grasped by a tremulous one and both stood in the moonlit shop and considered what they had just heard.

'I think your creations are magical, it's because of them that I came here, I'm... not an airhead – am I?' Poppy blurted out.

'Old spinster? How dare he! I think your designs are dynamic and modern. You are definitely a serious modern business cat, certainly *not* an airhead,' quietly hissed Miss Flossie.

They both stared at each other. Slowly, they gathered their bags and, silently, purposefully, slipped out of the store.

*

The new sign shone with the lustre of fresh paint as the three heads, cream, black and greasy, tilted backwards and admired the handiwork. The black scrolled paintwork on a pale grey background read:

PURRS

Perfect Underwear, Rather Ravishing Selection

The Feline Underwear Emporium

Felix clasped his screwdriver and leaned over to kiss Miss Flossie.

'See you later, naughty kitty cat.' He laughed at her confusion and swished his skinny tail as he disappeared inside.

The new store was an instant hit, bridging the generations and class divide. The shopping experience was fun, open to all and incorporated a claw bar and a complimentary supply of dreamy canapés. Discreet rooms were available for clients desiring this environment and a thriving postal service in plain brown wrapping expanded the empire further. A bespoke instore service of fur restoration whilst undergarments were being tried on proved popular amongst clients. Together with neck and shoulder massages it created a modern dimension whilst retaining roots in quality and luxurious standards of consumer care. With the profits from their business, Miss Flossie and Poppy set up body awareness sessions in schools and sponsored talented young cats through fashion college. With tails entwined and purrs richly vibrant, they finally read of the bankruptcy of M.D. Rowley, allowing them to buy their old store and installing the rather wonderful Monsieur Blanc, an elegant Persian, as Manager. M.D. Rowley lost everything and ended up in a dingy flat reeking of booze and fury in Hirsute-Ball Circle, a rather less than ravishing part of town.

A Drink Before Work

by Richard Barton

The pub door caught the December gale as it was opened and it crashed into a pillar.

'Get that dammed door clo...' The voice of Gilbert, the pub landlord, trailed off when he saw who was entering his establishment: five men, four of them huge brutes, clearly military types. The fifth was a smaller man, but he smirked at Gilbert, a smirk that said, 'I may not be big, but look at my friends and watch your step!'

'Sorry, gents,' said Gilbert, 'but we're trying to keep the warmth in. What can I get you?'

The biggest of the party gave Gilbert an unpleasant look. It was the only style he had to offer. 'Get us beer. And something hot to eat.'

'Hot broth? Made with our Christmas ham. And warm fresh bread with it? Have the table by the fire, get yourselves warmed up.' Gilbert glared at the old man who was seated at that table and flicked his head to indicate he should vacate the prime spot.

'The old man can stay where he is,' said the new arrival. 'We'll take that table, over in the corner. We want privacy. Beer, broth and bread too, quick as you like.' The five travellers clattered over to a table in a dark corner and arranged themselves and their equipment around it. The musician had stopped playing when the door crashed open but, after exchanging a look with

Gilbert, he began to strum softly. The beers were delivered, the temperature of the room recovered and the smell of the cold street outside was quickly replaced by that of the applewood, burning and crackling in the grate.

The biggest member of the group, clearly the leader, took his seat and said, 'Why do pubs think we want to listen to music when we're having a drink?'

'It's Christmas music, Reg,' suggested the smaller man.

'Christmas goes on for too darned long, if you ask me, Mauclerk,' grunted Reg, using the strange nickname they had given him.

'It's December the twenty-ninth – day five of the twelve days!' If Mauclerk thought this observation would mollify Reg, he was disappointed.

There was a pause before another of the group spoke, in an accent that had traces of the north country. 'I expect you're pleased to be back in Canterbury, Reg?'

'It's changed, Hugh,' grunted Reg. 'Grown. It was a much smaller place when I was a lad out at Barham.'

'It suffered during the war.'

'Everywhere suffered in the war, Hugh,' said Reg. 'That's what war's like. War's been over for years now, anyway.'

'Still, would be nice to see something of the city while we're here,' said Hugh.

'We're here to do a job, not go round gawping,' responded another of the party, this one with traces of the west country in his voice.

'I agree with Will,' said the fifth member of the band. 'I say we get the job done as soon as we know where he will be. Then we get out. The Boss will want to know what happens and what we get done here.'

'Richard's right,' said Reg, and that settled any debate. 'We'll see the cathedral. You can't miss it. But we'll do what the Boss asked and then get out.'

Gilbert started ferrying bowls of ham broth to their table, followed by hunks of gently steaming brown bread. The five men started eating noisily.

Will finished first so he suggested to his colleagues, 'Well, we're all nearly done here. Can't we get on with the job right away?'

'Soon enough, Will,' said Reg, who was taking his time with his food. 'As Richard has pointed out, we don't know where he'll be just yet. But we can be sure he'll be home for his dinner before he has to get back to his duties. Not long now. We'll catch him at his dinner and see if he's going to be sensible and come with us. If he's not, we'll catch up with him later, at his work.'

'Would it be sensible of him to come along with us?' asked Hugh.

By now Richard had also finished eating so he replied. 'Of course. If he comes with us, he's got a chance. He used to be best friends with the Boss. Really close, they were. If he comes along and explains what happened to the money, says he's sorry for being disrespectful, promises to be a good boy from now on, well, who's to say? The Boss might welcome him back and everybody's happy.'

'You know him best, Hugh,' said Will. 'Do you think he'll come with us?'

Hugh did know him best but did not want to commit himself to an opinion. He picked up a spare crust of bread and used it to wipe the dregs of his broth from his bowl.

After another pause, Richard spoke again. 'Reg, just to be clear, if he doesn't come with us, what will we do?'

Reg sighed. 'We've been over this so many times. I've told you. We'll find him at dinner, invite him to come with us to meet the boss and explain himself. All very friendly. Give him every chance to do the right thing.' He snapped his fingers at Gilbert, nodded at his finished drink and held up his splayed hand to indicate that another five beers were required. 'But if he wants to be stupid, that's his choice. We'll have given him a chance. If he's going to stick to his story that he's done nothing wrong and that he doesn't work for the Boss anymore, then we'll have to go back, catch him at his work, and finish it.'

'And by finish it, you mean…'

'You know what I mean!' thundered Reg. Then he lowered his voice as Gilbert placed the round of drinks on their table. 'He can't complain. If you're going to get close to people like the Boss, you know what you're getting yourself into. The company we all keep, well, it's not like all these lifelong clergy and monks and whatever they have here. It's a tough world and he was part of it long enough to know what's what. Besides,' he looked around the table, 'we've all killed before, what's the difference?'

'That was war, Reg,' said Hugh. He saw the look on Reg's face and quickly backtracked. 'I'm not saying… I understand what we have to do, the Boss made it clear.'

'Did he though?' asked Will. 'We're all quite sure what he wants?'

Reg slammed his fist on the table. 'He was perfectly clear! We all heard him! We know what he wants and we're the men to get it done for him.' He finished his drink. 'Right, I reckon it's about time. We'll bring our stuff with us and find somewhere to dump it while we see if he's going to be a good boy. If not, we pick it up and take the other approach.' He stood up. 'Right then, lads, let's get on with the job. This is our great day! From tomorrow, we'll be famous!'

'That's right,' simpered Mauclerk. 'It's a new year soon. I reckon 1171 will be our year, and no one will hear any more about that wretched priest Becket after today. Let's go!'

Of Human Tithe

by Guy Deakins

Blackstable had become *that* kind of town. Perhaps, it had always been destined to be *that* kind of town? Perhaps, it had *always been* that kind of town? Certainly, whatever veneer had been applied at some point in its long history was beginning to wear thin. Very thin indeed.

In pre-industrial days its affluent North Kent neighbour, the Cinque Port of Haversham, with safe harbour and Roman road to the City of Lunden, had the royal warrant to build ships for Kings. Blackstable was by comparison an insignificant shell-fishing village with too many pubs. Curtained on two sides by extensive marshes, it was a smut of raised land poisoned by copperas works and salt pans, a thick forest to the south hindering access to nearby Tercanbury. Things hadn't changed for centuries; however, as any student of history knows, *things* never stay the same.

The Georgians and later, the Victorians, keen to exploit their newly acquired industrial power, saw the land held promise and began to exploit its resources to the benefit of a burgeoning middle-class. Blackstable grew in size, resource and renown and it flourished for a century, nearly two, but, as with everything coastal, fortunes ebb and flow. By the 1960s, as shipped goods were containerised, it was evidently too small for a changing commercial world. The closing of the railway link to the harbour had not bode well. Stinking of boiling shell-fish and tar, the remaining light industries based around the waterside added a strangely piquant air to an unremarkable town that was trying desperately to escape the stigma of being fed by a cold muddy sea with nothing much to offer holidaymakers seeking sunnier climes. Yet, having tasted comparative success, it wasn't to be defeated and by the 1970s its fortunes were turning again.

As the grim reality of so many other geriatric waterside resorts was biting, Blackstable was bucking the trend – oddly by the decline of the very thing that had kept it alive. The port was being refitted for new enterprise – the main tarmacadam business moved elsewhere, the fishing fleet decimated by global trade treaties.

A new class of moneyed opportunist with a whim or a dream, boosted by a promised revolution of deregulation, were quick to claim what they saw as rightfully theirs. Despite the petty machinations of Tercanbury clerks (there remains no town council) hell-bent on establishing their fiefdoms in the brave new world of Blatcherite Britain – where the old middle class would be routed again and again into insensibility – Blackstable had kept enough odd charm through the years to be different. A charm that attracted a vanguard of people escaping. From what? Nobody was quite sure. Overpopulation in the great metropolis or cultural homophobia? To some, perhaps. From the imminent death of the old middle-classes? Most certainly, for like Monmouth's men they would be shown no quarter in the new world order of Laissez-Faire economics.

But there were other attractions to living in a small out-of-the-way town on a painfully slow train-line from Lunden. That it sat on the mouth of a river that fed into a much larger river held some sway. A tributary of a great estuary. It had a Dickensian romance that had somehow escaped the Dickensian squalor. People could pretend that they were in a quaint and unthreatening bubble, away from the harsh world beyond. Those escapees also liked to suppose it was sea they could see and no-one dared abash them for fear of offending the innocent incomers with much needed moolah. Truth be told, the sea proper, the official sea, the murderous sea created by the death of an entire country and who knows how many ancient peoples, wouldn't start for another seventeen miles further up the coast beyond Nimrod Bay. What these people had was the Swaill and beyond that, The Greater Tamesis Estuary.

Notwithstanding, the new locals used to like to pretend it was sea, lest they admit to themselves they had just moved a bit further up the same river than they had lived previously. Eventually, as the perfidious English are so practiced at doing, the lie became the truth and hungry hearts were sated.

But that is not the real story being told here. Nor is the story of the gently insidious *second* influx of rich interlopers from 'outside'. That wily group of punk-raised Lunden exiles that slowly and inexorably pushed the born-and-bred but admittedly under-employed locals further and further from *their* idyllic town into small pockets of resentful resistance, or for those that could not afford its increasing expense, who knows where and who cared? It was no longer their town. As with every other place in the sights of the post-modern university-classes (and those that aspired to emulate them), Blackstable had become a destination to be vaunted. It was no matter that these asset-rich apparatchiks lived within spitting distance of the increasingly aggrieved and disenfranchised poor. They were mere collateral damage in the great game of progressivism. No matter either that the main thoroughfare, Port Street, was 'Lundenderry-lite' on a Saturday night for many a year. No. That was just the dying of the light and would all pass as the proletariat moved on by their own volition. Assimilation would be their only other option. No. That is no story at all, merely a setting for the tale of new gods to come. (Is our preamble not the parable of all human history? Interlopers push out – or interbreed with – the resident population sending them into the oblivion of having 'once existed'? That is the way Homo Sapiens exploit and exist – in a constant state of narcissistic flux – looking for the next opportunity to prove themselves in an endless war against the guilt of knowing it is all quite meaningless to an indifferent Universe.)

The real story, the story that concerns *us*, begins one indolent January night when nothing much was happening at all. Not a soul stirred on the streets that were lit by the magnolia-enfiltered tones of the latest low energy LEDs (fully recyclable). Not even the urban foxes, once so proud to bathe in the harsh glare of sodium lamps, dared spoil the scene with their fritillaried scent. All was as it should be. Nice, neat and vaguely eccentric (in a cool, esoteric way). Which was the perfect time for Them to arrive. Of course, by the time the townspeople awoke to find They had arrived, nobody knew what or who They were except that They were very, very real with very real dangly bits and very real wobbly bits and all those oddly uncomfortable things good people are told to cover up with Dryrobes™. They were perfectly polite and the good peoples tried to accommodate, but truth be told, *They* were not Blackstable, *this* was not Blackstable. It would not do. The Police were called (out of concern, one understands) but they could do nothing because they could not see Them anywhere. Had They disappeared?

Most certainly not!

Discombobulated by the new arrivals and their apparent ability to be both seen and unseen, Blackstable's residents began to gather to discuss *Them*. At first in small cliques and gossip circles, then in larger groups. What to do? What could be done? Curtains were twitching, the children were imitating, old people embarrassed; worse still, people had begun to feel the fear so many of Blackstable's previous inhabitants had felt. It certainly wouldn't do.

A town meeting was demanded. A meeting was called. A meeting was arranged. It was to be held at the Bumbershoot Centre where a new town council would gather to listen to raised concerns. Posters were posted, leaflets distributed, emails sent, InstaTwatFace Groups set up. Tens, then hundreds, then thousands confirmed attendance. It'd have to be moved to a bigger venue. New posters were posted, new leaflets designed, emails sent, the InstaTwatFace groups just got on with it in their own toxic way. Weather permitting, the meeting would be held at 12pm (noon not midnight), on the date agreed, at the Saltpans Golf Course. All petitions would be received then.

The day, when it arrived, was fearfully cold, dank and dull. A north-east wind blew in straight off the water making the tips of anybody's fingers fool enough to leave the warmth of a pocket immediately hurt. Few turned up and the Bumbershoot Centre seemed like such a good idea to the only Tercanbury councillor who had braved the weather. It was not looking good as the forty or so complainants were joined by the merry band of Them.

There was an embarrassed silence as each party looked at the other. The wind blew harder.

'Bracing day!' opened one of Them in a most cheerful manner. The crowd looked comically perplexed.

A written sheet of paper was forced into the hand of the uncomfortably silent councillor. He stared at the words for a while, nodded and took a deep breath, held it for a good thirty seconds then noisily let it out. Taking another deep breath, he coughed to clear his throat, looked up, smiled at everyone, looked back to the first question and began.

'What do we call you?'

'I'm Geoff, this is Martha,' the apparent leader of Them said chirpily. He proceeded to point the others out. 'Ted, Graham, Lucy, Amanda, Alex, Alexa, Alexis, Alexandra, Alexindia, Xander, Xavier, Boat.' Geoff's smile broadened. 'We got fixed on the x for a while there.' The others waved a smile enthusiastically.

'Is there a problem?' the one called Geoff asked politely.

'We wondered...' The leader of the town meeting paused, looked to his notes, aware that the crowd was urging him forward. 'If you could put some clothes on?'

They looked to each other in that dumbfounded way that denotes pure unimagined astonishment and then at the gathering.

'Why?' they said in unison.

The council leader could feel his cheeks flushing red. He looked about for inspiration and spied a girl warming her hands. 'Are you not cold?'

Geoff stepped back slightly, his long dangly bits jangling comfortably between his legs. He looked to the others. 'No? Should we be?' They all nodded or shook their heads in total agreement.

Astonished, the councillor blurted out what to him was obvious to all. 'But you are naked!'

'Am I? How do you know?' Geoff was equally astonished at the assertion.

'Your…your…' The councillor was struggling. 'Your everythings are showing!' he jabbered, trying not to point lest he draw attention to them. Again They looked at each other and then at the heavily clothed crowd.

'No they're not,' Martha said, pointing and prodding at Their bits.

The town councillor stepped back befuddled. 'But…'

'Would you like me to show you my other bits?' Martha suggested with a mischievous expectancy.

Astounded at the possibility there may be other, bigger, even more dangly bits yet to see, the councillor held up his hand. 'No, no, no. We have seen enough! We just ask you…' What could he ask Them to do? Maybe the dangly bits and wobbly bits were cultural, or worse, racial. He couldn't dare, he wouldn't dare. He changed the subject as delicately as he could.

'Perhaps we could approach this differently… Do you… are you… gendered?'

'What is gender?' the one called Geoff asked innocently.

The councillor pondered the question, aware that children were in the crowd and mention of sex might cause issues elsewhere. 'Well, generally speaking, the differing physical attributes, in a binary process of a species' furtherment by way of offspring, create obvious differences in their characteristics, be they feminine or masculine or hermaphrodite...' He hoped he was still talking about sex but wasn't sure. He ploughed on, 'We use pronouns, He, She, Her, Him, They, Them... It...' He trailed off, suddenly embarrassed by the direction of the statement.

'Oh. We don't bother with all that. That's all a bit, well, you know, stereotypical. We are who we are.' Geoff shrugged.

'But your names. She's called Martha. He's called Graham,' said the poor man pointing.

Martha began to chuckle, the others joined her. 'Our names do not define us. We just like the sound of them. I don't suppose you know the meaning of your name means shit-for-brains in another language?'

Astounded, wounded, confused, the man struggled to find words. The crowd murmured a slightly hostile laugh. 'Does it?'

'How should I know? I don't believe you've said it? I'm sure the vowel sounds in another tongue refer to something entirely different. My point is, Who cares? We are who we are. Nobody else has the right to say otherwise.'

'Ah, okay. I see.' He looked down the list of questions, seeking one that wasn't about dangly bits. His eyes fixed on one and he looked up. 'May I ask. Are there more of you?'

'Oh, yes, yes. Many more. We are *The Many*. We, that is us,' Martha said pointing at the others, 'we are just the advance party. The scouting group. We'll report back soon. Your houses are so cheap and so near to the Divine, it's really too good an opportunity to miss!'

Suddenly aware what the statement meant for his beloved town, he grasped at straws trying to put off further incursions. 'Cheap?' the councillor rejoined. 'Cheap? Have you seen them? They cost far more than they're actually worth! The sea's going to flood them in a hundred years! Think of the rising damp!'

He heard a boo from the crowd. Then another. He'd gone

too far, said too much, misjudged the crowd's motivation. Something flew past his head. Suddenly reminded many people in the crowd prided themselves on their growing investments, he corrected himself. 'Of course, what I mean is, they are certainly not cheap! Reasonably priced for the right buyer...' The crowd settled.

'Your crypto-currencies are so easy to hack, eeeeverything is cheap!' Boat piped up before being hushed by the others.

'There's only one teeny tiny issue we can see,' Geoff offered, his over-large left hand raised as if holding a grain of rice between his fore-finger and thumb. The crowd hushed and leaned in, aware their whole world was about to change on this one small but not insignificant detail.

The councillor stepped forward as one would when gaining a confidence. 'Yes?'

There was a pause of immense gravity. The wind dropped, leaving the air crisp and chill.

'Can you stop eating our Gods please?'

A murmur spread through the crowd. What did he mean? Were they vegan zealots? Were they Hindu? Jainist? Would Blackstable suddenly be awash with holy cows traipsing and pooing everywhere they pleased with no regard for the school-run? It'd be hell! The crowd took the councillor quietly aside and consulted. Finally the conclave ended. The councillor returned to his original spot, the crowd close behind.

'Gods?' the councillor asked, unknowing the bear trap he had just quietly stepped into.

'I think...' began the obsequiously threatening reply, 'you call them Oysters?'

One Flew Over a Seagull Nest

by Oliver Whitefield

Note:

October 1908, Sir Bertram Gambill was reading an article that astonished him. The Director of the Daily Mail, Lord Northcliffe, announced he would offer a cash prize of £1,000 to any pilot fool enough who could achieve the first non-stop Channel crossing by aeroplane. Already, a few attempts had been made that failed miserably. Further in the same article, he discovered that a French aviator named Louis Bleriot was already in the starting block. He was not at all happy by the news as, at the same time, he was near completion of his biplane named 'Butterfly IV'. He also had eyes on the record and was praying for another incident from one of his adversaries.

That night, Sir Bertram Gambill couldn't sleep.

Of all the bad news he received recently, this was the worst. He couldn't face the idea that a foreigner, and French too, was on the verge of stealing his dream, his future, his holy grail. A few years back, he had used part of his inheritance to purchase a small bicycle firm based in Canterbury. He had big projects. He wanted to build aeroplanes. He first saw one of those heavy and clumsy creatures at Croydon Airfield two summers ago. He had a revelation.

His brother Procter was absolutely against it. The money left by their father was to be used to build a small three-cylinder automobile factory in Kent. They recently purchased a significant site in Maidstone, which used to be the main depot of The Kent & Medway Railway Company. As his brother said, the country needed automobiles and not motorized kites who fall into the ground at the first breeze. The logic was easy to understand. People wanted motorcars, the cost to produce them was low and profit was high.

He decided to prove them all wrong and aimed to re-establish himself back into local polite society after a couple of ill-advised investments. Against the opinion of the family accountant, he took his shares and rented a warehouse in Dover to house his new venture.

He had already established good contacts in the right place and was able to import, with the help of this father's agent in Germany, five 15 horsepower Benz engines, called aero engine 1, one of the most powerful at the time.

But what it gains in speed, it loses in consumption.

He also contacted a wood merchant who could supply top-quality oaks and poplars for the general frame and pilot basket. The fabric which covers the side-body and the wings came from London, and the piano cords, which give rigidity to the whole thing, came from Carters of Canterbury, a purveyor of the finest quality.

He learnt that Mr Bleriot had chosen the date of the 25th July for his endeavour. Sir Gambill himself decided for Tuesday the 20th. He hoped he would find the same optimal atmospheric conditions as last year. However, it was already at the beginning of March, and he still needed to start his testing program. He couldn't accept that what he was trying to do was a folly and required complete commitment in order to succeed.

Even his French counterpart knew too well that a hasty decision is often the open door to disaster. He took the time to assess each part in the development of his new Bleriot XI, the plan of which he started working on in 1907, taking the time to evaluate each piece. But no, our hero wanted to have his name in the history books and believed he had the perfect machine to do so.

The English Channel had been crossed many times by balloon, beginning with Jean-Pierre Blanchard and John Jeffries in 1785. But by aeroplane, it would be a world premiere. The candidates were many, but not all had natural abilities for success. Only a few had it, like Louis Bleriot.

The main obligation imposed by the race organizer was to take off at sunrise, which was not a big problem for him. He even had training in compass operating and visual navigation. The Royal Navy gracefully provided both. He wanted to put all the advantage on his side.

He was so confident that he didn't take seriously the warning of his chief mechanic concerning the size of the fuel tank. The poor man told him that carrying fifty litres of fuel was not enough, knowing the unpredictability of such a trip. He needed at least double the quantity to be safe.

Sir Gambill couldn't accept the subsequent weight increase created as it would destabilize the right size of the plane. No, he told him that his calculation would not change, and he was the only one who knew best.

He sent a telegram to the press to inform them that he would enter the Daily Mail competition to cross the English Channel and invited them on Sunday to explain all.

*

Understandably, the news came as a tsunami in Fleet Street. Journalists from all quarters came to Dover to discover for the first time the intrepid adventurer and his flying project.

Even if the day of departure was several months ahead, the multiple interviews given, and engagements from all quarters attended during this period, kept him away from Dover and his work for several months. He travelled to Wales, endured eight hours on the train from London to Scotland for just one invitation in Edinburgh, and even took the steamer from Liverpool to Belfast to be the guest of honour to the Lord

Mayor. All these events, although excellent for the ego, had a devastating effect on the project's advancement and our hero's commitment. And only two months separated him from the big day.

Aware of his more direct opponent, he sent one of his men to Calais to observe from a distance if Louis Bleriot's plans were on target. His envoy sent daily reports by telegram, and he was instructed to search the nearby countryside for a suitable landing ground. And what he discovered was that not only Bleriot was nearly ready but that he had even intensified components testing and had even spare time to recently compete in a forty-six kilometres race from Etampes to Orleans.

The latest message was interesting and gave him new hope. The day before, during a test flight, Bleriot badly injured his right foot, which made controlling a machine made of wood and canvas a near-impossible task, especially in a distance as long as 30 miles.

Sir Bertram was smiling. It was a sign from Mother Providence or Lady Luck. Whatever it was, he could waste no more time, and on the same day, took a direct train to Dover and spent the next month catching up on his schedule.

The Friday before the attempt, Sir Bertram gathered all his team around him and made a speech to motivate the men (and women) and to promise that success would be theirs.

Unfortunately, his audience was less enthusiastic than he was. They all knew something that our hero refused to see: the famous fuel tank problem. Nobody said a word about it, as debating the matter with the boss would be a fruitless endeavour.

He also wanted to complete a task which he had been postponing for years. It was something always at the back of his mind, like a strange little music. He invited his trusted family solicitor to Whitstable to discuss this pressing legal matter. He wanted to draft his will.

Weeks passed uneventfully and the weekend preceding his attempt, in recognition for their excellent work, he gave all his employees the whole weekend off. On the Saturday, with their families, they went to the seaside, all expenses paid by the boss.

Sir Bertram stayed at home to resolve the last few details.

On Sunday afternoon, he went on a long walk with his wife, Clara.

They were progressing gently along the coastal pathway, looking at the horizon. He didn't know why, but he needed to say sorry. Sorry for the long hours spent alone in their big manor. Sorry for his lack of patience and unwillingness to listen. Sorry to have missed so many school events. Sorry that his three children had little sympathy for him and were scared of his regular outbursts. The couple stopped near a small tree. She looked at him and, with a kiss, renewed her confidence in her husband.

She had met him when she was seventeen years old and contrary to her parent's' objections, agreed to marry him for better or worse. She would not let him down in this time of need. Sir Bertram was so troubled that he opened his heart to her for the first time in a long time. He told her that he was scared. All this external bravado, this so-called arrogance, they were for the press and the public. This success was so important to him, for his brother Procter, his family and the world. The afternoon was well advanced when they returned to the hotel near the airfield.

After a farewell to guests and family, he went to bed but couldn't sleep. He could see 'Butterfly IV' glistening in the moonlight through the bedroom window. It had on the right side the name of his dear wife '*Clara*' and on the left side, a large, coloured drawing of the gentle insect. He was proud of his aeroplane. As described by The Times newspaper: *'The endeavour of Sir Bertram Gambill is an embodiment of British industry and superiority, and his butterfly will fly high the flag of Britannia'.* He just hoped it was all true. He couldn't stop smiling. He felt confident in the future.

*

After a couple of hours of rest, it was time to prepare before the sun started to wake up.

The end of the night was fresh and calm. Forest birds and seagulls made a joyful sound around him.

The weather table printed daily in the Dover Chronicle newspaper indicated for Tuesday 20th July 1909 for the Southeast, clear blue sky with a gentle wind from the Northwest.

It was perfect for a ride above the English Channel.

He was fortunate that the wind was not strong enough to play the unwelcome guest. He put on his leather jacket and leather hat. He had his goggles in one hand and walked decidedly to his machine. His chief mechanic helped him to secure himself to the basket seat. Another member of the team was ready to turn the propeller. Not too far from their location, with a flag, a representative of the Royal Navy checked nervously his watch, waiting for the right moment. Departure was planned for 04.05 am exactly. Sir Bertram observed the official with attention, and then the flag was lowered in a fast movement.

Immediately the engine started in a colossal fume, and the aeroplane moved slowly from its location.

The pilot was waving goodbye to the spectators and family standing by the hotel's terrasse. He pushed the accelerator, and like an albatross, 'Butterfly IV' took off. He wished he had a more powerful engine.

Sir Bertram was ecstatic. The sensation of the morning cold air and the movement of his machine were intoxicating. But he needed to concentrate as he was in the most critical part of the flight. He remembered where he was supposed to land. His envoy did choose the spot well. It was a large grass field near Calais which, as per his written instructions and the help of a few hundred francs, had been prepared by a local farmer a couple of days previously. All he had to do was to keep the same direction on the compass and pray to the All Mighty. All around him was the sea, a dark blue expansion that seemed to know no land. After a while, he could see a couple of fishing boats returning to their port after a long night of work. He was not too high and could see men making gestures. Soon enough, he started to see the outline of the French coast on the horizon. He checked his compass and noticed he had been drifting at least five degrees.

No problem. He gently pushed the stick to the left, but at this exact moment, he heard the engine coughing, puffing, and then stopping. Immediately, he was stuck by the deep silence around him and the breath of the wind in his ears. Frozen by surprise, his brain was empty for a few seconds. Then, with all this strength, he tried to remember his emergency plan.

In fact, he didn't have an emergency plan. Now, it was him against the sea. At this moment, he realized the extent of his situation.

A quick look at the dashboard made things clear to him. No more fuel. It was entirely his fault, and he knew he had to face now the consequences, whatever they would be.

Fortunately for him, his aeroplane was solid and being a biplane, it would help him to descend in a controlled and smooth way. He scanned the water for ships nearby and saw on his right, at around a couple of miles away, what seemed to be a steamer travelling in the direction of France. Maybe it was the ferry that connected Calais to Dover five times a day.

With what remained of the altitude, he turned his machine to face the ship's bow. To attract their attention, he fired a round of red star flares. It had the effect of lighting the entire early morning sky in a dark orange tint.

After a few minutes, he went down engine first in the water. Although the speed was low, it had been sufficient to knock him out. He stayed unconscious on top of a dislocated wooden frame for a while. What was left of 'Butterfly IV' started its long journey to the bottom of the Channel. Drifting in and out from unconsciousness, he felt an intense pain from his left side. The only thing he could do was to keep out of the water as best as he could. He then heard a faint noise coming from the right. Noise of steam. Then, he fainted again.

*

Unknown to him, the 'Pride of Ramsgate' had already spotted him when Sir Bertram started to fall from the sky and was sailing as quickly as possible towards the spot of the crash. It was a lucky coincidence as the ship had left the Port of Dover very late due to a very unhappy bull. The creature didn't have sea legs and was not keen to enjoy the opportunity of a free trip. It was at the right spot, at the right time. The Second Officer ordered the pilot and his makeshift raft to be carried on deck. Sir Bertram was sent to the infirmary. The doctor was happy with his patient. He had only a few bruises and a broken leg. A fortunate man indeed. He arrived in Calais and was sent to the sailor's hospital in Sangate, and a telegram was sent to England to inform the authorities.

Sir Bertram had no idea how long he slept, but his first sight was his wife's blue eyes when he woke up. Clara was smiling. With her, his three children tried to attract their father's attention as best they could in a noisy but joyful way.

The sedative made him very tired but he was able to say a few words. His chief mechanic had also travelled to France. He was only too happy that his boss was alive after such an ordeal. The same week, his family paid for him and what was left of his machine to sail back to blighty.

He spent six weeks convalescing at his property in Kent under the constant care of Clara, the children, and the family doctor.

Then, the 25th July 1909 arrived.

Powerless, he was the indirect witness of the triumph of Louis Bleriot, who, after 30 minutes of a chaotic flight, landed on the downward slope of Northfall Meadow in Dover, breaking his undercarriage and coming to a rest in view of the castle, propeller and wheels snapped. He wanted so much to travel to Dover to see the achievement of his French colleague and adversary, but the doctor was clear. No excitement or cigars for the next six weeks.

*

It was not long before a crowd of local people were to join Bleriot at the landing site, close-marshalled by members of the Kent Constabulary. The epic had been achieved.

It is no more a dream. Goodbye small pioneers trying every possible way to elevate themselves into the sky, hello to the age of aviation and its captains of industry.

And it took just 30 minutes to cover the whole twenty-four-mile distance. Hours after his flight, Louis Bleriot travelled to London and left Victoria Station with Lord Northcliffe beside him. He was cheered by thousands of enthusiastic Londoners.

This triumph could have been Sir Bertram's. It was in his grasp and he knew it. Reminiscing on these last few weeks, he didn't make his mark in history books but realized that life taught him some precious lessons:

'Always consider others' opinions and always put yourself to the test to make sure that your way is the appropriate one.'

His recklessness could have cost him his life. He knew that very well and was so happy to still be able to breathe fresh air.

He was amused by a title of the Daily Chronicles written by the pioneer Alan Cobham about Bleriot performance: *'Britain must seek another form of defence besides ships.'*

Another from the Daily Mail: *'Great Britain is no longer an island.'*

*

Six years later, an event which would change the face of the world forever started on the 24th July 1914. The First World War.

Strangers

by Richard White

After loving I lay in his arms, keeping the silence that held us together, and waiting unwillingly for him to speak, which invariably he was the first to do. I hoped it would not be soon; these were rare moments, as he stroked my skin, telling me as always how perfect it was. This was the best of him, the closest of us.

Perfection has been my art of life since childhood, with a father so scrupulous that my mother ran away with a second-hand car salesman. I stayed with Dad of course, in Whitstable, messy as it was. We understood each other, if not always the world, and we both knew what was a nice neat house, as ours definitely was, and neither of us could stand things not put away. I wouldn't go to my school-friends' houses, which were far too messy. I thought there was nobody like my dad until he took me to the golf club and I met Savernake. He was different to the untidy men at the office. That first time I picked a hair off his collar, and he thanked me, apologizing. Savernake had standards. I know how to keep a nice house but it helps having a man to notice.

It took seven years to finish the house on Island Wall, his really but Sav insisted it was *ours*; the neighbours granted in the end that it was perfect. Over the years Sav had turned me into a goddess, writing me poems about my perfection. His eyes worshipped me even as I came out of the loo. His hands on me were a benediction, lifting me, always carefully, to our flawless heaven.

Until November the third, a quiet Sunday morning, when suddenly his hands stopped and stiffened. He clawed at something on my leg. I must have grunted because he reacted.
- What's this?
- Don't know, doesn't matter, can't you …
- It does. It's a lump or something.
- It's nothing. A spot I think.
- You never had it before, you were perfect …

And so the silence ended. My perfection was the thing he was proudest of in me. I did my best to maintain it, expensively but willingly, but I knew I could trust my own body. I would never let age spoil it, but today a crack had appeared between us, and when he wasn't looking at me, I slipped away to examine myself, and found a tiny grey-brown pimple, which I dabbed with peroxide. It made the gentlest movement beneath my skin, which I thought was an illusion. And the next day it was still there, but apparently not in the same place.

That night he found it again, before even going to bed. He said it was bigger. I knew it had moved.

It grew over the next few days and seemed unsure where it wanted to be. Sav started to panic. This thing was tiny but it grew into something massive between us. Of course we went to the doctor, who gave me a tube of something, and Sav came back with three more tubes from the chemist. There was a lot of wiping and rubbing and dabbing but there was no further change in size or appearance. Sav started to talk about it at breakfast,
- Did the pink stuff make any difference?
- Not really. Are you doing scrambled eggs?
- No I'm not! Your leg: I think we should be trying something stronger.
- Look Sav, this is *my* body. It's only a spot and…
- I have to look at it every day.
- No you don't. Can you see it now?

- I know it's there. It spoils your looks.
- Nobody has seen it but you, Sav.
- Well you are my most important consideration. You matter to me!
- Me or the spot?
- We don't know if it's the first symptom of something ... well, maybe terminal.
- It's a spot, Sav. I'll do scrambled eggs.

I wanted to forget about it, not that I had accepted this little spot; it was prising us apart. Our perfect life teetered. We went to a faith healer his mother knew, then to a skin specialist, then to a beauty parlour – anything we could think of. It wandered around my left thigh, easily escaping all the medication applied. My referral to the school of tropical medicine started a long succession of appointments, too slow for the advancement of the spot.

We lived together for almost a year, the three of us, him, me and the stranger. During all that time it never grew enough for me to be sure it was actually bigger, but its presence became the biggest thing in our lives. There was nothing more insistent or more disturbing to him. It haunted us on every intimate occasion, and on public ones too. It became the sour aftertaste of every argument. I insisted that it was me he should be concerned about, not a wandering spot. His obsession with my imperfection was unbearable. We didn't survive this incident, of course. He turned away from me in bed; I said if he could not ignore a tiny spot then clearly I was not the partner for him.

We had not spoken to each other for a week when I took over the tiny room that had housed our collection of netsuke. Sav was soon replaced by the spot in my intimate life. I would sometimes lie for an hour or more on a sunny afternoon and gently push the spot and it would nudge my finger and sometimes wandered around my finger-tip to settle where it had been before. I was soon at peace with the spot, and came to quite like it. Still a stranger, it was part of me and we developed a slightly guilty but very private relationship, the sort I had with myself when I was first discovering my own eroticism. By September, after a series of consultations with specialists in parasitic medicine, Sav had found a skin specialist who was prepared to cut it out with a scalpel, but I had not liked the hungry look in his eye and had refused to keep the appointment. The spot remained our subtext.

- You said you wanted tea but you haven't drunk it.
- I said I didn't want it. You don't listen!

There was a silence more in shock than in anger. I knew we were at an impasse. I made the decision.

- I think we should spend some time on our own – a break from each other.
- You mean for a week or so?
- Well, maybe longer.
- But the skin specialist…?
- I can go on my own.
- But you won't, will you?
- Listen Sav, I want a little time away from…
- So that's what we have come to? It's me that you're really worried about?
- It's not you. It's *the stranger … and you*! You give me no peace, Sav.
- Huh! So I'm as bad as the stranger?
- I didn't say that.
- But it's what you meant!
- Please Sav!

Another silence, disturbed by him.

- Alright, I will have a cup of tea. But not that Lapsang piss of yours!

Our last words for seven months. I finally gave him my two netsukes so that the other seventeen of his would not be lonely. In a conservatory belonging to Libby, least untidy of my friends, too hot in the summer and nearly impossible to sleep in even with an eye mask, I was left alone with my *stranger*. I started to talk to it. It became first a he, then rather old and grumpy, and finally it got a name. It had to be Nick. He seemed to respond to his name, and wiggled about to answer. He tickled, but not unpleasantly, and while he had often moved considerable distances around my leg, once I told him to keep still he complied. It was quite nice having someone to talk to who was not obsessed with my appearance and who never nagged me. Among the girls at work, who had never seen him, Nick became my new boyfriend. I told them he worked as a talent spotter. They didn't laugh.

Then my boss Angela suggested we all go out together for dinner, with our partners of course. I told them Nick was busy. I was seated opposite a gorgeous man named Nathaniel, rather an old-fashioned name I thought but he was attentive and funny, there was something clean and nice about him, and he said my skin was beautiful. We had already exchanged numbers when I noticed. Nobody else did. It was obvious from the way he kept wriggling his left shoulder and touching his forearm with his right hand. So when he took off his jacket for the heat, it was not even a surprise.

– Oh! What's yours called?
– You mean my...?

I nodded, my eyes pointing to his arm. I had to come round to his side of the table to show him my leg. He laughed.

– Mine's called Ethel.
– An old-fashioned name.
– She's a bit like me – only partially modernised.
– Do you think they'd get on?
– I felt mine jump.
– Mine too.

It was a new life from that night, if not really a relationship. He was good looking and had a fabulous collection of antique flint-lock guns, but he was too involved with his spot to pay much attention to me; but my own spot was always consoling. Within a week our spots had moved us in together. I knew Nick was happy, he had a way of squirming softly when I touched him. We sat and gazed at each other's little friends,

me and Nathaniel, and we could not resist comparisons.
- Does Ethel like curry?
- Hates it. She goes all wiggly and coarse. Gives me an itch.
- Nick has a sweet tooth. I now have to give him two sugars in tea, or he gives me a jab.
- You mean he scratches you?
- Well, it's more a tiny tingle. But he's very accepting otherwise.
- Would he like a drink now?
- Ooh yes, have you got Campari soda? More soda, please! Too strong for Nick.

Then Nathaniel introduced me to other sufferers and from then on I never held anything against Nick; spots were an inexhaustible subject, from colour and movement to their reactions to other people who hated them.
- Jealousy, of course.
- They don't know how sweet and gentle a spot can be.
- You either love 'em or you hate 'em.
- D'you think they have feelings?
- Mine certainly does. Emotions too!
- Have you heard about that book?
- You mean 'Spotted' by the woman from Nepenthe in California?
- I couldn't take the stuff about reaching term over years and being born in your liver.
- Like Alien, you mean? Pimples from space? Nah, rubbish!
- You don't have to believe everything you read!
- Well I believed most of it; until the bit about an intelligent parasite.
- She thinks we are the privileged ones, carrying and giving birth to tiny colonisers.
- Ridiculous!
- Well, you must admit, they are intelligent.

And then we all lived in a commune in the Stray Marsh, south of Minster on Sheppey. Nobody came near us. The few locals were all terrified. They thought we were infectious. In May a reporter came down from London. Nathaniel was ready to see her off with an eighteenth-century musket, but fortunately some of the others managed to persuade the reporter that she had the wrong commune and the one she was looking for was a long way off in the other Minster Marshes, near Pegwell Bay.

It was only a matter of time of course, they were closing in. The commune members were defensive and belligerent and we had become like an obscure religious cult. Some of them had started holding weird rituals and they were even said to be worshipping some celestial entity sending creatures down to earth to save humanity. Activities like these had pushed me to the outside of the community. I had originally felt a sense of belonging. We all had. But some part of my head was reminding me that we were probably doomed.

Every week I felt a little more estranged from these people. I carried the same mark, making me one of an elite species, and I was welcomed by all of them, but I felt different. I could see them all as if I were an outsider. Now I could not leave; we were seen as unclean and some kind of a menace. There had been announcements in the news about us, accompanied by warnings to people to keep a distance. If I left the camp, I was at risk from anybody who recognised me.

The most distressing aspect for me was that I no longer had the simple and close relationship crowned by adoration that I knew before. A man had worshipped me and now he would not pick up the phone. Finally I was the stranger. Other commune members were like mothers with new babies. When I joined I had no intention of staying but now I felt under siege. We lived in a ragged collection of old caravans and huts, some members even surviving the winter in small tents. I made the best of it but I could not make it meet my own standards. I looked out over shining marshes. Nothing moved but sheep.

I listened to what others said, having to square it with my

own common sense. People here who had seemed sensible were now shockingly altered. Even their eyes showed signs of paranoia. Suspicion, originally maintained only for people from '*beyond*', now began to focus on their own members. I no longer felt safe even in another spot lover's company.

My greatest loss was intimacy. My life had been a long intimate honeymoon. Now I was cursed by everyday habits and necessities: water came from two taps sprouting from the ground in what was once a camp site, and one of them had been shut off by a neighbouring farmer who claimed we were illegal, and it was four miles to the nearest shop. At first I liked the candles, oil lamps, camping gas stoves and evening fires. I had sung and told stories with the rest. Now my thoughts strayed into escape routes.

Then the bubble burst.

The moment was just after the second of the police raids. There was widespread suspicion of our camp, and the first may have been a mistake, because people from the surrounding area, knowing little of what *the spots* were, thought of us as some kind of gypsies, and not being able to chase us off the land, tended to blame us for every kind of crime or deception they had heard of.

On the second raid two men were arrested, one of them Nathaniel. Although he was the first spot host I had met and I thought of him as a kindred spirit, he was also the most aggressive defender of the territory, and his exploits were the ones that first brought public attention to us. He had seemed personable, but his temper and violence against outsiders alienated me from the whole group. When the police car took the two away, there remained a group of policemen interviewing our members. One of them, obviously senior, came to chat.

- Better move along there, luv, you don't wanna get involved with these people.
- I am involved.
- What you? You got one of those spots, then?

It must have looked like the start of a striptease as I raised my skirt. His eyes, already wide, seemed to protrude from his face. He soon became uneasy and seemed to wonder if he'd catch something.
- I see ... well it's only little.
- They are all about this size.
- You didn't look like one of those ... people. Had it long?
- Over a year.
- Why don't you get rid of it then?
- I've tried. It's hard to catch.
- If you want I can send someone who can do it for you. Got any money?
- £50 cover it?
- Well it might. Have to ask me brother. His name's Gregory. Give me your number.

I got a text the next day, **BE OUTSIDE YOUR GATE THURSDAY 8 AM. HAVE CASH READY. £50. GREGORY.** And he was. I woke up when I heard my name shouted. I knew he wouldn't come in. He had a doctor's bag. I showed him my left leg, he looked at it warily, wiped the area with something cold, then knelt down and I felt a sharp scratch.
- Has it gone?
- It won't trouble you anymore.

He stood up and handed me a card as he took the money, then said 'OK now,' and turned to leave. The card said Gregory Grindley, Veterinary Surgeon.

The next day the swelling started to rise. The day after it was a roaring red lump. I went to Sheerness to the doctor's surgery.
- Where did you get this?
- Sheep tick.
- Are you sure?
- What else could it be?

The doctor's eyebrows rose, he looked at me with a worried expression, then gave me the antibiotic scrip. In three days it had gone down, but the spot remained, perhaps a little smaller. I spent a long time looking at it, because while it was still there, something was different about it. That night, when I fell back on my habit of nudging the little monster around, I realised what it was.

The spot was dead. I felt a bit sad. We had been together a long time. It had become a friend.

Things changed rapidly after that. First the spot dwindled, then one day only a tiny scar remained. I started to wonder whether I could get in touch with Sav again. I decided no, but then I knew that there was nothing keeping me in the commune any more; in fact, if they knew that I had killed my spot, I'd probably be lynched.

I got out just before the big police raid, the third one, following an all-night ritual in the camp, with fires and whooping dancers. It looked a bit like a Ku Klux Klan ceremony. That was too much for me. It was also the best moment to escape.

I never saw anyone from the commune again, nor did I see Sav. I didn't want to, but I have never thrived on my own; being imperfect was hard, but it's so much nicer not having to be perfect. Nobody has ever noticed my tiny scar, nor ever asked me about *strangers*.

I met a man in Sittingbourne just after I found my way off Sheppey Island. He was my sort of man, even if I don't have a very good record in judgement. He didn't seem to have any spots; I know the symptoms pretty well. He stood there and looked at me, and I could see it in his eyes: *perfection*!

He was there to collect his vintage Sunbeam from an expensive bodywork specialist. He drove me to Whitstable in it, before even asking me where I lived. On the way he talked about the spot business that had been on the local news. I said I knew nothing about it. So where could he drop me?

- I don't live in Whitstable.
- Oh! I thought everyone did.
- I used to live on Sheppey.
- God, I wish you'd said. That's a long way now.

— But I don't live there anymore.
— I've got a big house on Island Wall. Plenty of room if you fancy it.
— Well I don't!
— So where are you going to go? It's pretty late.
— That's my business.

He looked alarmed. I know that look, people recognise a stranger. I gave him a thankyou and goodnight, and headed off down Oxford Street. I turned after a hundred yards and he was still looking at me. Island Wall was a great temptation, but perfection can be dangerous, and I have never found anybody who understands my need for silence. But I have a friend who keeps a nice house in Swalecliffe.

Also I have a slight tickle on my left forearm. It's probably nothing but I think I just felt it move.

The Lady in the Lane

by Aliy Fowler

I was fourteen and a half, and Tom sixteen, when our parents moved us from the bright lights of Whitstable (I say this tongue in cheek) to a smallholding on Graveney Marshes. Our new home was a low-slung cottage, a few hundred years old – timber-framed and rough-plastered, with a roof of cratered Kent peg tiles, and inadequate wooden casements that admitted little light, even on the sunniest of days. It was a house built for winter. When the wind howled and the rain battered the grimed-glass panes, there was nowhere better to hunker down, thick velvet curtains pulled against the draughts and a fire roaring in the grate.

We lived on a dead-end lane, surrounded by scrubby grassland. The nearest village, if you could call it that, was a 25-minute walk away. It had a small post office-cum-convenience store, which never seemed to be open when we needed something, and a pub which served passable scampi and chicken in a basket and would provide part-time employment for Tom. Our closest neighbours were farmers. They kept sheep and chickens – and largely to themselves.

As an introverted, bookish child, I didn't mind the isolation, but Tom abhorred it, resolving from day one to have his driving licence as soon as he was legal. In his free time, if he wasn't playing Space Invaders on his beloved Atari, he would be in Father's second-hand Land Rover in the field behind the house, practising high-speed reversing, handbrake turns, and other skills far beyond those required in a standard driving test. It was no surprise when he passed the week after his seventeenth birthday. From that day on, whenever there was an errand to be run involving a trip out in the beleaguered Landie, Tom would volunteer.

One fateful evening in the run-up to Christmas, we ran out of eggs. Mother needed them for supper and had nothing else in, so it fell to Tom to drive to the neighbouring farm for supplies.

'Come with me for the ride, Jen,' he said.

But I didn't like those narrow, twisting lanes, when the sky was December-dark and every blind corner threatened a brush with an escaped sheep or a mud-splattered tractor, its headlamps casting less light than a tallow candle.

Tom had been gone for forty-five minutes before it occurred to us to worry, and at an hour Mother said we should ring the Andersons to find out if he was still with them, or at least what time he had left. But as Father stood to make his way to the telephone, in the tiny, dank room that passed for his office, we heard the Land Rover crawl into the yard.

Mother hurried to open the back door and it was clear that only a single beam emanated from the front of the vehicle's chassis. We watched Tom clamber from the cab and limp across the concrete towards us. As he drew near, we could see that the lower half of his face was covered in blood.

Mother was mute.

'Jesus, Tom!' I said, looking first at his ghoulish countenance and then beyond him to the poor Landie, whose left wing was scraped and crumpled.

'Tom?' Father was right behind me, his tone more stern than concerned.

'I'm okay. I hit – hit a tree in the bank, d – down near the end of Sandbanks Lane.' He shivered. 'The eggs didn't make it.'

'Darling, never mind the blasted eggs,' said Mother, finding her voice. 'Are you hurt?'

He wiped a finger over his upper lip and held it out to examine the blood that still trickled from his nostrils. 'I think I bashed my face on the steering wheel.'

'What happened?' said Father. He still exuded more suspicion than sympathy to my mind but, knowing my brother, this was not unreasonable.

Tom pushed his way past us into the kitchen and took a chair at the table, flinching as he sat.

'There was a woman in the lane,' he said. 'I wasn't speeding, she was just there – totally out of the blue. I have no idea where she came from, I swear. I had to swerve and the front tyre went up the bank. I thought the Landie was going to flip.' He let out a shuddering breath.

Father stood opposite him, leaning in, both hands on the table. 'You didn't hit her?'

'No. God, no. But…'

'But what?'

'She disappeared. I mean literally disappeared. I got out to make sure she was alright and she wasn't there. Not on the road, not on the banks. There were no gateways. There was nowhere she could have gone. Shit.' He was blinking rapidly. 'I even looked underneath – but she'd vanished.'

Father lifted a single eyebrow. 'She can't have simply vanished.'

'I know, but she did.'

'You'll have to pay for the damage to the Land Rover.'

Tom winced. 'Isn't it insured?'

'There's a hefty excess on the policy,' said Father. 'And I'll need to hire something while it's out of action. You can pay me back in instalments.'

I watched my brother's face fall. He was counting on saving every penny he earned from his part-time job in the pub. He was so desperate to get himself a car – nothing fancy, an old banger, something that meant he wasn't reliant on parental lifts or the sporadic village bus service when he needed to escape the parochialism of our marshland hideaway. That dream was as crushed now as the Defender's left wing.

*

The man who owned the local garage owed us a favour, which meant Father had his precious vehicle back within the week. Since it suited him to have Tom run errands when not at school or clearing glasses in the Four Horseshoes, he was soon allowed behind the wheel again – subject to stringent conditions regarding his speed.

And so it was that in the week leading up to Christmas, we found ourselves waiting, once more, for Tom to return from whatever evening mission he had been tasked with. He wasn't particularly late – just enough to put Mother on edge after the recent incident. She was chopping vegetables on the kitchen table and was so obviously not concentrating, I was sure she was set to lose a fingertip.

I was about to offer my help, when the Land Rover rumbled into the yard, the full complement of headlights blazing through the kitchen window as the vehicle was reversed into the lean-to opposite. And then we waited. It was a while before we heard the cab door slam, and Tom seemed to take twice as long as usual to cross to the house. I saw Father shoot Mother a what's-he-done-now look and caught her sigh before she turned back to her dicing.

Tom walked into the kitchen and placed his rucksack on the table. No blood. No flinching.

'There you go,' he said. His voice was flat and his fists clenched. I was sure his lips were quivering too. He made to leave the room, but Mother caught him by the arm as he passed.

'What's wrong, Tom?'

He shook his head, lowering his gaze to avoid eye contact.

'Tom?'

'I saw her again.'

'Who? Who did you see?'

'The woman.' He pressed his lips together, so tightly they lost all colour.

'Sit down, lad,' said Father, releasing him from Mother's grip and coaxing him onto a chair. 'Take your time.'

Tom leant over and rubbed at his thighs. 'It was at the bottom of Sandbanks Lane, like last time – near those cottages by the creek. She appeared in the road, right in front of me. I swear she came from nowhere.'

Mother was sitting beside him now. She clasped his balled hand in hers.

'Are you sure it was the same woman?'

Tom nodded. 'Yes, she was all in grey, the same as before, with long, straggly hair – blond or white – it was hard to tell in the dark. And she seemed to move without moving. I can't describe it properly.'

Father, who could see Tom was shaken, did something I rarely saw him do. He walked to the dresser at the far end of the room and took out a whisky tumbler and his precious bottle of Islay Malt. He poured a generous measure and placed the glass in front of my brother. Tom peered at it, making no attempt to pick it up.

'Go on,' said Father.

Tom allowed himself a reluctant sip, then knocked it back.

'She came to say sorry,' he said. 'I know it sounds crazy, but she did. She held out her arms to me, just staring. Then she crossed them over her chest. She looked so – I don't know – remorseful, I suppose. I could see her lips moving. She wasn't making any sound, but I know she was saying *Sorry*. And then, like before, she just wasn't there.'

He sniffed, and I honestly thought my big brother was going to cry. I wondered how I would react if I'd seen what he had. The thought that he'd encountered something otherworldly – something supernatural – was both enchanting and chilling. I determined there and then never to be alone on Sandbanks Lane at night.

'I owe you an apology too,' said Father. 'I was wrong to doubt you. I can see how much this has upset you.' He tilted his head and smiled. 'You needn't worry about the rest of the money.'

Tom's brow furrowed. 'I'll help, Dad. Honestly.'

'No, I won't hear of it.'

Father put a hand on Tom's shoulder and Mother breathed a sigh of relief, then took up her vegetable knife again.

*

I dined out on Tom's story for years afterwards. He didn't like to talk about it, but I had no such qualms. My brother had experienced a ghost. An actual ghost. A bona fide highway haunting. Other stories of strange occurrences on Sandbanks Lane emerged after Tom's sighting – mysterious incandescence, ethereal forms and disembodied shadows – but nothing a sceptic couldn't explain away. Usually, the observer had enjoyed a little too much of the hard stuff or had simply seen headlights, veiled in fog, flickering between tree trunks on the winding road. One blustery evening a boyfriend, on his way to collect me, was adamant he'd seen Tom's lady near the railway bridge at the near end of the lane, but when we drove that way twenty minutes later, the phantom turned out to be a polythene feed-sack, pinned by the squall against a gnarled old birch and shimmering in the moonlight.

The sightings all added to the romance of our isolated part of Kent and I cherished our time there. Tom never really warmed to it, and after university, he escaped to London and a high-flying job in finance. He met his wife-to-be, Sarah, and together they bought a flat in a large Georgian house in Camden. It had high ceilings and period mouldings, and sash windows through which the wind whistled when it blew in the wrong direction.

The night of my first visit to their new abode was a wild one, with frequent, booming thunderclaps and heavy rain, and a howling gale that forced its way through the many invisible gaps in the glazing. Sarah had filled the dining room with candles, whose flames flickered wraith-like in response to the draughts. Halfway through our meal, a particularly violent gust extinguished an arrangement of tapers on a console by the window.

'Sorry,' she said, mock-grimacing. 'I was going for a cosy atmosphere, but I seem to have achieved borderline sinister.'

I laughed. 'It's nothing compared to a stormy night on Graveney Marshes.'

Sarah paused for a moment then asked, 'Have you ever seen a ghost?'

'No,' I said, 'But Tom has, of course.'

'Really?'

I was surprised he'd never told her. 'Yes, when he was seventeen – not far from where we lived.'

Tom shook his head.

'Oh Jen'_– he took a greedy mouthful of Bordeaux – 'there was no ghost. That was just a ruse to get Dad off my back.'

I stared at him, open-mouthed.

'But – but – your description of how she reappeared to you – to say *Sorry* . . .'

'All part of the fiction, Sis. Dad was going to take all my pub earnings to cover the cost of me dinging the Landie. I'd never have been able to afford my own car. The first spectral appearance didn't cut it, so I had to come up with something else.' He shot me a grovelling smile. 'I couldn't come clean with you in case you let it slip.'

'Tom!' I frowned, kicking him hard under the table. 'I could never use Sandbanks Lane on my own after dark. All those bloody years I've avoided it!'

He refilled my glass and winked.

'All those years you've had a great story to tell!'

Stranded

by Lin White

It all started for Daniel with a visit to the Seaside Museum in the October half term holiday. He had been in town with his mum one day when it started to rain heavily, and they took shelter in the little museum in William Street, Herne Bay. It proved to be bigger than they'd expected, and in the end they spent over an hour wandering around, looking at the display of memorabilia from the town's past. Mum liked the photographs in the exhibition room, but Daniel found himself drawn to the fossil area, gazing with interest at the various exhibits on display, including a huge pair of mammoth tusks found off the coast one particularly low tide. He even stopped in at the children's area and spent a few minutes combing through the tray of pebbles and sand to find the sharks' teeth hidden there.

As they walked back through the shop on their way out, Daniel gazed longingly at the sharks' teeth on sale. Mum shook her head. 'You could just as easily find your own,' she said.

'How? Where?' The idea of finding sharks' teeth appealed to him. And maybe he'd find a fossil or two. He thought of the mammoth tusks and shook his head. That had to be a once in a lifetime find. Or did it?

'Off the coast of Reculver. You need to go at low tide, but there's all sorts of bits to be found there.'

And so next day, which thankfully dawned dry and bright,

Daniel carefully locked his bike to the rack outside the coffee shop at Reculver and made his way down to the shore, his bag slung over his shoulder. He had checked the tide times and knew he would have a good couple of hours of good searching time. He walked out, his boots squelching in the soft mud, and started to study the ground beneath him, looking for the teeth and other things his research had told him he might find.

*

For Callum, it started with being stranded at his grandparents' caravan at Reculver for the week – a dead-end place in the middle of nowhere with nothing to do and nowhere to go. And now Grandma was feeling ill so they couldn't even go to the wildlife park as he'd been promised. Yesterday had rained heavily all day, so he hadn't even been able to leave the caravan, and it was so cramped there was no space for anything fun. They didn't have any games consoles, the battery for his Switch was flat, the games on his phone were boring and all Grandad could suggest was a game of cards.

'Why don't you take Snowy for a walk?' asked Grandma in the end. 'He could do with some exercise. But not too long, it's supposed to rain later.'

Callum scowled. The dog was a horrible, yappy little beast that was always under his feet. But at least it would give him something to do. Reluctantly he clipped on the dog's lead and accepted the roll of dog bags Grandad forced on him. As though he was going to pick that disgusting stuff up!

In a hurry to get out into the late autumn sun, he forgot to pick up his phone, but had almost reached the towers before he realised, and couldn't be bothered to go back for it. He didn't need it anyway – all his friends were busy and there was no one else to call. He kept going, his anger driving him forward.

The towers were about ten minutes away from Grandma and Grandad's place, and he walked across the grass and stopped to stare up at them. They formed an imposing sight, two rectangular towers standing on the edge of the cliff at one end of a ruined building that a notice board informed him had once been a church.

'Hey!'

He looked back to the path and saw an elderly woman gesturing to him. 'Your dog just messed. Better clean it up!' Her dog, a spaniel, stared at him from his position at her feet.

He looked down at Snowy, who cocked his head on one side innocently. Behind him sat a steaming pile of dog crap. 'You're a damn nuisance,' he muttered. Maybe he could pretend he hadn't heard or seen.

'Isn't that Snowy? You must be Eleanor's grandson. I thought you'd be more responsible than that.' The old woman's voice was strident and carried clearly. Shit, what if she told Grandma?

A man and a woman who had been wandering around the ruins hand in hand stopped to stare at him. Swearing under his breath, he fished in his jacket pocket for the dog bags.

'Go on, lad, you've been told,' the man said. 'You kids are all the same these days. Disgusting! Shouldn't have a dog if you can't clear up after it.'

The roll of bags was jammed in his pocket, and he struggled to free it. Snowy decided he wanted to move on, and started pulling at the lead, almost knocking him off balance.

The man and woman were walking towards him. 'Better clear it up, lad,' the woman said.

'I'm trying to!' he snapped back. 'Don't need to keep on.'

The woman gave a small scream. 'It's trying to attack me!' she said, as Snowy jumped up to greet her. She pushed the dog's muddy paws off her elegant trousers and rubbed at the stain left.

'Keep your bloody dog under control,' the man said. 'Or I'll report you to the police. Are you even old enough to be out on your own with a dog?'

By the time Callum had managed to scoop the disgusting mess into a bag, his temper was boiling. He stomped off to the nearby dog bin, dragging a reluctant Snowy after him, and thought rebelliously about taking the dog back, but he couldn't bear the thought of being stuck indoors again. It was all his parents' fault – why couldn't he have stayed home? Then he would be able to hang out with his friends instead being stuck here.

The woman with the spaniel was walking further along the path towards Minnis Bay, so instead he headed to the other side of the towers, past the coffee shop.

On the eastern side of the towers, towards Minnis Bay and Margate, the sea wall was just a step or two above the gentle shingle slope down to the sea, but this side the cliff rose up beyond the coffee shop, leaving a long drop to the ground. At high tide the sea would come right up to the bottom of the sandy cliffs, but right now the tide was partway out, leaving a large, flat area and an inviting pebbly beach and rock pools to explore.

Partway along the path, there was a gap that led down to the beach. The way down was narrow and uneven, and Snowy kept trying to pull him off balance, so in the end he unclipped the lead. The dog sped away, delighted to be free, and Callum finished climbing down to the beach in peace.

The area was peaceful, apart from the faint swoosh of the water in the distance. No one else was around apart from a solitary figure bent over the ground near the water's edge. The ground was uneven, a mixture of sand and pebbles with rockpools scattered around. Callum picked up a stone and threw it as hard as he could. It made a satisfying splash in one of the pools, and he threw another and another. Snowy ran from him to the sea's edge and back again, barking excitedly, and Callum began to calm down a bit as they progressed along parallel to the cliffs.

Then he heard shouting. 'Hey, get away, you thief!'

Looking over, he saw the distant figure waving his arms and shouting, while Snowy jumped and barked. He called the dog, but he took no notice.

'Get your dog away from me, he's trying to steal my food!'

The boy was about the same age as Callum, and had a

backpack slung across one shoulder. A bucket stood next to him, and he had a small plastic spade in one hand.

'Aren't you too old to be building sandcastles?' Callum taunted as he approached.

'I'm not building sandcastles, I'm looking for sharks' teeth and fossils.'

Callum's mood was too dark to be interested. He laughed scornfully. 'What a waste of time.'

'I'm not asking you to do it,' the boy retorted. 'Just to keep your dog under control.'

'He's not doing any harm,' Callum said. 'Stop being mean to him.'

The boy shook his head and turned away, taking a few steps along the beach and then crouching down again to look closely at something on the ground.

Snowy barked and jumped, and the boy toppled sideways into the edge of a rock pool. Snowy pounced on him with delight and the boy shouted and shoved at him, struggling to get back to his feet. 'Keep your dog away, I said!'

Callum swallowed down the feeling of guilt. It wasn't his fault the dog was stupid and didn't do as it was told. And anyone who came out to the beach like this was asking to get wet. 'It's not my dog. And serves you right for being such a weirdo. I hope you're soaked.'

The boy swore, and Callum laughed awkwardly and turned away. Striding furiously along the beach, he hoped that Snowy would follow him. And if he didn't – well, it wasn't his stupid dog anyway. It was Grandma's fault for being ill, she should have been walking the stupid mutt herself.

He passed an outcrop, out of sight of the boy, and was grateful when the dog caught up to him. Guilt washed over him; Grandma would have been terribly upset if he had gone missing.

The two encounters had put him off balance; he knew deep down that he was in the wrong, but didn't know how to handle it. Instead he kept walking, losing track of time. Snowy ran on ahead, along the bottom of the cliffs, and Callum followed, still fuming at his encounters and generally in a foul mood.

They rounded another part of the headland, and ahead of him a rocky outcrop promised interesting findings. He made his way across, but slipped and his ankle twisted underneath him. Swearing, he sat on the rock, promising himself that it would be better in a moment.

To make his ordeal even worse, the sky had darkened dramatically in the last few minutes and now he felt the first of the heavy raindrops. He tried to stand, but his ankle was agony every time he tried to put weight on it.

He heard barking, and looked up to see Snowy appear around the headland. To his horror, the sea was coming in quickly and was starting to surround the rocks he stood on. The strip of land between the cliff and the edge of the waves was no more than a few metres. Even as he watched, the next wave reached closer to the edge of the cliff before receding. The wind was getting up now, and he could feel spray from the waves in the air.

He was injured, he was about to be cut off by the tide and he didn't even have his phone on him.

Truly frightened now, he began to yell for help.

*

Daniel had been retreating closer and closer to the cliffs, and now he gave a glance over to the incoming tide. It was time to end his fossil hunting trip and head home out of the rain that was starting to fall. He had made some good discoveries – several sharks' teeth and a couple of other fossils. Maybe tomorrow he would take them to the museum and see if they could help him identify them. It had been a peaceful morning, apart from that kid with the dog who had pestered him. Thanks to them, his clothes were soaked and filthy and the papers in his bag had got damp. He was grateful he had left his phone at home; Mum would have been furious if it had got ruined in the seawater.

As he was thinking this, the dog in question appeared, barking around his feet. 'Go away,' he growled, but the dog wouldn't stop. He looked around for its owner, but he was nowhere to be seen.

Daniel trudged back in the direction of the path from the beach, but the dog was still on the loose and there was no sign of the boy. Daniel wanted to get home. He wanted to study his findings, get his papers dried out. But something was bugging him. He looked at the dog, who had now started running into and out of the waves that were approaching, and then along the cliff, where the boy had disappeared round the headland.

The boy was an idiot. Surely he knew there was a danger of being cut off by the tide, or of a cliff fall, especially after that heavy rain yesterday. He had been nasty, and Daniel owed him nothing.

But somehow he found himself walking the other way, along the cliff. Just to check the boy was okay.

As he got further along the cliff and was beginning to think he needed to turn back before he got cut off himself, he heard a voice. 'Help! I'm stuck! Help!' And then he saw that the incoming tide had surrounded an outcrop of rocks, and on those rocks, completely surrounded by water, was the boy.

*

Callum felt an intense sense of relief when he saw the boy from the beach appear around the headland, but when all he did was wave his arms, shout something and then turn away again, a sense of terror washed over him. That was it. His only hope of rescue had turned his back on him.

He guessed he deserved it. He had been nasty to him. He had been horrible to the people by the towers as well. And to his grandparents. And now he was going to die out here. He shivered; the water was cold and his ankle was throbbing and now he was soaked with spray and rain. He stared at the shingle that filled the gap between the sea and the cliff, trying to work out how far up the water would come. He was sure it would cover the rocks he was on. Maybe he could swim to shore? But the wind was increasing and the waves looked fierce, and he could hardly move his foot without feeling sick with pain.

He wished he could start the day again. He would have helped with the washing up; he would have played cards with his grandad. He would have even read a book; studied for his exams; anything but storm out of the house with the dog and no phone, get shouted at by people for not clearing up crap and get injured and trapped on rocks at the bottom of a cliff with the tide coming in.

A sudden thought made him look up; what if there was a landslide? What if earth fell on top of him, and he was buried alive? Would they ever know what had happened to him?

While his thoughts had been wandering, the sea had started to lap over the top of the rocks, and the wind had increased, dark clouds threatening a return of yesterday's heavy storm. Already the rain was steady, and his clothes were soaked. Grandma had been right about the weather after all, he thought gloomily. He should have stayed in. As much as, hours before, the caravan had felt like a cage, now he longed for the shelter and warmth and company.

He could hear Snowy barking again, and then the dog appeared around the headland, but the area between him and the rocks was already deep in water. What if he tried to swim, and got washed away? Grandma would be heartbroken if anything happened to the dog. He wished he'd kept him on a lead. He wished he hadn't come to the beach. He wished a lot of things were different. He felt sick and scared.

Snowy disappeared, and with him Callum's hopes of rescue, but then the boy he'd seen earlier appeared again instead and Callum yelled and waved his arms. 'Help!' His voice was hoarse from all the shouting he'd been doing.

'You'll be okay!' The voice travelled faintly over the surging waves.

'No, I'm stuck and I've hurt my ankle!' Callum was crying

now, convinced that this was it; that he would either drown or be knocked off his feet and dashed against the rocks, as the tide started to pull at his legs.

But the boy seemed to be pointing out to sea. Callum looked in the same direction.

Was that a boat?

As it drew closer, he realised it was indeed a boat. It was orange, and the people on it were looking in his direction.

It was a lifeboat!

He waved his arms, the relief flooding him like a warm bath.

By now the boy was as near as he could get without paddling, standing on a flat rock well away from the edge of the cliff. 'My name's Daniel,' he called across. 'Don't worry, they'll soon rescue you.'

The lifeboat slowed a short distance away and he could see three people in yellow and orange on board.

As they cautiously got closer and Callum began to dare hope that he wasn't going to die out here, he remembered something else. 'Snowy,' he called across to Daniel. 'Where's the dog? Grandma will kill me if anything happens to him.'

'It's okay,' Daniel called back. 'There's a lady here, says she knows the dog and knows your grandparents. She was going to let them know. She's taking your dog with her.'

Callum gave a sigh of relief. Maybe, just maybe, he would get out of this okay.

'Hello,' said the nearest lifeboat man as they got close enough to talk properly. 'My name's John and this is Nick. We're going to lift you aboard, okay?'

It was a struggle, and his ankle hurt even more by the time he was seated in the boat, but he sobbed in relief that he wasn't going to drown.

'Let's get you a little warmer,' Nick said. 'Then we'll take you along the beach a little to where we can get you ashore safely.'

They wrapped him in a blanket on the boat and he hunkered down out of the wind, trying to warm up a little, while John checked over his injured ankle. 'I don't think it's broken,' he said. 'Just a nasty sprain. But you'll need it checked out.'

The lady who was driving the boat took them along to the other side of the towers where it could pull in close and he could climb out onto the beach. John steadied him as he staggered on shaky feet, and to his surprise there was a small group of people waiting for him. There was Grandad, and Grandma, and the woman who had yelled at him about Snowy. She now had her dog and Snowy at her feet, and she waved at him cheerfully. There were several other people he didn't recognise. And Daniel had jogged around to join them.

Just at that moment an ambulance came around the corner and stopped by the group. Lifeboat man Nick went to talk to them, while John helped Callum across the beach.

As Callum reached his grandparents, he sank to his knees, shaking with relief and cold. 'I'm sorry,' he said over and over as Grandma wrapped him in her arms and held him tight, ignoring his soaked, icy clothing under the blanket.

The people from the ambulance checked him over and strapped up his ankle. Before they loaded him into the back for a ride to the hospital for an X-ray, Grandad brought Snowy over to see him. 'We're so glad you're safe,' he said.

'And Snowy raised the alarm,' Daniel said from just behind him.

Callum reached out and stroked the dog. 'Sorry, Snowy,' he sniffled. 'I'll take you for a better walk as soon as my ankle is better, I promise.'

He looked up at Daniel. 'You saved my life too,' he said. 'And I was so nasty to you. I'm sorry.'

Daniel smiled. 'Don't worry about it,' he said awkwardly. 'I'm glad you're okay. And maybe tomorrow you could help me check through what I found? You know, to make up for it?'

Callum thought for a moment of the week stretching out before him. A friend would be good. 'I think I'd like that,' he said.

The Golden Owl Flies to Whitstable

by Joanne Bartley

We saw the elderly couple standing close to the caged pebble wall at Dead Man's Corner. They ignored the harbour fishing boats and studied the stones.

'I think they're looking for a clue,' I said.

'They can't be,' my husband said. 'They're old.'

The woman crouched to study the wall at close range. The old man considered his printed sheet of A4.

'They have to be,' I said. 'They're in the right place.'

My husband was already jumping up the wooden steps.

'Are you looking for clues?' he asked. 'My wife made this treasure hunt.'

No, no, no! It would be awful to talk to strangers who were stuck and frustrated all because of me. My husband waved an arm. I was expected to join them. Should I pretend to be busy and in a hurry to get somewhere? No, there was no easy escape.

'So, you made this thing?' the old man said. 'We're really stuck on the clue by the Tower Tea Gardens.'

'We go for a walk every day,' the woman said, frowning. 'We've walked that way so many times now.'

'I'm sorry,' I said. 'It's hard to get the difficulty level right.'

I'm a treasure hunter and a treasure hunt creator so I

understood their exasperation. I felt bad that I'd tormented this confused couple with a fruitless daily walk.

What was I supposed to do? It wouldn't be fair if I gave them the answer. People would think it was cheating. There was a prize at stake.

The tea garden clue involved finding a padlock engraved with the maker's name PERRY fastened on an old wooden gate. It was easy to walk down the wooded path and miss this small thing. These people were old and their eyes might be bad. Perhaps I *should* tell them where it was?

'Don't worry,' the old man said. 'We're having a great time. We like the difficulty level. It's quite a challenge. It's given us something to do on our morning walks.'

'Thanks for making this game,' the old woman chipped in. 'We'll find the right way in the end.'

She turned away, her eyes scanning the pebbles looking for the right stone.

The pebble with the flower picture was up a bit and to the right. I hoped she'd find it in the end.

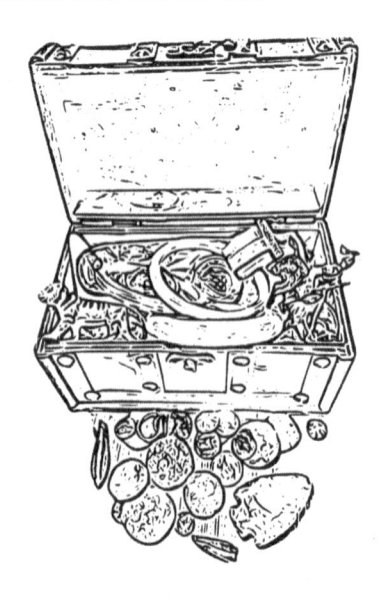

I've always enjoyed looking for things. I collected cacti as a child and loved seeking new specimens in flower shops. I played with our family tree hoping I'd find the birth records of long distant ancestors. I like looking for butterflies too. There are only 59 species in the UK so of course I wanted to spot them all.

It's the seeking, not the finding. It's the hope that makes it special. It must be some overdeveloped hunter gatherer thing. In cave woman days I'd have trekked for miles and miles seeking bison hoof prints. The mix of seeking, trying, hoping, this is my drug.

But on a dark night in Fontainebleau Forest it wasn't about the seeking, it was about holding the prize in my hand. The golden owl prize. The fabled prize of the Chouette d'Or treasure hunt. The owl is a symbol of wisdom and, for me, solving this mystery would be my symbol of smartness and success. The prize is also worth life-changing cash.

Some people might question how a Brit who can't speak any French thinks she can solve a French treasure hunt. A treasure hunt that's been running thirty years, to boot. Well, I think of my French-free methodology as an advantage. I would never get tangled in unlikely anagrams, or subtle word play, no 'jeu de mots' would lead me to explore some rabbit hole of a bad solution. My failure to speak French is my superpower, as long as no clues *are* actually solved with French language tricks. The truth is no one knows how to solve the clues, and that's because Max Valentin set the clues and he took their secrets to his grave.

Max Valentin; even this nom de plume is an enigma, is it a clue? Max published his book of clues in 1993. His text was illustrated with cryptic pictures like a cockerel on a map, a sword in a stone, a walrus and a ruler. What do these things mean? Max buried his owl in a secret location, and tragically died in 2009. No one will know where the owl is buried until the clues are solved and the golden owl unearthed. The fact the treasure hunt creator died on the exact anniversary of the owl burial is a detail that drives conspiracy theorists mad. I ignore this nonsense and work on the puzzles.

Max's fans have been contemplating his book of riddles for thirty years and there's still no sign the owl will be found any time soon. If you know what the 'spiral with four centres' means you're doing better than most. Spirals are everywhere, just not the four centred sort. Online forum factions wage wars over whether Apollo's arrow landed in the town of Dabo or not. No one can make up their mind whether 'the black perched nave' is a church or a ship, or possibly a church-shaped ship? There's a church this shape in Dabo. The mayor was recently forced to issue a warning to try to stop people digging owl-sized holes.

Traditionalists stockpile eBay copies of the Michelin 989 map of France and shun the use of Google maps. I'm with the old school owlers; the only way to draw X marks the spot is on a thirty-year-old map.

In May 2023 I drew my map lines with a film crew watching. I declared that the owl would be found 5 steps north of the 'Point de vue d'Orphée' in the forest of Fontainebleau. I folded my old map, it was time to dig. I regretted agreeing to the documentary, worried my empty-hole shame could be broadcast to the world.

'Doesn't that rock remind you of something?' Guy D'Arcy said. 'I mean the shape.'

I put down my shovel and studied the lump of rock. It was a huge thing. It probably had a name like most of the boulders in the forest. Claude-François Denecourt, a dwarfish map maker and tourism entrepreneur, named every feature of Fontainebleau Forest in Victorian times. Can you still say 'Victorian' when you're in France?

Guy's rock had nothing to do with my solution. I didn't care about this lump of stone.

'No, I don't think so,' I said, putting down my spade. I wished the soil wasn't quite so solid. I was getting nowhere because the earth was full of roots. 'It just looks like a rock to me.'

Guy was tall and tanned, a former golf pro turned documentary maker, who was used to getting his own way. His film crew were just out of film school and regretting taking this job.

'I think it looks like a heart,' Guy said. 'You know, the aorta. Is that what they call it?'

I looked at the rock, I thought about hearts. If it was supposed to look like a heart wouldn't it be a comic book heart like the ones on valentine's day cards? It was true that real human hearts were blobby roundish things, and this rock was a blobby roundish thing. But weren't all rocks roundish blobs?

Guy was excited because the clue said, 'it's the right path only if the arrow points to the heart.' We'd found a perfect arrow-shaped rock that pointed straight down a path. My dig was at the heart of the short path. I was sure that Guy's rock that looked like an aorta had nothing to do with anything. Was aorta even the right word?

'We're running out of battery, and it's getting dark,' Casey said. She was the no-nonsense camera woman.

'I don't have much memory,' said Peter, the sound man, checking his equipment. 'How much longer do you need?'

Guy considered the complaints from his crew. We were all feeling demoralised. I'd already explained that I was unlikely to find the owl due to my knowledge that the owl was buried under an oak tree. The arrow was great, the path was perfect, but the 'Point de vue d'Orphée' was in birch woodland. The hole I was digging was pointless.

I felt like the worst ever adventurer. I'd got everyone lost in the forest, heading east instead of west, and we hadn't brought torches. We left them in the car because we were supposed to be digging in daylight not dusk. We'd journeyed pointless extra miles, with the poor crew carrying heavy equipment, before finally finding the right place. Sitting at home looking at clues and drawing lines on my maps was my strong point, not the adventurous bit.

'I think Casey's right,' Peter said. 'It's going to be too dark to film, and we don't have torches.'

He was a skinny giant from Scotland who rarely spoke; we

had to take his point seriously.

'Okay, this is hopeless, let's go,' Guy said, and marched away.

No one expected this development. Casey and Peter exchanged glances and started packing their equipment away as quickly as they could.

I looked at my hole, barely three inches deep. The film crew were grumbling and packing up but they were some way away from leaving. I made a snap decision. I threw my spade in my backpack and followed Guy.

'Guy, wait,' I shouted after him. 'Don't you think we should wait for the others?'

'I'm going to the car, they can catch up.'

I was a very amateur adventurer but weren't people supposed to stick together in the wilds? It would be dark soon, we had no torches, there was no phone signal in the forest. We'd got hopelessly lost finding the route in the daylight, did Guy think it was an easy trek to the car in the dark?

'I know the way,' Guy said, striding onwards.

I looked back. No sign of the others. What should I do? The young keen crew were my allies on this awful trip. The filming was all takes, re-takes and bad interviews, but they laughed about it and made it all okay. I'd rather wait for them, but Guy was limping onwards.

He had a hip replacement operation in a month. I had a vision of him falling in the rocky forest and being eaten alive by wolves in the dark. Okay, he might not be eaten, but it was wrong to leave him alone. I ran to catch up.

'So, your solution was wrong,' Guy said as I joined him. 'Your lines on the map looked good, there was the rock shaped like the arrow. It was shaped exactly like an arrow. So what did you do wrong?'

The owl had been buried thirty years. This was the longest unsolved treasure hunt in the world. Did Guy really expect me to solve it? I'd seen his excitement as I plotted my map lines revealing a shape of a ship. Then I showed how the light from Apollo's arrow marked the spot at Fontainebleau Forest. He was dreaming of filming the historic moment the golden owl was pulled from the earth.

'I don't know why the solution was wrong,' I explained. 'There was no oak tree. Everyone's seen the leaked photo and those stupid acorns. It was pointless even digging, it wasn't the right place. But I couldn't know that until I got there.'

Guy stopped at a crossroads.

'It's straight on, isn't it?'

I didn't know if it was straight on. I hadn't paid attention. Casey had taken control when my navigation skills proved inadequate. She'd calmly taken the map from my hands, planned the best route, and I'd been hugely relieved when we finally found the rock of Orpheus.

Guy noted my indecision. 'Yes, it's straight on,' he said.

It was dark, and the path went on and on. The trees and boulders all looked the same, there was no way to tell if the path led to the car park. I felt sure we were heading deeper into the forest.

We walked on and on, with Guy's limp getting more pronounced. He stopped to take a drink.

'It's a good thing we trust each other,' he said.

Trust each other? What! Why would I need to think about trust? Was I supposed to trust that he didn't murder me in the dark forest, or…? No, I shouldn't go there. It's like being challenged not to think about the colour blue. You think of it.

There was movement in the bushes, a sound moving closer. Guy screamed. It was a beast, a monster! Guy ran into the trees. The shaggy furred monster stopped in the path, watching me. It had a bulky head, horns, a snout. It was a wild boar. The creature vanished into the undergrowth.

I was unsettled by Guy, frightened of angry wildlife, and I wasn't convinced we'd find the way out of the forest anytime soon. It would be scary to spend the night in this wild darkness.

We reached another junction. Guy held his lit-up phone to illuminate a sign pinned to a tree. 'Route de La Chouette,' it said.

'Christ no!' Guy said. 'F***ing Owls.'

The owl sign was mocking us, but it had a worrying meaning. The route we'd travelled from the car to the dig spot hadn't led us this way. We'd seen a few signs on the trees, but I'd have remembered this one. Someone was bound to have joked that the chouette was hidden on the chouette path.

This sign meant we were lost.

'Do you know the way?' I asked Guy.

He rubbed his sore leg, then downed some pain killers. I felt bad that he was suffering. We'd already walked miles further than we needed to because I'd got us all lost. I'd dragged Guy all the way to France to film the digging of an empty hole. But so much of this was his own fault; he should never have trusted me to have the correct solution.

Perhaps it was no disaster anyway? He could change gear and make a humorous documentary about an English eccentric who thought every clue linked to Greek myths. He could end with a tragi-comic picture of me looking foolish and desperate as I shovelled dirt. I didn't mind. I was already looking forward to returning to my clue book to correct my missteps.

Maybe 'the arrow aims for the heart' referenced Diana? Did the goddess of the hunt have a bow and arrow and some love interest? Maybe I should find a rock of Cupid? Claude-François Denecourt had a thing about naming rocks after gods. I was eager to seek the answer in my Guide to 'Sentiers de Promenades de Fontainebleau.' Was Cupid a Greek god or was he Roman? I would soon find myself lost down enjoyable Wikipedia rabbit holes.

'So much of that solution was right,' Guy said. 'The spiral, the argonaut ship, the way the arrow lands exactly on Dabo.'

This was true. I wasn't going to throw my whole solution in the bin. I was glad I had a signed non-disclosure agreement. Guy could forget my spiral and ship, I would take it from here.

'Have you got a signal on your phone?' I asked. 'I've nothing.'

'I know the way,' Guy said, marching onwards. His straight-legged gait was almost funny, but it was mean to think it.

We reached a stone staircase. It was a huge steep hill and Guy was in a lot of pain. Orpheus coped with the Underworld and now we faced our own hellish challenge. Guy winced his way up every step, as I struggled behind, carrying bags. We finally reached the top of the hill and could see the distant car park.

Casey and Peter were waiting by the car. We'd been missing so long they'd persuaded some drunk boulderers to call the police. The boulderers cheered, and the search party was cancelled.

'I knew the way,' Guy said. 'We were never in any danger.'

He slammed the door as he got into his car. Casey rolled her eyes. Peter mouthed the word 'wanker.'

I like the seeking, trying, hoping, but looking for a car park in that dark forest was no fun.

Guy still hopes to secure funding for his documentary

project. I have my doubts about it all.

Last week he popped up on WhatsApp.

'Do you think this could be the nave?' He shared an image of lines drawn on a map.

In the end I don't think Guy was trying to make a great documentary, he was looking for a buried owl that's been underground for thirty years. He was seeking a solution to a wonderful mystery. He was one of us.

'Wish us luck!' the old man at the harbour said, as my husband and I went on our way. 'We're determined to find your treasure.'

I'd bought a chest-shaped box and filled it with the kind of treasures I could afford. A Victorian marble, Roman coins, arrowheads, an old toy soldier, a medieval ring. I enjoyed my treasure hunt shopping.

In the end a charming, grateful family solved my Whitstable treasure hunt. The final clue led to a spot in the undergrowth beside the Favourite oyster yawl. I wonder what that family have done with my lovingly assembled collection of low-grade collectibles. I mean treasure.

My Fontainebleau adventure was exciting, that's for sure. I'll never forget the moment we spotted the arrow-shaped rock. It really was shaped like an arrow and it fitted the clue perfectly. It was Guy who spotted the rock first. Does that rankle? Of course.

I'd decided 'the arrow points to the heart' meant the centre of the path, but what if the aorta stone was actually the heart? Maybe I should go back and dig in a different spot?

My owl adventure should shine like gold in my memories, but strangely, the day I met the old couple shines brighter. I made a treasure hunt, just like Max Valentin! A treasure hunt that was all my own. I wrote the clues, I tried to make them clever, I looked to see if it would work. I hoped people might enjoy my game. It was that heady, addictive mix of seeking, trying, hoping. Did people like my clues? The answer was yes. That's my treasure right there.

The Golden Owl Flies to Whitstable

And here I am again. Writing words on a page. Are they the right words? Will they find approval? Seeking, trying, hoping once more. Will these words bring me reward?

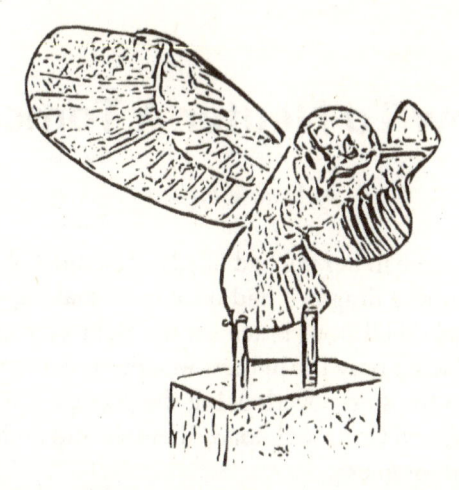

Names, places and facts have been changed to turn my treasure hunt story into fiction, and before you grab a spade, the golden owl is absolutely, definitely, not buried at the Rock of Orpheus in Fontainebleau Forest.

How To Neuter A Tomcat

by Duarte Figueira

When Ella came in her tail had filled out so much it reminded me of a Chinese dragon I had once seen snaking along in a Soho festival. She'd been bitten on the right paw and moved gingerly, placing only the lightest weight on it as she climbed the stairs to the study overlooking the postage stamp garden of our terrace on Cromwell Road. There she hid under the sofa bed we kept for guests.

It was the third time she'd been bitten that year. I knew it was probably the slim black cat that had sprayed several rooms in the house until we'd installed the microchip cat flap. Now he ruled the garden and attacked her whenever she was caught unawares, which was seldom.

'We have to get the damn thing neutered, John,' my wife Mary said.

This was several hours later. She had pulled Ella out by the hind legs and examined her paw. Ella had already licked away a patch of fur and exposed pink skin with the ugly bulge of an infected bite. Someone from the local cat protection group had told her that if we caught the black cat we could get the vet to neuter it. I'd asked the vet if this was true as I held Ella and watched him give her an injection later that same day. He'd shaken his head.

'If you bring him in I'll do it, but you'll have to register him as yours.'

'And you will know that is not true.'

'But the owner will not be able to take action against me,' he said.

He smiled as he pulled out the needle.

'You know, it's pretty common to have a tomcat like this around in this part of Whitstable.'

Back home I sat on the sofa and thought about the options. We could sub-contract the problem back to the RSPCA. Might they take away the black cat and re-home it after neutering it if we claimed it was ours? But I realised that if they were approached by the real owner they would finger us as the guilty party just as the vet had said.

I then considered more extreme scenarios involving the cat's demise and secret burial or dumping some way from our area. I remembered my mother telling me that when she was a child she had seen her father drown unplanned puppies in a weighted sack. But this sounded risky and involved the trapping of the cat followed by a potentially messy execution. The implications of discovery involved prosecution and my family would never sanction such action.

The existence of the intruder nevertheless tied my stomach in knots. How dare the bugger deny our cats their legitimate property rights with his cross-garden raids? I scoured the net for advanced tech that would stop him in his tracks, but for some reason Mary refused to countenance low-voltage electric wiring over zoo fencing. I don't want to live in a secure facility, she said.

Perhaps a sustained campaign of aggression then, with me targeting the cat with slingshot and water pistol until it considered our garden too dangerous to approach. But this also had its downsides. I'm a water engineer and there would be many times when I was out checking some site. That would reduce the cat's perception of danger and I had no idea of its appetite for retaliation against our own cats while I was away from the house. Plus Mary would no more accept this solution than the kill-and-dispose option.

Nevertheless, I played around with softer versions of this strategy for a number of weeks, charging into the garden every time the black cat came into view on the sheds at the bottom of our garden or when his presence outside our back door was signalled by our cats fleeing at high speed though the cat flap. My counter-attack was accompanied by blood-curdling yelling that would have put an Iroquois war band to shame.

None of it worked. The cat sensed the implied powerlessness and futility of these mock assaults and was effectively trained over time to disregard them. Eventually, it would sit on the shed staring through the glass of our lounge French windows. Behind them our two cats stared back at him in terror, while I hopped about beneath him like a demented shaman. I abandoned my failed strategy after the Brackens, our elderly but right-on neighbours, complained about the din. Not very cool, man, they said. I conceded the battlefield in disgrace and sloped upstairs to my study.

Mary tried a different tack of seeking to win his trust by feeding him. While our cats were kept locked up elsewhere in the house, she would sit in the garden close to a bowl of dried cat food just distant enough from her to allow him to feed and escape capture. Gradually, she fell back into the lounge and placed the bowl just outside the French windows. Eventually, it was placed just inside them on the doormat, while she sat on the edge of the armchair and said soothing things to him while he fed, one eye on the open door behind him.

Meanwhile, I sat upstairs in my eyrie metaphorically licking my wounds. Over time, I convinced myself that I was spiritually above all this and no longer concerned myself with the cat problem. I had no idea of Mary's eventual plan, whether it was to trap the cat in the lounge or to simply seek to douse his violent instincts through a sort of domestication. The only time she involved me was when she cried out one afternoon and I walked down to the lounge to make sure she was all right.

The cat scurried out and sat halfway down the garden slabs licking himself.

'He let me stroke him! And he ate from my hand!' she said.

I looked again at the disgustingly healthy jet-black sheen on the cat. He glanced up at me for a moment, dismissed me and carried on his cleaning.

'He's a darling really, and very natural of course,' she said.

'Are you going to catch him and let the RSPCA have him?'

'I don't think I could now. We'll just have to keep the cats in more.'

But that didn't happen. The black cat disappeared soon after, though given its unpredictability his absence was not noticed immediately. A couple of weeks later I asked my wife whether she had fed him recently.

'No – he's not shown his face for a while. He'll turn up, I suppose, unless he has had an accident.'

'At least the cats can have their garden back, and no more vets' bills,' I said.

'I do miss him, though,' she sighed.

In truth, our cats never displayed their previous confidence in the garden after the black cat was gone. The male, called Robbie after the poet Burns, had become nervy and extra alert, dashing through the cat flap and upstairs every time the wind moved the leaves on the bushes. Whilst Ella, who was a tougher character, would sit sentinel-like on the shed staring at the direction the black cat normally came from. The depressing thought occurred that she was pining for him as well.

Then one day he was back. Creeping over old Mr Bracken's shed next door, then over the trellis fence before leaping softly down onto our mock Indian garden slabs. I was home alone, working in the study and watched with something resembling horror as he approached the cat flap.

I crept downstairs and peered round the door into the kitchen. I could see him worrying at the flap. No chance, mate, I thought. But suddenly he pushed in and was out of my sight.

I stepped into the kitchen. His head was dipped in Robbie's food bowl.

He looked up at me without fear.

Bastard.

'Who do you think you are?' I screamed.

He was out of the flap in a millisecond. I watched him leap the wall and disappear and then walked to the drinks cabinet for a stiff whisky. And then another.

At dinner I told my wife.

'Yes, I know. I leave the cat flap open and he pops in for a snack. He belongs to Martin from Reservoir Road. But it's not...'

I interrupted.

'Martin? Who is Martin when he's at home?'

'Martin Larsson. Lovely man, moved to the town last year. He's Norwegian and a musician. He's very successful, apparently. Has his own studio.'

I met Martin about a week later when I found him sitting

in our basement having a glass of wine with Mary. He was a handsome, bearded man in his early forties, dressed in a black leather jacket and matching tight jeans. He reminded me uncomfortably of Viggo Mortensen. He smiled up at me, displaying his perfect teeth.

'Darling, Martin has come over to borrow some cat food and we got talking. Guess what? He is going to give me some guitar lessons.'

And so that was it. Every Saturday afternoon over the next few weeks I would listen to her laughter and his low powerful voice downstairs between the most basic strumming and painfully slow and ragged chord changes. Gradually over a period of weeks I noticed that the musical content was decreasing and the conversation element growing. My wife always glowed when the class was over and Martin would sometimes give me an enigmatic smile as he passed me in the hallway on his way out.

Then one Saturday I came downstairs to make a cup of tea and found him holding her hand over the kitchen table. He glared up at me before slowly releasing it. My wife could barely look at me as they packed up their guitars.

'How is the cat?' I asked.

'Thor?' he replied, 'well, he's no Loki, that's for sure. I might as well have had him neutered.'

I stopped him.

'So isn't it the same cat, then?'

'I tried to tell him,' my wife said, 'but does he listen?'

'Loki disappeared. When he did I went spare and knocked on every door in the neighbourhood. It was then that I met Mary and she suggested I get another cat.'

I looked at my wife's back as she stared through the window at the garden.

'Why didn't you have Loki neutered? He was a dreadful nuisance,' I said.

He looked at me with thunderous contempt.

'Because that is not natural. How would you like it if I cut off your balls?'

'Yes, don't be ridiculous, John,' said Mary.

Well, I felt joyously released. I had come to imagine that the cat had miraculously regained consciousness, somehow clawed its way out of the nylon sack, then grimly dug itself out from under several feet of silt and muck in the Gorrell Tank before crawling home. But no, he's still there, thank God. And now Martin would have to join him. Bigger sack and more rope of course, but my trusty pipe wrench would still do the job, so no difference really.

'Quite right,' I said, retreating to the study.

A Whole New World

by Richard Barton

So this afternoon he could tell her about himself! He had the go-ahead to reveal his big secret.

They had met just ten days ago in Dane John Gardens. This park, within the city walls of Canterbury, had a coffee shop which Simon liked. Just being able to buy a decent coffee from a normal person and enjoy it in such a special place was (he smiled at the common usage of the word) magical.

He got talking to Judy as she was waiting for her drink. She suggested he try one of the syrup flavourings. It seemed so easy and natural. They strolled around the gardens together talking about their surroundings, Canterbury and nothing in particular.

They were walking along Castle Street when Judy said, 'Well, this is me. Break time over. Back to work.'

Simon looked at the building she was about to enter. 'You work in here? What do you do?'

She giggled. The large windows were covered with pictures of houses and flats, along with their details. 'What do you think I do?'

Simon avoided the question. 'I'd like to see you again.'

She considered him for a moment. 'OK. Give me your number.'

'My what?'

'Your number. Your mobile phone number.'

'Oh. I don't have one of those.'

'You don't? You're a strange one, Simon. Well, tell you what, stop by here next Tuesday at three. I finish early and we can continue our walk.'

So at three o'clock the following Tuesday they had met outside what Simon had discovered was called an Estate Agents. He found out about her – a Canterbury girl, born and bred, interested in music and history and a 'Friend' of both Canterbury Cathedral and the Marlowe Theatre. But when she asked about him, Simon had to be evasive. He couldn't say anything about his world, not without permission. He had felt able to tell her he lived in the countryside between Canterbury and Littlebourne, where he grew herbs and other plants. For a living, he had explained that he used the plants to create remedies which were sold up and down the country and sometimes abroad.

'Remedies?' she asked. 'Do they work?'

'Well, yes, or people wouldn't buy them.'

'It could be placebo effect. Or clever marketing. Have they been subjected to clinical trials?'

Simon did not understand what Judy meant by any of this. He didn't know what she meant when she asked him about things called Netflix and Facebook. When she asked him where he went to school he answered, 'A boarding school. Up north. You wouldn't have heard of it.'

'You are a mystery, Simon. Living on a smallholding, growing herbs for your remedies. No mobile, no internet. I like you but... I'm not sure I want to be with someone who's so secretive. What is it you're not telling me?'

They walked on a few paces. 'Judy, I want to tell you. I just need to – to check something. I'm sorry if I'm being secretive. Listen, can we meet again at the same time next week? I'll try to have everything arranged by then and I'll tell you all you want to know.'

She had agreed so Simon contacted the Ministry as soon as he got home. They had been very efficient, as they generally were these days. He had gone up to London to be interviewed and he was sure someone had been sent to Canterbury to take a look at Judy.

By Monday night he was getting anxious – what would he say to Judy the next day if he had not received approval? But early on Tuesday an owl arrived with all the documentation, rules and procedures.

So it was with a light heart that Simon waited outside Judy's place of work. He had never before revealed his world to someone from outside it (Simon did not like to use the 'M-word'). When she came out she kissed him on the cheek and said, 'You look giddy as a schoolboy!'

'Yes! I can tell you all about myself! I don't have to be secretive anymore. But you must promise not to tell anyone about me, about what I'm going to tell you.'

'Hold on! I'm not sure I can promise that! If we're going to, well, be a couple, I'll need to tell my friends about you. My Dad will want to meet you.'

'That's OK, I can meet your friends and family. We'll work out what we can tell them. Come along, there's a pub I want to take you to, a pub used by my community.'

'Your community?' There was a note of disappointment in her voice.

'Yes, it's called The Black Cat and it's not far, it's in Longmarket.'

'I've never seen it. I thought I knew all the pubs in the city centre.'

'No, well, you won't have been able to see it. But you're with me now, Judy, so I can guide you in.'

Simon led her at a brisk pace through the city to Longmarket. Suddenly he turned into a doorway she had never seen before and she found herself in a dark and shabby pub, lit only by candlelight. Strangely dressed people sat at some of the bare pine tables. There was no music, just the murmur of low voices. A man in long purple robes approached them.

'Simon Ganderstone?' They shook hands. 'And you must be

Miss Judy Barnes. Welcome. I'm Maxilbert Fennerstraat. Call me Max. I'll be here if I'm needed.' He left them and sat at a corner table.

'OK Simon, just tell me what's going on.'

'I'm a wizard, Judy. I can do magic. Everyone here can. There's a fair number of us witches and wizards living in and around Canterbury. This is our pub and through the back there is a shop where we get our stuff.'

'A wizard. Magic.'

'Yes, let me get you a drink and I'll tell you all about it.' He bought two glasses of something that tasted a little like beer, but Judy found it syrupy and much too sweet. They sat at a table and Simon asked, 'So, where shall we start?'

'If you're a wizard, show me some magic.'

Simon pulled out a wooden stick and pointed it at the candle on their table. It rose a few inches into the air.

'Very good,' said Judy. 'You've got it attached to a fine string.' She waved her hand over the candle to try to find what was lifting it up.

'No, it's magic. How about this then?' Simon shook his stick again and light shone from it, brightening up their corner.

'Good, this place could do with better lighting. Your stick is really a torch, then?'

'No, honestly, this is magic. Watch the candle again.' He waved his stick and the candle turned into a white rat.

'Charming,' said Judy. 'That one is a clever trick, I'll give you that. Can you make the stick light up again, it's a dark place you've brought me to. Don't they have electricity here?'

'It doesn't work properly around us. Most of your electronical things go wrong if there's one of these –' he held up his wooden stick '– nearby. That's why I don't have a mobile and can't use your internet thing.'

'How do you get messages to people?'

'We use owls. They carry our letters.'

'Owls? You mean... you have to write letters out by hand? And then owls carry them for you?'

'They don't seem to mind.'

'Hmm. How long does it take to get a message delivered by owl?'

'Oh, they can get about, you know. If I sent one to London it would be there within three hours.'

Judy laughed. 'With this,' she held up her mobile, 'I can talk to anyone in the world. I can send them messages and pictures, which they get immediately.' She looked at the screen. No signal. Fairly normal for Canterbury. 'Well, I don't have a connection just now.'

'Too much magic around,' said Simon. She let him have that. Maybe it was the explanation for Canterbury's notorious problem with signal coverage.

'If you don't have the internet, what do you do for entertainment? You can't have much: no streaming services, no e-books, no social media…'

'Oh. I don't really know what those are. We do have books, though, and the wireless.'

Judy laughed again. 'Wireless? Don't you mean radio?' Simon shrugged and Judy continued, 'How do you get about? Do you use cars or buses or trains?'

'We have one train. Oh, and there's a bus, but I don't like using it. We can use your buses and so forth if we want. But otherwise we use broomsticks.'

At this Judy guffawed. 'What? You sit on the handle of a broom? I can't imagine how uncomfortable that must be!'

Simon felt somewhat offended at this remark about what he saw as a central part of the culture of his community. 'You get used to it.'

'Really? Sounds like the definition of a pain in the arse!'

'Look, we have other ways of getting about! I can flit between fireplaces in different buildings, for example.'

'Fireplaces? Well that's great if you want to get somewhere that has a fireplace. It won't help you get to Sainsbury's, will it?'

'Sainsbury's – that's one of your shops, I've seen Sainsbury's.'

'But you've never been in one?'

'No need! We have our own shop. Let me show you.' They had finished their drinks so Simon led Judy out of a back door of the pub and into a little yard, from where a gateway led them into a strange, dark shop. 'Everard's Emporium!' said Simon proudly. 'Nothing like the range of shops we have in London, but our people can get everything we need here.'

The shop was dark and cramped, although there were few other customers. Simon showed Judy around. She was unimpressed by the range of animal products. 'I'm no vegetarian but I would draw the line at some of these,' she said.

Next they looked at the range of jokes and pranks for sale. 'These are horrible,' said Judy. 'Really cruel. Who would find it funny to play these tricks on another person?'

Simon showed her a shelf stacked with his products. 'These are what I make, see? Making such things was my top subject at school. They sell here, and at other wizarding shops, and some by post.'

'Do you make a good living from these concoctions?'

'I get by.' The truth was Simon was never going to get rich selling his products. 'I grow food at my cottage and I keep a few chickens and goats.'

'I see. So, just for a moment, suppose I believe you. There are magical people living up and down the country, in secret. What if I decided to tell everyone about you?'

'Well, I have to ask you to sign a contract that says you won't.'

'And if I refuse?'

Simon looked awkward. 'Um, well, that's why Max is here. Unless you agree to keeping our secret, he's going to have to erase your memory.'

'He's going to do what?'

'Not all of it! Just your memory of me and all this.' He looked around the shop.

Judy looked cross but then her face relaxed. 'OK. Well, again, just supposing any of this is true. I can see you would have to protect your privacy. You'd never be left alone if the rest of us knew there were people among us who could fix our problems just by waving a stick. If you've got your own world and it's peaceful and happy, I can see why you'd want to keep it that way.'

'Well, I should say it's not always peaceful and happy. We have bad people too. We had one a few years ago, a really terrible person. He attracted a following and started a war. Loads of people were killed.'

'Oh, how terrible! What happened?'

'Well, luckily, we had a teenager who was able to finish him off.'

'A teenager? You relied on a teenager to stop a mass murderer?'

'Yes, well, him and some friends, Actually, it's a terrific story, but not one for now. Shall we go back to the Black Cat and see if they have anything to eat?'

'You mean they might not? No offense, Simon, but it's a bit gloomy. Have you ever been in one of our pubs?'

He had not, so they walked past the Cathedral and the Marlowe, then through Solly's Orchard to the Miller's Arms. Simon was hugely impressed: the food, the drinks, the service, and the cleanliness. Afterwards they walked along the river to Sainsbury's and Simon was agog at the range available. He had never seen so many different types of food and drink. The fruit and vegetables on sale put Everard's Emporium to shame. Simon had never heard of a ready meal before. Judy collected a few things she needed and Simon could not understand why she did not have to hand over bulky coins, as he had to in his shops. Instead, she waved a small card and that seemed to take care of everything. Judy explained that she did not even have to come to the shop; there was a thing called an app, which meant she could order everything she wanted and have Sainsbury's deliver it to her home. It was better than magic.

Nineteen years later
The doorbell rang at precisely eleven o'clock. Simon closed the lid of his laptop and opened the door of the cottage. The

representative of the magical school was admiring the garden.

'Lovely flowers, Mr Ganderstone.'

'Thank you Professor.' The herbs and other special plants had all gone. The goats and chickens were absent as well. There was no need for any of that now, so the garden had been turned to flowers and ornamental shrubs. 'Do come in. Would you like tea?'

They sat down with their drinks and Simon offered her some cookies – Tesco Finest.

'These are good,' she said. 'No one else here for our meeting?'

'The girls are at school and Judy had to work this morning. But we've agreed what we're going to say.'

The teacher seemed determined to make more smalltalk first. 'I haven't seen your remedies on any shop shelf in a long time.'

'I gave that up. It was a huge amount of work for very little return,' answered Simon.

'What do you do now?'

'I got a job in a bar when Judy and I got married. Now I manage a restaurant. It's going well.'

'You don't use magic at all?'

'Sometimes, to water the garden. But never in the house, it interferes with the Wi-Fi.'

He could see that the schoolteacher did not know what that meant. She moved swiftly to the purpose of her visit.

'I came here five years ago to offer your elder daughter a place at my school. You said she did not want to attend.'

'That's right. She wanted to stay with her friends and go to the same school as them. Besides, she's always been interested in science and you don't teach that. Do you know, she told me the other day that magic breaks something called the laws of thermodynamics, and that by creating new energy we could be contributing to climate change.'

'No regrets, then?'

'None. I assume you've come here to talk about my younger daughter?' The teacher nodded. 'She wants to stay with her friends and go to the same school as her sister. She says she wants to work with AI technology to create soundtracks for video games when she grows up. Going to your school isn't going to help her with that.'

Simon could again see that the teacher had little idea what any of this meant. He knew the feeling, from his own introduction to the non-magical world all those years ago.

'So, you're sure you don't want to introduce your daughters to our world?'

'Quite sure. Why would we? Their tech is better than our magic. Their world offers a better standard of living, it's more fun and, frankly, it's safer than yours. No thank you.'

All was well.

Gridlocked in Whitstable

by Gillian Rolfe

Sebastian Sproggett had been Keeper of the Grid at Tankerton Slopes for so long he could barely remember a time when he wasn't. He didn't mind, not really; after all, who wouldn't want to live in a place like this all their life, patrolling the slopes above the beach and eating ice-cream? The day-trippers and locals didn't suspect a thing and there had been almost no breakthroughs since the great floods of '53. He licked appreciatively at the luscious ice cream he was holding. The concoction, sticky with bobbles of strawberry sauce, dripped onto his wrinkled hand.

He had stumbled into the job, as a young lad, one sun-soaked afternoon whilst kicking his football on the Tower Slopes. After a magnificent shot the rubber ball, on its downwards trajectory, rolled into an earthy crack in the stubby turf. He was not unduly concerned as the brittle sun-baked grass always gaped open along the Tankerton Slopes during the summer months, the moisture evaporating in the heat, like a sunny forehead without a hat, causing the turf to shrink.

Peering into the fissure, he had been startled to see a giant eyeball looking back at him. It was attached to a face, obviously, but Sebastian could only see a close up of a pupil and a white patch turning an angry pink colour where his football had bounced on it. He wiped his hot hands down the legs of his grey school shorts, paused, then leant down to retrieve his football.

'I wouldn't if I were you.'

'What...' stuttered Sebastian, glancing up at an approaching small figure shadowed by the sun, but he withdrew his hand thoughtfully. The person came nearer.

'You're not frightened then?'

Sebastian peered up into the old woman's face.

'Um...'

She tapped her teeth gently against the handle of her walking stick, assessing Seb's small, grubby persona.

'I suppose it has to be you then.'

And that had been that, no opting out, just an acceptance of a job that must be done, that only he could do, that he had done for many years.

*

Further along the greensward slopes, a small girl drew patterns in the grass with the toe of her red trainer. She glanced at her father. His frame was bent over in the concentration of his task. He straightened up and smiled at her solemn face.

'Finished! That was fiddly, still, done now. With this technology, we can be airborne! Here you take the kite over there so it catches the wind, be careful of the GoPro camera, we don't want it falling off.' He grinned encouragingly at her.

So, to please him, she dutifully trotted off and released the kite into the air. The salty wind whipped the nylon fabric from her fingers with ease so she ran back to her father and together they looked at the live-feed on his phone.

'Look at that, a birds-eye view! See the beach huts? Those diamond patterns of drainage channels under the turf look great from up here, like a sepia harlequin effect,' he enthused.

The little girl looked at the screen and her mouth opened in a perfect 'oh' shape. She then looked at the green stretch of turf in front of her through narrowed eyes. She walked several paces away from her absorbed father and raised her foot to push into the cracked brown earth.

Sebastian Cornelius Sproggett crumpled up his sticky ice cream serviette, pushed it into his jacket pocket and ambled over to her.

'I wouldn't do that if I were you.'

The girl stared at the old man with her head to one side, then placed her foot back down onto the grass.

'You're not frightened then?'

'Um...' she murmured glancing at her oblivious father absorbed in his phone, then shook her head.

'I suppose it has to be you then.'

A Fluttering of Doves

by Peter Quince

Saskia sits at the window of her third-floor flat in Hugh Place, a flower-strewn, canyon-like alley which runs off Faversham's Marketplace and is quaintly secluded from the bustle of the town centre. She watches doves on the Tudor roofs opposite; barley-twist chimneys give the view a beguiling, timeless air. She has always thought so and considers herself privileged.

Until a week ago she would sit here drinking tea with Rufus as they gazed at the doves together. She would sketch them and he would observe her as she did so. It was a way of passing time beyond the boundaries of conversation when words became redundant, and when the tribulations of their relationship became impossibly tangled and they each needed a breathing space.

There was something therapeutic about listening to the cooing and, as a couple, observing the frantic fluttering and the courtship dances. Now Saskia watches the doves' antics alone, and she doesn't pick up her sketchbook anymore.

She cradles a mug of tea in both hands. What else is there to do? He's gone now. Not far, but far enough to break the spell. Rufus has returned to the Thames barge which is moored on Faversham Creek just a few yards upstream from the Oyster House, an iconic building complementing an equally iconic sailing vessel. He has joined the rest of the crew in preparing the barge and ensuring that it is seaworthy.

Saskia wonders if she should pursue Rufus, wonders if the Grendel has sailed yet. She can't quite remember the date. She wants him back despite the latest and most violent altercation yet. But pride roots her to the spot in the shadow of the doves. He'll return when the barge returns. When the doves fly.

She sits in the window and wills her mind to drift. It is an indulgence she cannot resist, although it pains and saddens her. She recalls that time they stumbled into St Mary's Church dressed in their gardening rags and found themselves in the midst of a wedding ceremony and couldn't help but laugh and all the guests turned and they were ushered out as vagabonds. And then she is startled back into the present moment.

One dove balances on the back of its submissive partner and flaps its wings furiously in a show of dominance and desire. It is all a matter of instinct; it worked that way with Rufus: they fought and then they loved. She sips tea and gazes up at the sky above the complex of massive chimneys. It is cirrus, fair-weather cloud she sees, ideal for sailing out into the Thames estuary, west towards London or east past Whitstable and around the Kent coast and on to Rye Harbour in East Sussex. Rufus has sailed that way before, loves the weird landscape of Dungeness, the way the coastline changes, the women in Rye.

She recalls the time they dug plots together in the Abbey Physic Community Garden and he told her what a beautiful place this was, a fragment of paradise in the middle of a market town, a sanctuary for seekers and sufferers and those in love who sit on benches saying nothing, beyond the trivia of speech. They had ended by hurling compost at each other and giggling like naughty schoolkids and the garden manager had glared at them and told them it was out of character with the serenity of the place.

A dove alights from mossy roof tiles and circles a chimney stack and comes to rest in precisely the spot it flew up from. What is the point of that? Saskia thinks. But that is what Rufus does on the Thames barge: sails up the Creek and into open sea and comes back again to the very same mooring. It is life – for doves, for sailors, for those who wait. Circular and ultimately meaningless.

She remembers taking him out to Harty Ferry, a few miles beyond the town on the cusp of the estuary. How charmed he was by the abundant bird life. 'I've only ever seen these marshes from a sailing boat; a totally different perspective,' she recalls him saying. She said, 'I want to show you the natural spring. The water travels underground all the way from Bavaria. People come here to collect water in demijohns and cart it home and swear by its health-giving properties.'

'Minerals,' he had said. And they had stood side by side holding hands, staring at the gushing outflow and marvelling at the rose blooms and daisy chains and peacock feathers that water-gatherers had left as spiritual offerings.

Saskia drains the last of her green tea from the mug, but keeps it firmly clasped as if it were some kind of anchor, a still point. She sits by the window frozen to the spot, although in May the air is warm and the open sash allows the doves' soft symphony into the room and charms it. 'Good sailing weather,' Rufus had said. That was before the final, acrimonious argument.

She brings to mind their carefree strolls along Abbey Street, resplendent in sunshine, with its astonishing display of Tudor houses and medieval remains on both sides and, halfway down to the quay, Arden House, where the mayor of Faversham was murdered deep in winter and dragged through snow across the back garden, leaving a trail of red against the white. Rufus enthralled her with the story. 'One of the finest streets in the whole of Britain,' she recalls him remarking. 'They make the occasional film here, you know. Get shot of the cars and cover up the road signage and you've got a convincing, more or less intact medieval street.'

The doves' commotion – there is now a flight of half a dozen of them – dislodges little scraps of moss from the uneven roof tiles. They tumble into the black gutter fifty feet above the canyon which forms Hugh Place. Saskia looks down into her empty mug and reads the tiny flecks of tea, which are sage green and tell her nothing she didn't already know. But she doesn't see the base of the mug for more than a few seconds; she sees Rufus hauling ropes on the Thames barge, preparing to sail. She thinks it's into the unknown.

She resurrects the final argument, tries to piece together the way it went, the exact words, analysing, hoping to make sense of it and reassure herself that all is not lost, that their relationship has not hopelessly run aground.

'So what is it you want, Saskia?'

'You.'

'But you have me.'

'Not anymore.'

'What do you mean?'

'Now I have to share you with a bloody barge – and the barge wins!'

'Only once in a while.'

'Frequently! It's become an obsession!'

'Come with me, then.'

'No. You know I hate sailing. It makes me sick, I've told you – shown you.'

'I'll be back.'

'When?'

'In a week maybe.'

'Where are you going this time?'

'Rye.'

'Again?'

'Again.'

'Where you met Georgia.'

'A friend, nothing more.'

'Oh?'

'Yes – oh.'

It went something like that, she recalls; almost verbatim but not quite. But then he threw in another subject, a counter-punch, and blindsided her.

'And this flat, Saskia.'

'What about it?'

'It's full of clutter – *your* clutter.'
'You have clutter, too.'
'I don't have art materials scattered all over the bloody place!'
'It's my hobby, same as sailing is yours.'

She sits and, recalling the gist of the argument, cannot help but find herself flooded with the same emotions she felt at the time: resentment, anger, sadness, regret, despair, by turns, admixed and confusing. And then he shot up from the chair and shouldered his backpack and said, 'I'm going or I'll be late.' She sat passively as she heard him thunder down six flights of stairs, the sounds gradually diminishing into a reverberant silence. And then she sat back and closed her eyes and the cooing of the doves returned as if they would soothe her with a lullaby. But, this time, she felt detached from them. And from everything.

It is still early morning, the dawn sky awakening, expanding, lifting the lid on darkness. Saskia finally swallows her pride, suppresses a simmering resentment, turns away from the Tudor rooftops and the doves, and dashes down those same six flights of stairs. She crosses the cobbles of the Marketplace, skirts the Guildhall with its imposing clocktower and glances up at the time. She rushes down West Street, turns right past the Shepherd Neame brewery, breathing in the aroma of hops and malt, and finds herself, breathless, at the Creek bridge.

High tide shows that the waters are almost at flood level on both sides of the bridge, ideal for casting off in a big sailing ship. Momentarily she pauses, leans against the parapet and contemplates the Grendel in all its brown and tan glory. It is a magnificent piece of maritime architecture, a triumph of human ingenuity and design. She recalls sketching the Grendel and proudly showing the result to Rufus. He said something bland like, 'That's nice', and promptly ignored it. And then, later, he said, 'It's the real thing I crave, not some representation. I prefer experience to art.' That hurt; it was cruel and unnecessary and showed a boorish side of him.

Saskia can see men on deck preparing to sail. She watches

from the Creek bridge with a kind of numb reflection, as though she has been left out, abandoned, surplus to requirements; as though she inhabits another world far from his. But she feels a desperate need to speak with Rufus before it is too late; before that final argument solidifies; before the Grendel reaches Rye, with Georgia no doubt waving to him from the quayside. *A friend, nothing more.* She cannot know; she can only speculate. What does it matter in the end? He would come back or he wouldn't come back. It is all the same in the final analysis.

She walks over the bridge and turns along the creekbank in the direction of the Thames barge. It is now perhaps a hundred yards away. She hears shouting on deck; they must be on the point of sailing. She catches sight of a figure clambering up the main mast with simian efficiency, fixing a rope to a spar. It isn't Rufus. She is glad it isn't him. She needs to speak earnestly, eye to eye at ground level. Preferably on the wharf alongside the ship where no other sailors would be intimidatingly close.

A man looks down on her from the considerable height of the guard rail; he notices her rapt curiosity. He cups his hands around his mouth because there is a considerable clamour all around him.

'Can I help you? We sail soon.'

'I need to speak with Rufus.'

'Rufus, did you say?'

'Yes.'

'Okay.' He gives her the thumbs-up.

The man disappears beyond the guard rail. Saskia lingers self-consciously. She can hear the urgent gutterals of men's voices, but not Rufus's. She gazes beyond the smooth blank hull of the Grendel to the open water of high tide. Two swans are gliding towards the Thames barge; they look regal, nonchalant. They are as brilliant white as the doves on the Tudor roofs.

Rufus's voice hits her; he sounds annoyed.

'Saskia? What do you want? We're about to sail and I'm busy.'

'I need to speak with you.'

She sees him raise his eyes in a gesture of exasperation, then he vanishes behind the guard rail. She is sure it's the last she'll see of him. But suddenly he is striding down the gangplank towards her. Her heart does a somersault; she feels weak and a sense of panic overcomes her.

'What is it, Saskia?'

She is not sure what to say, how to hold his attention. 'I... I wanted to wish you a safe voyage.' It sounded vacuous the moment she said it; it would alter nothing.

He stares into her eyes with subdued ferocity; she can see the clenched muscles of his jaw move, as though he is grinding his teeth. She recalls the final, explosive argument. *Now I have to share you with that barge.* She thinks he'll simply turn on her, storm up the gangplank, as he stormed down those six flights of stairs.

But he says unconvincingly, 'I'll be back.'

'Don't see that woman in Rye, eh?'

'I don't intend to.'

A friend, nothing more. That was what he said. But when he returned last time he was full of her. He couldn't help but sing her praises. Saskia remembers feeling humiliated.

'Okay, Rufus. Enjoy the trip.'

'I will – I always do. But I'll be back.'

They stare into each other's eyes and the stare lingers. They stand six feet apart, Rufus on the lowest rung of the gangplank, Saskia stranded on the quayside. She yearns for him to give her a parting hug, but he turns and walks up the gangplank and vanishes beyond the guard rail.

Saskia watches the Grendel pull away from the quay with laborious slowness, the wind of the open sea yet to fill her sails. She stands and waits for Rufus to appear at the stern and wave; but he does not appear. No one does. Two white swans accompany the Thames barge down the central channel of Faversham Creek, an improbable escort. It passes the Oyster House on the right on its way into open country before entering the Swale estuary. The Grendel diminishes into nothing more than an indistinct brown smudge. Saskia imagines Rufus somewhere in the hold, or working the ropes with his shipmates.

She lingers a long time on the quayside, but finally turns and walks from the Creek past the brewery into West Street and the Marketplace. It is busy now with stallholders selling bread and flowers, clothing and hot food. But such a colourful scene for once means nothing to her. The undoubted vibrancy of the town leaves her cold.

In her flat above the canyon of Hugh Place, Saskia sits in her wing-back chair by the window; the matching chair is empty. She gazes out at the blueness of the sky. Only a wisp of fair-weather cloud spoils the otherwise perfect blue. *Good sailing weather*, he'd said. *Need to get away.*

Half a dozen doves cavort on the sloping mossy roof tiles, several fluttering around the barley-twist chimneys. Saskia notices fragments of white down gently sliding down the roof and drifting over black guttering. She thinks it looks beautiful, like froth on a windswept sea. A loud noise reverberates through the canyon of Hugh Place and sends the doves winging away in a panic. They leave behind nothing but a few dislodged feathers. *Maybe a week*, he'd said. The doves will return by evening; she is certain of that.

But Rufus never did come back. The last she heard, from a crewman on the Grendel, was that he had settled in Rye. Saskia sits alone in her wing-back chair and gazes out of the window onto still, mossy rooftops. A way of passing time when there is no possibility of conversation, when words become redundant. She waits for the doves to settle between barley-twist chimneys but, oddly, they do not return that day.

If You Go into the Woods Tonight

by Aliy Fowler

September 1969, the month Johnny Buller turns seventeen, is unseasonably warm. And October, gliding in on its predecessor's coattails, remains mellow. Resplendent in its reds and golds, it is one of the mildest Octobers anyone can recall.

On the last Saturday of this month, one of their group – Johnny can't remember who – suggests they take blankets and beers, and whatever else they can get hold of, and head out above Whitstable into Benacre Wood.

Johnny decides to bring his guitar. He has a new number to show off, *Bad Moon Rising* by an American band called *Creedence Clearwater Revival*. The song reached the top of the charts on the day of his birthday and he's been practising it obsessively ever since. It's a great number, punchy and full of energy. The lyrics are kind of apocalyptic, but the tune is so upbeat you don't notice.

At dusk, the six friends set out from the bottom of Duncan Down. They're carrying torches but they don't need them. The night is clear, with a full moon, luminous as the mast light on Johnny's dad's trawler. Chattering and whooping, they cross the down, following a winding path that Billy knows, way up into the woods beyond. He leads them to a clearing, obscured on all sides by tall trees whose gnarled limbs remind Johnny of an Arthur Rackham drawing. Billy and Stuart set a fire, while Kathy and Grace lay out blankets. Jeanette, whose father is a butcher, produces strings of sausages folded together in greaseproof paper.

'How are we going to cook them?' Stuart asks, opening a beer and swigging from it.

Jeanette brandishes a bunch of long metal skewers with wooden handles and gives Stuart a how-could-you-doubt-me look.

Grace has brought Babycham, lukewarm and sickly sweet. The girls mix it with brandy from Billy's dad's flask and take short, greedy gulps. It amuses Johnny to see how quickly they become giggly.

He removes his guitar from its case, which has been sitting too close to the fire. The metal clips burn his fingertips. He presses them against his beer bottle. It's only slightly cooler than the air, but it helps. The guitar itself has not got hot. *Thank God*, he thinks. He positions himself on a weighty log and begins to strum, reflecting on how perfect this all is – the musky-sweet scents of autumn, the balminess of the night, the bright faces of his friends illuminated by the crackling blaze as he plays.

He runs through most of his repertoire and finishes with his rendition of *Bad Moon Rising*. The girls, perry-fuelled and exuberant, are gushing in their enthusiasm. The boys are more restrained, nodding their approval, and he suspects they are a little jealous.

'What's it about?' Kathy asks.

'Werewolves, I reckon,' says Billy. 'It's a warning not to go out when there's a full moon.' He points at the silvery orb ballooning above the trees and grins at the girls.

'Yeah, right!' says Grace, rolling her eyes at him. 'Hope you've got your crucifix in case we run into a vampire later.'

With it being so close to Halloween, and with the moonlight and dancing flames casting eerie shadows at the fringes of the clearing, it seems inevitable that the group will start sharing grisly stories.

When they stop laughing at Grace's remark, Stuart asks if anyone has ever seen a ghost.

Jeanette goes first. *She* hasn't actually seen one, but she tells the others of the time her grandfather encountered two Roman soldiers at Reculver. 'It was on the site of the old fort,' she says. 'They materialised right in front of him. And then they just vanished into the mist.'

Stuart is next, describing his cousin's brush with the phantom of a French railway worker, who haunts the platform of the old Whitstable train station. Grace becomes quite animated, saying she knows of at least three other people who've seen him.

Kathy tops these tales with a first-hand account. 'I've seen Sarah of Chestfield,' she tells them. 'She was a maidservant at the manor there, and Bishop Odo had her hung from an oak tree when she reported him for raping a stable girl.'

'Oh God,' says Jeanette.

'Where did you see her?' Johnny asks.

Kathy clasps her hands together. 'On the golf course. The tree was where the pond is now, and poor Sarah's spirit wanders from there across the 18th green. There've been lots of sightings.'

When it's Billy's turn, he asks if anyone has heard the story of the Dismembered Man of Benacre Wood. No one has, and he explains how – about a hundred years ago – a local landowner starved his hounds prior to an important hunt to make them more voracious. But when they were released, they attacked the first living thing they came across, an innocent farmhand on his way to see his sweetheart. 'The dogs were half-crazed with hunger and they tore him apart before the huntsmen reached him,' Billy says. 'And now, when the moon is bright, he roams the woodland in search of his missing limbs.'

This is a new one to Johnny, and he suspects Billy has invented the tale with the sole purpose of frightening the girls.

Not long after this, the fire begins to die down and the air temperature drops. Jeanette announces that it's getting late and Kathy says she's cold. Stuart offers to accompany them both home. Johnny knows he's hoping for a snog from Jeanette once he's dropped Kathy off.

Billy and Grace both want to stay a little longer, and Billy throws another piece of wood onto the lacklustre flames.

'Can you play 'Bad Moon Rising' again?' Grace asks Johnny.

He's happy to oblige, but as he reaches the second refrain of the chorus, Grace inhales sharply. 'Shit, what was that?'

'What was what?' asks Billy.

Johnny stops strumming and follows the direction of Grace's gaze, but he can see nothing except the dark shapes of trees, black against the purple sky.

'There!' She points. 'Something floating above the path.'

'You're imagining things,' says Billy, putting his hands on either side of her shoulders. Johnny knows he's always been a bit taken with her. 'I'm sorry if I scared you with that story.'

Grace doesn't shake him off. She asks, 'Was it true?'

Johnny is convinced it's not, but he's pretty sure Billy isn't going to waste this opportunity.

'How about I take you home?'

Grace nods and smiles at him. There's a self-conscious coyness in the way she holds her head.

Billy helps her to her feet, although she is quite capable of standing by herself despite all the Babycham she's had. He folds the blanket they were sitting on, then turns and winks at Johnny.

'You can catch us up, yeah?'

The wink means '*not too quickly*'.

Johnny has to put his guitar back in its case. It's fiddly in the gloom, and he can't get the clasps open at first. Once he's stowed it, he realises he needs to put the fire out. The weather's been dry and he can't risk leaving burning embers. There isn't any water so he empties the last two beers onto the smouldering wood. It sputters and steams and finally surrenders, the hot ashes turning to dank mush.

When he looks up again he sees how dark it is without the orange glow of the flames. He feels in the pocket of his coat for the lamp he took from his brother's bicycle, since he doesn't have his own torch. He flicks the switch and a feeble beam emanates from the bulb, illuminating only a couple of discarded bottles close enough to kick. It gutters, dims further, and goes out. Johnny curses. He has no idea where the path is. He knows if he heads downhill he'll reach the town eventually but, in places, the brushwood between the trees will be impassable.

He makes for the lower bound of the clearing and stops. He can hear rustling, as though something is forging its way through the undergrowth in the thicket further down. And then a different sound, sporadic, like heavy breathing but animalistic. In the enveloping blackness, it's disquieting and an uneasiness begins to seep in at the edges of his consciousness.

The large cloud, which has been veiling the moon since Johnny extinguished the fire, has shifted now and watery shafts of light penetrate the woodland where the canopy is less dense. He sees something – a pale shape, not twenty yards away. It's half-obscured by a broad trunk, but it seems to be hovering seven or eight feet above the ground, bobbing in the most unnatural fashion. As it moves into the clear it resolves into a shape that cannot be. A torso. A chest and the stumps of arms that stop mid-bicep. There is no head, and no legs to support it, but it continues to levitate, weaving through the trees in a jerky motion that makes Johnny feel sick.

He tells himself this can't be happening.

He tries not to look.

But the thing – the limbless body – is almost luminous in the moonlight and Johnny watches, rooted, as it comes closer, its ghastly motion hypnotic. He can't run – wouldn't know where to in any case. He lets his guitar case fall and he drops to his knees in the scrubby underbrush, hoping he is hidden.

He covers his head with his hands and screws his eyes tight shut. He presses his palms against his ears to block out the bestial panting.

But the sound becomes louder and louder – and then there is hot, fetid breath on the back of his neck and the dull thump of something heavy landing in the vegetation just a yard away. Fear pools around him. He wants to scream, but his lungs won't take in enough air. It's as though he's inhaling stagnant water.

He feels himself shake.

No.

He is being shaken. Something – someone – has a hand on his shoulder. Firm, but gentle. And there's the glare of a torch in his face.

'Hey, hey. Johnny isn't it? You okay, man?' The languid, sing-song voice, the soft Jamaican lilt – it's reassuringly familiar.

Johnny shields his eyes. 'Leroy? Is that you?'

'Leroy Hamilton, sure as sure.' The man lowers his torch so that it points downwards, the beam picking out sooty patches of grime on his dark denim jeans.

'What you doing hunkering in these woods all on your own?'

'I dropped my light,' says Johnny, unable to let on to Leroy that he was hiding from the abominable thing in the trees.

'You find it?'

'Huh? Oh, yeah. But it doesn't work.' He flicks the switch to demonstrate the lamp's defectiveness. It's only a half-lie.

'You want me to take you home?' says Leroy. 'Bucephalus here can easy take two of us.' He plays the torchlight over the withers of the large stallion that is standing noiselessly behind them.

Johnny starts. In his relief at seeing Leroy, he's failed to notice the animal until now.

'Is that your horse?' he asks, then reckons it sounds as though he's doubting a man of Leroy's means can afford such a mount and he regrets the question.

But Leroy chortles and shakes his head. 'I work weekends at the stables over at Court Farm – for a little extra brass.' He taps the side of his nose with his index finger. 'Helps me pay the bills. I get to exercise the horses when I want.'

'It seems a strange time to do it,' Johnny remarks. He's trying to keep Leroy talking, keep him here as long as possible. To give *The Thing* time to be gone.

'I like it the best,' Leroy says, in his leisurely drawl. 'When I was about your age, there was this tree-covered hill above Port Antonio where I used to ride bareback with my friends on clear nights. We weren't strictly meant to borrow the horses, that's why we took them out after dark – but we figured we were helping keep them in good shape.' His eyes flash. 'Ever since, I've always been a sucker for a moonlit ride. Takes me right back home.'

He glances over at Bucephalus, a wistful smile on his lips, then turns again to Johnny. 'Anyway, you going to hop up?'

Johnny wants to cry Y*es!*, but he's never ridden a horse and he thinks it will feel wrong to sit pressed so close to Leroy. The man is twice his age and he only knows him to nod to down at the harbour.

'I'll be fine,' he says and does a half-decent job of pretending.

'Then you take my torch,' Leroy tells him, forcing the chrome handle into Johnny's hand.

'Thanks,' says Johnny, more glad of it than he's willing to admit. 'I'll return it.'

He watches Leroy place a foot in the stirrup and pull himself onto the saddle. He makes it look effortless. He dips his head in a parting gesture and spurs Bucephalus on.

As he re-enters the wood, this time on the uphill side of the clearing, Leroy Hamilton, with his ebony skin and his inky jeans and his borrowed black stallion, disappears into the night. All, that is, except his pristine t-shirt, its white cotton slub catching the moon's silvery light, so that the garment appears to float between the trees – seventeen hands high at least.

And Johnny laughs as relief crashes over him like a warm wave. He switches Leroy's torch back on and begins to make his way towards the town.

Magic Touch

by P.J.Ferst

It's 05.40 on a cool October morning in Whitstable and there is a faint rosy hue in the east which suggests that sunrise will be soon. Miss Kemp is resting on a bench a short distance from Seaview Cafe, which is popular with both locals and the people often referred to as DFLs, (Down from Londons). It is where she prefers to relax after her energetic early morning walk: first from her flat in Tankerton to this area known as The Slopes and then onwards in the direction of Swalecliffe. This morning she has been walking into a north easterly wind and is glad she had her old but still serviceable camel wool coat to protect her from the cold. Her sturdy brogues have enabled her to enjoy the springy grass and her walking cane to ensure good balance as she follows her daily route – the seaside path that leads first to Long Rock Beach and then to Herne Bay and beyond. However, Long Rock is always the place where Miss Kemp turns round and heads back to her favourite bench, having completed her target of approximately one mile. Back on her bench now, she has spotted a pair of seagulls far below her scavenging in the sand as the tide recedes and then perching on one of the wooden groynes which divide each beach. What, readers may be wondering, is fuelling this lady's persistence in taking such daily exercise and why so early in the morning?

Well the answer to the first question is twofold. Firstly Miss

Kemp is determined to follow the guidelines put in place by the government during the 2020-2022 Coronavirus pandemic with its Delta and Omicron variants, one of which was exercise in the fresh air. Of course, she is well aware that some time has gone by since restrictions have been lifted but she is resolved to continue her well-practised routines. She is also resolved to continue wearing one of her large collection of masks on the rare bus and train journeys she takes, besides using hand gel when she's picked up post put through her letter box or when the Sainsbury's van driver delivers her weekly shopping. Just in case. However, readers, the question of why she feels compelled to take her exercise so very *early* in the morning remains to be answered ...

Now, sitting and relaxing on her favourite bench, Miss Kemp can just make out on her left the mist-shrouded outline of the Isle of Sheppey. She sighs as happy childhood memories flood back – of the place where her beloved grandparents used to live and with whom she and her sister spent their summer holidays in the 1970s: birdwatching on the wetlands, crabbing and swimming, whilst their wealthy parents went off on world cruises. On her right, Miss Kemp can see that the sun is starting to spread rosy streaks over Herne Bay Pier, or rather the remaining part of it that adjoins the shore. The sight of the pier head always tends to prey on her mind, for part of the pier was separated from the rest by a savage storm in 1978 and its isolation always seems to echo that of her own.

There is, however, a practical reason why this lady chooses to take her exercise at dawn. It stems from her knowledge that the warmth of the fully risen sun acts like a magnet which draws certain types of people to the Slopes – including the type of people whom she desperately needs to avoid. It isn't the early morning joggers or the cyclists, who flash past her at a distance on the pavements or the grassy verge, intent on upping their fitness levels. It is a different type that she is eager to shun. The type who present a threat because they bring danger along with them. That is why, dear reader, that after exercising, Miss Kemp feels the need to leave Tankerton Slopes when the sun has fully risen in order that she can make her way to her flat, like a homing pigeon bent on flying back to its loft as speedily as possible.

Miss Kemp is now nervously checking her watch and is greatly relieved to find that it is only 6am. She knows that today's sunrise will take place at 6.20am. Twenty precious minutes remain for her to breathe in the briny Tankerton air that she loves so much, to savour the sunrise, to hear the dawn chorus. And now she turns her head and scans the area behind her seat and on each side of her. All seems to be well and she breathes a sigh of relief. There is no traffic on the road and only one human being in sight – a red-faced young man jogging energetically along the pavement at least a dozen yards away. So she takes a few deep breaths and gradually manages to relax. But the slowly rising sun has started to cast its soporific glow over Miss Kemp and the desire to doze becomes overwhelming. When at last she wakes up with a start, she checks her watch and is alarmed to discover that it is 6.50am! The very first thing that she sees is a man some thirty yards away on her left hand side – a man wearing a navy raincoat and carrying an umbrella. But the man is not alone. Horror of horrors. There is a dog following him!

Miss Kemp can feel her heart begin to race. This is the type of person she has succeeded in avoiding. Up to now. The dog is not even on the lead, though thank goodness, at this moment, it is making its way to the bushy area at the edge of the Slopes and is busy sniffing near holes in the ground. This is a place she knows attracts dogs that are able to pick up the scent of voles or rats in the long grass. Miss Kemp is fervently hoping that the man and his dog will turn left here and walk in the direction of the harbour. Then there will be time for her to make her exit from the Slopes. But to her dismay she sees that the man is turning right and his dog is trotting past him. Indeed, it seems to be heading for her bench. And it is now only about twenty yards away.

Panic-stricken, Miss Kemp drops her precious cane onto the ground. She tut tuts in annoyance, then leans down and swiftly snatches it up, her mind in a whirl. Can she get up from the bench fast enough to make a successful retreat to the pavement and head home, or will the dog chase her? Fortunately, a Shakespeare quotation memorised from her grammar school days leaps into her mind and answers her question: 'Discretion is the better part of valor.' No, she will not act hastily. She will stay on the bench and defend herself. The dog is a large muddy brown mongrel, the size of a Labrador, but it's rushing to and fro in the boisterous manner of a terrier as it approaches ever nearer. Growling and making straight for her. Now she can hear it panting and see its tongue lolling out.

*

Miss Kemp is starting to tremble and feel faint. However, despite the pounding of her heart, she is just about able to lift her arms, hold her palms out in front of her and shake her head sternly. But the animal appears to misinterpret her gestures and keeps on advancing. Now it's near enough for her to see the sharp scary-looking teeth. Just in time, she is able to swing her legs up onto the bench. She glares at her foe with all the courage she can muster and brandishes her cane like a sabre. To her relief, the dog comes to a complete standstill a few yards away. It tucks its tail between its legs and stays there motionless, its eyes following the movements of her cane. Meanwhile, its tall, grey-haired owner is hurrying up, puffing a little. He stops a few yards in front of her bench and clips the lead onto the dog's collar.

'I'm so ... so very sorry,' the man gasps. 'Alina won't hurt you. She's actually very sweet-natured.'

Miss Kemp purses her lips as she looks up at the dog's owner. 'Yes, I can see that *now*.'

There is a short, uncomfortable silence. 'She's a rescue dog from Romania and was badly beaten when she was a puppy. She must have been terrified of your stick. I certainly wouldn't have let her off the lead if she posed any risk, I can assure you. Of course, it takes her a long time to trust people. But that doesn't excuse me for not keeping her under control. Are you feeling all right?' The man looks worried.

Miss Kemp swallows. 'Yes, I'm feeling better now, thank you. I'm sorry to be so pathetic. It may seem silly to say this but I'm scared of dogs – in general.' She looks at her watch. 'Good gracious, it's half past six. I'm usually home by now. I must have fallen asleep.' Tentatively she puts her feet back on the ground and blows her nose on a tissue. All of a sudden, rain drops start to fall and there's an ominous rumble of thunder.

'Which way do you usually go home?' the man asks.

'Oh, I walk along the Slopes in the direction of the Royal Hotel.'

'That's the same way I go. Would you like to share my umbrella? Otherwise you'll get soaked.'

'Thank you. That's very kind of you.'

'And don't worry about Alina. I'll keep her away from you.'

In ten minutes' time, the pair have almost reached the wooden hut opposite the Royal Hotel when the rain becomes even heavier. The hut is one of several shelters on Tankerton Slopes with benches on all four sides.

Shall we sit down in there till it stops?' the man asks her. 'Or are you in a hurry?'

'No, that's fine.'

The man folds the umbrella and sits down on the middle of the bench, making the dog sit on his right-hand side and motioning Miss Kemp to sit on his left.

'Phew!' The man smiles. 'By the way, my name's Brian. Brian Morgan.'

'Mine is ... M-Margaret. Margaret Kemp.'

'I believe Kemp is a Whitstable name, isn't it?'

'Yes, it is. I was born in Whitstable – at the cottage hospital down the end of Pier Avenue.'

'My goodness. I've heard it's one of the oldest in England. But I still haven't really explored the area yet. I'm a bit of a newbie. I only moved down here a month ago from Maidstone. Perhaps you can enlighten me about this area some time. Where do *you* live, if you don't mind me asking.'

'No, of course not. I actually live in Pier Avenue itself.'

Brian claps his hands. 'We're practically neighbours then. I live in Ellis Road.'

*

And that's how it all started. Two strangers meeting by chance one October morning on Tankerton Slopes. The swapping of names and histories. Margaret's dread of dogs ever since her teenage years, due to her being attacked and badly bitten by a Jack Russell. Brian's claustrophobia that started during childhood when his father punished his misbehaviour by locking him in the cellar; the therapy he later sought; his loneliness on becoming widowed. Margaret's desolation when her sister died of cancer three years ago; her own loneliness and fears.

*

The following Saturday afternoon, Brian invites Margaret to his bungalow in Ellis Road with its spacious back garden. They have both decided that today will be the day that she and Alina will finally conquer their fear of each other. First he brings out a tray of coffee and biscuits and Alina sits beside him, eyeing the biscuits. Later, Brian gives Margaret some dog training tips. He shows her how to use the launcher for Alina to retrieve the ball. Alina trots off and returns with the ball in her mouth but she keeps dropping it at Brian's feet. Brian refuses to pick it up but after eleven throws, Alina finally drops it at Margaret's fee, the cue for Margaret to say 'Good dog!' and slip Alina the treat Brian gave her.

'Well done, Margaret! – and now it's time to stroke her. Are you up for the challenge?' and Margaret nods.

'Remember what I told you – tone of voice and type of touch.'

Margaret smiles. 'Good dog, Alina,' she murmurs. '*Very*

good dog!'

As Margaret bends down, Alina's soft toffee-coloured eyes gaze up at the lady who has begun to stroke her – hesitantly at first and then more confidently. And oh, the relief that Margaret feels as Alina wags her tail. She feels free of fear at last – and all due to Brian's help. Now Brian throws the ball right across the garden and while Alina races after it, to his surprise, Margaret puts her arm round his waist. 'Brian, I can't thank you enough.'

'Nor I you.' And Brian turns towards her and kisses her cheek.

*

Margaret and Brian are now planning their future. In November they are going to explore the Isle of Sheppey as Brian has never been there before. Margaret is looking forward to showing him the sights and the places she had visited during her holidays with her beloved grandparents. Naturally Alina will be coming too. Moreover, in December, the couple will be celebrating Margaret's sixtieth birthday at the well-known Whitstable restaurant – Jo Jo's dog-friendly Meat, Mezze and Fish restaurant. And it's just across the road from Margaret's favourite bench …

The Last

by Guy Deakins

Well. That was that. The last oyster to come from the Whitstable oyster beds had been harvested. Oliver looked at the pathetic specimen in his hand and wondered what it'd be like to eat. Of course, he couldn't afford to eat it. Since the acidification of the North Sea had reached a critical point all the shellfish had started to sell at a premium. Was it worth it? It hardly had a shell left; a paper-thin concretion was all it had mustered in the few years it had existed. A thin calcium crust around a delicate body of digestive tissue and muscle. Did it have a brain? He hadn't thought of an oyster in that way before and now it didn't matter. It was the last of its kind in these waters and that made it rare and anything rare had immense value. Some ridiculous kleptocrat would buy it for some ridiculous sum – probably more than their ridiculously valued mountain home – and eat it while it still lived.

He'd read somewhere Queen Cleopatra used to digest pearls in vinegar and drink the soup as an aperitif. Perhaps the lucky buyer would have this oyster digested in some thousand-year-old rice vinegar first. Allow the shell to gently dissolve, the tender flesh inside cooking in the acid. Who knew? It didn't matter. None of it mattered anymore. Now he was holding the most valuable thing he had ever held in his shaking hands and wondering was it all worth it. Oliver certainly didn't think so.

He looked across the scaffolds of once-prosperous oyster

beds and then out across the estuary. They were almost flooded, even now at low tide. The ice sheets had melted, the sea had risen, the land claimed. Once this whole place had teemed with life. You couldn't move for life. Birds, fish, crustaceans. Vertebrates and invertebrates. All had been such an everyday occurrence that one quickly learned to ignore, even be annoyed by. Now, without the sounds, the smells, the tastes, it all seemed empty.

Carefully putting the oyster back on a trestle, he reached down into the water and into the soft mud at his feet. Fumbling around in the silt, he picked up a stone and brought it into the light. The beach was so quiet. No puckering and popping sounds of life as the water receded and the mud breathed. All the aerating worms that used to filter so much human rubbish had long since vanished. Now the mud just smelled of airless, pungent wrongness. The town smelled the same.

It had been such a glorious place to live and work. The seabed had been full of clams, winkles, cockles, shrimp, prawn, crabs, squat lobsters, all delicious, all available. Whitstable, quietly reliant on the vast estuary it sat next to, had been bustling and vibrant; said to be 'a great place to visit' nestled on the North Kent Coast. It was world renowned, a space to write about and to explore and to covet. Now it was an oily stinking desert, the seafront properties, glorious though they once were, now home only to the Watermen who inhabited the relatively dry first floors. Everything else had been left to decay. He looked across at the old beachfront pub, now a half-ruined shell, the old sign swinging sadly in the breeze. Neptune had claimed a new empire.

Oliver rolled the stone between forefinger and thumb, contemplating the events. The floods, when they first came, were surprisingly unexpected – though warnings had been given for decades. A cold winter night, the bitter north wind and a gibbous moon had delivered the first subtle punch. A gentle overtopping of the sea defences went unnoticed by most. It had rained and people were sensibly asleep. A few insomniac dog walkers had mentioned it, but nobody quite believed it. A folktale in the making and nothing of concern. A once-in-a-century event so insignificant it didn't merit further discussion.

The next augury was a little more serious and much less than a century later. A stronger storm, a full moon and a high tide, perfectly timed for mid-afternoon in October. There were still tourists milling about, wondering what the hell was happening to their glorious beachfront hidey-hole. Basements were flooded and shingle removed in vast gaping sections. The local paper picked it up, but quickly buried the story somewhere near the sports section when moneyed interests warned of dire consequences if they made a big thing of it. The council, out of cash and out of favour, didn't repair the beach defences.

A few years passed and the October storm was forgotten. A rumour built on improbability. The seaside was such a delightful place and with the increasingly year-round warm weather, Whitstable was a special place to call home. But, as was the way with the increasingly unpredictable climate, soon came the coup-de-grâce.

An August squall, traditionally marking the start of Autumn, turned into a deepening front that swept along the coast of East Anglia and across the Thames, bringing with it a storm surge of immense height. A normally tame sea was a mighty maelstrom topping five metres above its norm. The sea wall, wooden in places, un-kept and unrepaired, offered little resistance.

Of course, the money men had blustered and quailed, trying to reassure those that needed reassurance, but the storm damage had been twofold. So quick had it rolled in, the drains couldn't cope; the clay hillsides, bone dry and set like concrete, offered nowhere for the runoff. The old town was flooded from above and below. People, important people with a voice, had died. The fishing-village life fairytale had ended. Other people, people who thought they were important because they had a following on some useless echo chamber app, didn't want to live there anymore; the charm of a waterside retreat where the water was supposed to be over there, no longer offered such an illusion. Life in wellies and waders was not a lifestyle of choice.

So it came to pass. Whitstable was a different town. A hillside town with rills and runnels and waterways leading down to the muddy, stinking remains of what was a bijou urb for the London glitterati. Oliver looked down to his hands and the pebble.

It had all been such a wonderful place.

Doctor Dieterle's Patented, Practical & Complete Cure for Sorrow & Sadness

by Nic Blackshaw

Those seen dancing were thought mad by those who could not hear the music:
often attributed to Friedrich Nietzsche

'I can cure pain,' the doctor said.

It was a bold claim, the product of either breathtaking arrogance or epic delusion. I'm sure he'd rehearsed the line, perfected the timing, the slight pause between 'cure' and 'pain'. He knew to leave the statement hanging, trust my imagination to do the heavy lifting. Did he think he'd hook me so easily? Like the killer chat-up lines you see on certain websites, designed to snare savvy girls wary of wolves offering them everything they've ever wanted.

I'd heard similar claims over the previous few months. Every quack or new-age guru offered their own particular twist, depending on their belief system, but all with the same general idea. Happiness guaranteed or your money back.

There's an entire industry catering to people like me, lost in the impenetrable thickets of bereavement. Since my wife died

I'd been staying in bed all day and crying all night. I needed help badly.

But this isn't a story about me. I'm sure my woes are of little concern to anyone. This is a story about the good doctor and his cure.

I should introduce the man in all his splendour. His name was Doctor Ernst-Pieter Dieterle. It's a grand name, inspires confidence, resonates nicely with those Teutonic tropes of precision and efficiency embedded in our national psyche.

His full title included half the alphabet, arranged after his name in upper and lower case, an untidy jumble of letters like the random sequences social media sites generate when you want to reset your password. That is until you split it into its constituent parts. He'd done a whole lot of learning. I'm sure it got him a good table at the swankiest West End restaurants and drew patients or, as he preferred to call us, happiness-seekers, to his plushy practice.

I met the Doctor at his Harley Street clinic. Visitors were buzzed in off the street, thick plate-glass doors swishing aside to permit them into the cool dry air of the climate-controlled interior, and closing with an airlock *whoosh*, street-noise excluded, exchanged for the reverent hush of thick carpet and wood panelling. Only the very privileged could this way come. That should have been a warning.

His office took up the entire front of the building. Facing the vast windows were portraits of eminent Victorians lit by brass overhead lamps: earnest black-suited medical men posing with the paraphernalia of their profession – microscopes, stethoscopes, and test tubes – offering their silent endorsement.

He cut an unassuming figure, steel-grey hair and thin-framed glasses suggesting a clever technocrat, not a master of business.

He gestured for me to take the chair in front of his desk and, after only the briefest of preliminaries, delivered his extravagant line about curing pain.

He sat back, watching for my reaction.

'Well, Ms Brown,' he said. 'What do you think?'

His gaze was penetrating but not unkindly. Nevertheless I regarded him with what I hoped was an expression of polite but firm skepticism.

'How's that work?' I asked.

'Quite so, Ms Brown – bring me to the point. Put simply, I condition your brain to reject sad thoughts.'

'Then presumably you pay a percentage to Dr. Pavlov's estate or you're infringing his patents.'

'The technique involves triggering Pavlovian responses but it's…'

'High street hypnotists offer similar therapies.'

'I was about to say I work at a much deeper level. I will reprogram your mind, using targeted full-spectrum narco-inhibitors, specifically designed for your neuro-chemistry and character type…'

I had no idea what any of that meant. Scientist or shaman, they all deploy mumbo jumbo to impress the uninitiated.

'What's your success rate?' I wanted to cut through the flimflam.

'Of course. Results. Would it surprise you when I say: 100%?'

I gave him a sardonic smile.

'It would.'

But nothing I said was going to throw him.

'Figures verified by the regulatory authority. I can supply a copy of the report. Are you impressed now, Ms Brown?'

'What's it all cost, Doctor?'

He laughed.

'There is no pulling the wool, is there, Ms Brown? A series of treatments at the Vogler Institute, a very pleasant facility by the sea and…'

'I'm sure it is, Doctor – but what's the cost?'

'The full course of treatment is £20,000.'

I grabbed my handbag off the floor and stood up.

'I'm sorry I've wasted your time, Doctor, but there's no way I can afford that.'

The Doctor waved me back into my seat.

'There is another option, Ms Brown. If you can arrange your own accommodation and come as an outpatient, we can provide the therapy for £2,000. There are a few conditions but...'

He brushed them away like fluff on his perfectly tailored trousers.

'... nothing that should trouble you. Will you trust me to cure you, Ms Brown?'

*

A month later I took the train to Whitstable. Within a few days I had found a room-share in a large house, close to the High Street, and a job in a coffee shop. And I had three weeks to settle in before the first round of treatment.

*

The days flew past. Back in London I could go days without speaking to another human being. In Whitstable I couldn't stop – work, home, all day long I was surrounded by people.

When it came time to start the therapy, I had second thoughts: I felt happier, really I did. I told the Doctor, at the pre-treatment assessment in his office at the Vogler Institute, but he had an answer ready.

'Of course, Ms Brown,' he said. 'You left a place you associate with your wife, and come somewhere you are not reminded of her. It is natural. But believe me when I say you have not finished grieving. The pain has not gone.'

I wanted to say perhaps we could postpone, see how I felt in a few weeks, but the Doctor had more to say.

'I understand your uncertainty, but first let me demonstrate what I mean. What makes you saddest?'

'I don't know,' I said, taken back by the question.

Is it possible to grade grief, assign greater value to breakfast in bed on a Saturday morning to the way she ever so delicately ran her finger down my spine to wake me? And I didn't want to share those memories with the doctor.

He must have seen my face harden.

'I know, I know,' he said. 'Is it possible to separate one moment from another when you shared so much happiness? But I know there is something, something you regret, that gets you...' He indicated his stomach. '...right here.'

I glanced out of the window. The Vogler Institute is a glass and steel building shaped like a ship's hull, pointing out to sea, but Dieterle's vast office overlooked the High Street. Down on the pavement I saw a mother pushing a buggy, a toddler strapped in the seat, pointing his tiny finger at every object they passed.

I felt tears welling and took a quick breath.

'It's all the things we were going to do, that we'd talked about, dreamed about; like starting a family. I'll never have that now. It's the life we could have had.'

The mother had stooped to talk to her child.

'I see mothers like her and feel cheated of my chance.'

I brushed away a tear and looked directly at him, half-expecting a triumphant smile, that he'd made his point. But he handed me the box of tissues, his face full of compassion, and I felt able to shed a few more tears.

'What time do you need me here?' I asked.

*

The following week was a blur.

Day 1: shuttling between treatment rooms, blood, saliva and cognitive tests, and then x-rays, CT scans and electrocardiogram.

Day 2: sitting in an oversized dentist's chair for neuroimaging with a conical machine pointing at my head, answering an endless stream of questions: what makes you happy, what makes you laugh...? as they mapped my neural responses, identifying which area corresponded to which emotion – happiness, hopefulness, sadness, desire and despair.

Day 3: sensors plastered all over my head, a light shining in my eyes, tracking optical movement and the same questions: what makes you happy, what makes you laugh…?

Day 4: a kind of helmet on my head, the Doctor's patented virtual reality headset, cannula connected to a drip, administering the Doctor's patented cure, watching a series of clips: colourful balloons floating up into a clear blue sky, clowns tumbling in the ring of an old-fashioned circus, dolphins leaping through ocean waves, each with its own music soundtrack and the pop of a party popper, the crack of a circus cannon, or the squeal of a dolphin announced the cut from sequence to sequence.

Day 5: repeat of Day 1, more tests.

*

The Doctor hovered throughout the process, supervising. He took me aside toward the end of Day 5.

'I ask only one thing, Ruth. May I call you Ruth?'

'It's my name,' I said.

'You must relax this weekend, Ruth. It has been a tiring week. Forget about the tests and the treatment. Do something that makes you joyful. Eat ice cream on the beach, watch an old movie, whatever gives you joy.'

Everything had been so impersonal, the treatment clinical and emotionless, that this one moment of human kindness really affected me. Perhaps using my first name made it a personal conversation, so I turned the question back on him.

'What gives you joy, Doctor?'

It surprised him. He took off his steel-rimmed glasses and polished the lenses, using the time, I imagine, deciding whether to share something personal with a patient.

'I swim,' he said, putting his glasses back on. 'Whenever I'm here, I swim in the morning. Cold water is most invigorating, most beneficial to the immune system. My grandmother was an ardent advocate of cold-water immersion, said it was the way to a long life. And she lived to 97 so perhaps she was right.'

He chuckled, amused at the memory. I was about to say

something but he was already turning away.

'Have a pleasant weekend, Ms Brown.'

*

I don't remember climbing the stairs or opening the bedroom door. I woke at about ten o'clock on Saturday morning, feeling incredibly contented. Usually when I stretched out my arm I half-expected the sleeping form of my beloved but this morning, coming into contact with the coolness on the other side of the bed I felt only happiness that the weekend had arrived.

The feeling didn't last. I glanced at the clock and realized I had only half an hour to get ready for my shift. But it felt a long way from the days when, numb with grief, I'd pull the duvet over my head and stay in bed.

The morning rush was on when I got to the café. I tied my apron and stood at the espresso machine for the next couple of hours, making coffee after coffee. It was hectic but the banter with my colleagues kept me smiling.

One of the girls, Dawn, tapped me on the shoulder and said she'd take over for a while, let me stretch my legs. I picked up a cloth and a box tray and bustled around, clearing tables.

Head down, focused on the job at hand, I barely noticed the customers but the excited squeals from a baby in a high chair drew my attention. She was waving her dummy with one hand and a spoon with the other, a big smile on her face, when the dummy flew across the room.

I stooped to pick it up, saying something like, they're always doing that, aren't they, meaning to clean the dummy and bring it back.

The mother gave a hollow laugh.

'Sounds like you been through it yourself.'

It reminded me I'd lost my chance for a family. I mumbled something – God knows what the mother thought because, as soon as the feeling arrived, I heard a little pop and the sound of gentle laughter, Frank Sinatra began singing about the

Summer Wind, balloons floated up – blue, green, red, yellow – like I was at a summer ball, the balmy breeze of a summer's evening, the hickory-wood smell of a sizzling BBQ, and a warm and fuzzy feeling like I didn't have a care in the world.

I let out an enormous sigh. Later Dawn said it was the longest *aaaghh* she'd ever heard, like someone sinking into a warm bubble bath.

*

Over the weekend it kept on happening. Every time I had a sad thought something wonderful happened: the smell of candy floss and popcorn, 'Alborado del Gracioso' played on marimbas, the taste of salted caramel and hazlenut chocolate, I saw unicorns trotting down the high street, clowns with streamers came tumbling out of shops, balloons floated over the harbour.

*

There was something else, but I was so pleased to escape from the sorrow, I didn't really think about it.

After every experience I felt compelled to spend money. Usually it meant ordering something over the Internet – a watch, a book, an item of clothing. I found myself trying to book a holiday and had to stop myself clicking 'complete' on a £2000 Caribbean cruise.

I mentioned this to the Doctor when I went for the next round of treatment but he deftly danced around the question.

'Often feelings of well-being are accompanied by a desire for something tangible, something you can hold in your hands. You were simply transferring a happy feeling to an object, hoping to preserve the sensation. Is that so foolish?'

'I suppose not.'

'And have you bought anything you didn't want?'

'I was never a fan of Jeffrey Archer but, now I have his collected works, I've realized how interesting the British Constitution really is.'

'Excellent,' he said, disappearing into his office.

*

The following weekend made the first weekend seem a gentle introduction and I was glad I cancelled my shifts at the coffee shop.

The images came so fast and frequent I found it impossible to tell appearance from reality, real from fake emotions. I lived in a world where fairies walked hand-in-hand with acrobats, where balloons and bubbles emerged out of chimney pots, where brightly coloured umbrellas spontaneously opened, shielding me from jellybean rain, and always a new song on the soundtrack.

By Sunday night my bedroom looked like the studio of a shopping channel, cardboard boxes and bubble-wrap and an array of products – foot massager, lava lamp, spice grinder, yoga DVDs (x2), gold chains (x5), novelty china mugs (3).

The doorbell seemed to ring every few minutes and my mobile phone pinged constantly with texts confirming delivery times.

I told Dawn. She'd not long broken up with her girlfriend and I hadn't wanted to offload my troubles when she had her own sadness to deal with, but I had to tell someone.

She told me I'd every right to press Doctor Dieterle for answers.

'Don't let him blind you with science.'

*

When I went to see the Doctor he was sat behind his desk, eyes closed, head tipped back, a record playing on his hi-tech turntable. I came in quietly and pulled the door closed, not wanting to disturb him.

Instead I ran my eyes over the room, the Charlotte Perriand shelving unit against the sidewall, the photos of Dieterle with Bill Clinton, Dieterle getting an award shaped like a double helix from the Queen, Dieterle in black swimming trunks and

[Doctor Dieterle Patented Practical & Complete Cure For Sorrow & Sadness]

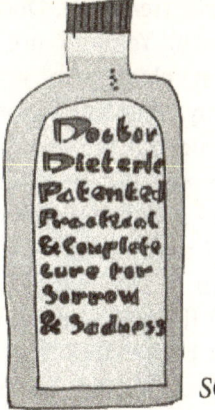

SC

black swimming cap, standing over the glittering dark of an ice hole. There was a Norwegian flag fluttering beside a sign that read South Pole.

The Doctor opened his eyes but didn't lift his head. He waved for me to sit but closed his eyes again as the soprano began to sing, 'Ich bin der Welt abhanden gekommen'.

Eventually he directed a remote control towards the turntable, pressing pause.

'You will forgive me, Ms. Brown. I cannot interrupt the Lieder until the soprano has sung the first line. To do that would be to deny myself one of the great pleasures.'

'It's very beautiful.'

'It is sublime, Ms Brown.'

'If you say so, Doctor.'

'There is much argument whether the song is best for a male or a female voice. But there is no right or wrong, it is a matter of taste. I would always choose a woman's voice. And, in my opinion, nobody captured the poet's melancholic tone better than Jessye Norman.'

'It's not the sort of music I listen to.'

'Ah – a shame. But perhaps you will learn to appreciate it.'

I nodded but, to be honest, I couldn't see that song on my

playlist.

'I need to talk about the treatment, Doctor.'

'Of course, Ms Brown. You did not come for a music appreciation class. I'm pleased to say the treatment is progressing satisfactorily. Most satisfactorily.'

'I'm happier, that's true, but the spending is out of control and it's getting dangerous. Whatever I'm doing – cooking dinner, running a bath – goes completely out of my mind until I've made a purchase. I return to my senses and find charred remains at the bottom of the pot or... I can't take baths anymore because I left the tap running, went off to order an exercise bike, and came back to find I'd flooded the bathroom.'

'A regrettable side effect, perhaps, but there is a cost for any cure.'

'Right now, it's not a cure, it's a curse.'

'Come now, Ms Brown.'

'I want you to stop the treatment.'

He smiled the way doctors do when they're questioned by someone who doesn't have eight university degrees.

'You're having a very strong reaction to this aspect of the treatment: much stronger than usual. Most happiness-seekers are able to control the urge to buy and vitiate the effects, according to their needs and their taste. But it seems, my dear Ms Brown, that you are the one per cent who cannot mitigate the impulse.'

'I need you to stop it, Doctor.'

'We must let the treatment run its course. The impulse will diminish naturally. Be patient, Ms Brown – the important thing is the therapy is a success. Now, I have a rather busy schedule so, if you have no objection...'

'That's not good enough, Doctor. I can't afford to continue like this. I spent the last of my wife's life insurance paying for the treatment. My wages from the café barely cover my rent and living expenses.'

'I'm sorry, Ms Brown – there's nothing I can do. If I could, but – once you start the treatment...'

'There must be some way.'

'It is already too far progressed.'

'Perhaps I should speak to the Medical Council or whoever supervises you.'

'You signed the consent form – all the relevant information was included in the contract.'

Finally the penny dropped. I'd been suckered.

'So that's it, Doctor. You're what my grandfather would have called a shyster.'

The smile disappeared. Had I got under his skin?

'Did you think you'd receive expensive treatment without giving something, in place of money?'

'What have you done, Doctor?'

He stood, his jaw clenched.

'There is no such thing as a free ride, Ms Brown.' His lips curled a fraction. 'There is always a price must be paid.'

Now I saw the true arrogance of the man.

'What have you done, Doctor?'

'Nothing that was not specified in the contract.'

He handed me a sheaf of papers. I saw my signature at the bottom.

'Here,' he said, 'in black and white print, Ms Brown.' He sat down. 'Perhaps you did not read it as diligently as you should have. That, however, is not my fault.'

My heart sank. I felt like Faustus when he realized Mephistopheles had him bang to rights and I half-expected a trio of little devils to spring out – just like the balloons and unicorns and the other mythical creatures that wandered through my subconscious. But it was just the Doctor and me, sat across from each other in a steel and glass box inside the Vogler Institute.

'Let me explain,' he said. 'We have a similar business model to social media companies or music streaming sites. You get the service at a reduced cost and, in exchange, carefully selected advertisers are permitted to sell products targeted specifically to your tastes. We can only offer the budget version of the treatment because advertisers pay the remainder. They are all carefully screened to meet our exacting moral and ethical standards.'

After he dropped the bomb he waited for the dust cloud to subside. I felt my cheeks redden. How could I have been so naïve? Numbed with grief, I'd signed my soul away for targeted ads from carefully selected advertising partners. If only the Doctor had made it clear, I'd never have gone through with the treatment.

'I want it out. Turn it off – whatever it is you need to do to…'

'I'm afraid that's impossible.'

I stood up. I don't know what I was going to do, throw something at the photos or smash the record player. He must have seen the crazed look in my eyes because his tone suddenly softened.

'I wish I could remove the conditioning but there isn't an on/off switch. However, at the end of treatment, as pain responses become less frequent, so does the advertising. Fewer episodes means fewer advertisements.'

'How long will that take?'

'Two months – perhaps three.'

Another three months I'd be penniless. No, worse: I'd be drowning in debt, maybe even living on the streets. He came around the desk.

'We can stop the treatment now – you have only one round left. At least that will shorten the affected period.'

He threw out his arm, like a nightclub bouncer directing punters off the premises. I was furious but what more could I do? I bit my tongue and said nothing. I walked towards the door.

'Unfortunately,' he said, 'I cannot offer you a refund for the last round of the treatment.'

I swung back but before I could say anything he gave an apologetic shrug.

'There's really nothing more can be done.'

Nothing I could say would make any difference. As I walked

across his vast office the Doctor pressed play on his remote and the song picked up from where it had stopped.

As I reached for the door handle Dieterle spoke again.

'I'm booked on the noon flight to Zurich.'

I turned to see him talking into his mobile. He'd swivelled his chair around and was gazing at the grey, choppy sea.

'I'll have time for a morning swim, before I leave for the airport.'

I closed the door and walked away.

When I told her what had happened Dawn put her arm around me. She suggested doing something special the next day, something I'd never done before, guaranteed not to bring back unhappy memories. How about walking along the coast to Herne Bay? If we met early we'd have the coastal path to ourselves and she'd treat me to a slap-up breakfast at the greasy spoon on the front. I agreed. At least it would take my mind off everything. I said I'd meet her at Tankerton Slopes, near where she lived.

*

The weather was fine that morning. Hardly anyone about apart from a swimmer, some way out, black swimming cap bobbing up and down. Was it Doctor Dieterle, I wondered, out for his morning swim?

The sun was slowly burning away the thin mist and everything was crisp and fresh and new. I don't know why – memory's a funny thing, isn't it? – but I thought about Celeste. Even though we'd never walked along this beach, something made me think of her. Maybe it was just that I'd have liked to share the moment with her – this perfect morning, pregnant with possibility, the waves hesitating before they rippled onto the shore, like the whole world was holding its breath, waiting for something magical to happen.

And, as the emotion turned from joy to sadness and that old, familiar ache that she was gone, I heard a shout from out beyond the oyster beds.

I felt myself drifting away even as I scanned the water. I heard a dolphin's squeal and straightaway a smile began to form: ah, dolphins are lovely, I thought as I gazed, vaguely, across the white-tipped waves, surrendering to the now familiar euphoria. The last thing I remember was the black-capped swimmer waving his hand, then disappearing underwater and rising briefly to wave his hand again. Three times he dipped beneath the waves and reappeared but, the fourth time, a dolphin's fluke broke surface. Wonderful, here they come, I said to myself: oh, the joy of it!

I heard an oboe playing a beautiful melody. More dolphins joined the fun, leaping through the waves, the water cascading in little waterfalls, glinting in the sun. A clarinet took over the melody and the orchestra swelled and the dolphins leapt, trailing rainbows. The soprano's voice rose above the clicks and squeals of the dolphins, 'Ich bin der Welt abhanden gekommen', she sang.

I thought, I know this, it's the Doctor's song and, you know what, he's right. It really is sublime. I floated off the beach and into town, swept along by the music and the aroma of hot popcorn and vanilla ice cream. There was shopping to be done.

*

When I met Dawn on Tankerton Slopes I was wearing a red cotton dress I'd bought at a boutique in town, carrying a red parasol and a delightful wicker basket, a baguette sticking out of it and, buried under the blue-and-white cheesecloth, a plethora of wax-paper packages.

Dawn smiled and it was like the sun coming up.

'What you got there?' she asked, lifting the cloth.

'I thought we could have a picnic breakfast.'

A red helicopter climbed above Whitstable beach. For a moment I thought it an illusion, part of the treatment.

Dawn must have read the look.

'The woman at the kiosk said they pulled a man out of the

sea. He must have got cramp, the water's still really cold.'

She laid her hand on my arm to soften the news.

'I'm sorry, Ruth,' she said, 'I think it was your Doctor. If only someone had seen him and raised the alarm, because by the time help came, they were too late to save him.'

'Oh well,' I said, putting my arm through hers. 'There's really nothing more can be done.'

Taken For A Ride

by Harry Harrison

Tim gathered a heap of birthday cards from the doormat but slipped the letter into his pocket. His fate in an ordinary brown envelope. Down the hall, French windows opened to Laura's sunlit garden. Seagulls calling and the sweet blossom of Spring filled the kitchen.

As Laura turned towards him, he forgot everything else as he did when first he caught her smile so many years ago. A familiar joy overshadowed by worry. Not fearing death but causing her pain.

'More cards,' Laura said. 'Made breakfast, and the weather's going to be sunny. Scrambled eggs and Italian coffee.'

'Not like Skiathos.'

'Can't go every birthday. When you're better.'

The scent of fresh toast. Ordinary things having sensual vibrancy.

'Next year, we'll have my pension and swim naked in deserted coves.'

Thinking him childish, but funny, Laura wondered if they would travel together again.

Spooning the last of his Greek honey from the Sporades Islands, Tim licked his finger and thought, why now?

Looking through the windows, amongst the jostling roses, he saw a black shape. A bicycle with a red satin bow on the handlebars. Despite the jaunty decoration, the bike brooded, dark and exciting.

'An e-bike,' she said, happy for him. 'Press this button and pedal like hell. Soon overtake me.' Smoothing her hands down her jeans, her eyes flitting around the kitchen, she hoped he'd like her present.

Wrapping his arms around her, he hid his tears, wiping them away before standing back and holding her by the shoulders. Laura giddy with the prospect of picnics and forest trails.

'Still need my morning to myself,' he reminded her. A solitary walk or bike-ride was routine on birthdays, now harder every day. Laura revealed, with a mischievous grin, a new, stone-coloured helmet.

'I'll go for a spin along the coast to Reculver.'

Upstairs, he opened the envelope, expecting regretful opening words and practiced kindness from his consultant. So soon. At least the prognosis was clear and involved no long months of suffering. Too hard for Laura to bear caring for him. After hiding the letter, lacing his trainers was easy but sitting upright again made him dizzy. If only Sandy was here, wagging his plumed tail, ready for any adventure outdoors.

Walking had been his chance to talk, and his collie sat listening to his dilemmas and proposals. Sandy's only interruption was to cock an ear or nudge Tim's hand to walk on. Under a pear tree where once Sandy chased squirrels, they buried the dog deep to frustrate the ravening foxes.

Laura came out to say goodbye. By the door sat Sandy's steel water bowl neither wanted to throw away. Laura cleaned it each morning, watching robins and thrushes sip and flutter in the cool water.

'Don't be late for lunch. Friends, remember?' Kissed him. 'Don't fall off. Got your phone?'

He nodded, patting an empty pocket. An ending today, on the crumbling clifftop at Reculver? Turn towards the sea, switch the engine to sport and use his last strength to pedal off the cliff. A geriatric Thelma or Louise, crashing down to the rocky beach. Man meets a stony end.

Curious, he thought, how thinking about ways of ending things brought up vivid moments. Last Winter, Sandy splashing in the freezing surf, heaving at an ancient wooden stake on the deserted foreshore. Everything on the beach glistened. Reculver Towers in stark silhouette against a paper-white sky. The post turned to stone by the invasion of sea minerals from surging and ebbing waters over the centuries.

'Sometimes,' said Laura, 'I have no clue what you're thinking, Tim,' and went inside.

'Bye Laura,' he waved, but she was gone. A stupid idea to throw himself off the cliff. The skylarks in the field would be nesting, startled, and Laura, who loved the lark's song, would never forgive him. He would tell her tonight and share his stark news.

The clifftop spread out before him; the flinty sea streaked with turquoise, swathes of rough meadow, and the sentinel towers of Reculver guarding the entrance to the Wantsum river and Thanet.

After decades walking here, the glowing landscape was still breathtaking. Not a soul in sight and all this to himself. Between the paths, the skylark rising, hovering, and singing until sunset.

Dropping the power to eco, he drifted down the track. The bike sprang into life when he pedaled and pushed him up hills. It had a life of its own.

Inland, trains clattered East and West towards each other on the straight track to Margate. He imagined them colliding, but they swept past each other, windows glinting. At this early hour, hungover revellers woke beyond their station, stumbled off at Birchington, crossed the iron bridge, and waited for a returning train.

'Come here,' he called aloud to the wraith of Sandy trotting alongside and stopped by a bench for a rest. Remembered running his hand over Sandy's bony head.

Not far from here, Laura lost her sunglasses collecting sloe berries, and the next day Sandy found them, snuffling through the grass. Sitting and panting, a paw on the tortoiseshell frame. Laura hugged Sandy with delight, overcame her dislike of dogs too late, for Sandy died weeks later. Keeled over, as if stunned.

'Old age,' said the vet. 'Happens to us all,' the young man added.

Out to sea, calm descended. A landscape, often dappled by scudding clouds, had a new stillness. The sky a perfect dome of luminous blue. Sand martins swooped over long grasses with the joy of flight. The sea lay flat and sullen. Odd weather, he concluded. Something's up.

In the valley below, a lone cyclist plodded uphill. Another grandad squashed into tight shorts. Stupid bloke should go back to golf before he kills himself. What an old git, he thought, just like me.

The biker crested the rise. An old jacket and jeans. An e-bike too, the way he trundled uphill without effort. How odd. Only two of them in this deserted landscape. Old men on bikes. The same grey helmet too.

'Are you Tim?'

Standing to greet the stranger, puzzled, he gasped as the other man lifted off his helmet, sat heavily and astonished. Winded.

'Astounding,' agreed the rider, propping his bike on a stand. 'I'm a bit overwhelmed as well, and I was expecting *you*.'

Speechless, Tim gaped at a perfect image of himself. Lanky, with a crown of grey hair and the same wry smile. Different to the worn-out old face surprising him in the mirror each morning, but precisely like himself in videos Laura took to send to the children. What was happening here? Impossible he had a twin, but the voice was like his own.

'Once in all our lifetimes, we pass our own selves,' the man began, although Tim was still too shocked to listen.

'Passing each other in the busy high street, unnoticed, or we walk by our *other* on a crowded train. Few of us recognise the top of our own heads and in any case, distractions happen. Going through a tunnel.'

'This change in the weather?'

'More of a compromise, between your climate and mine.'

'Did you say, meeting our *other*?'

'Yes, my name is Tim too, and in this,' he hesitated, stretching out his arm, 'in this emptiness, impossible to miss one another.'

Baffled, Tim wondered if he had died, or if this was a bizarre breakdown.

Grinning, his twin turned, and two sets of blue eyes met. Tim shuddered.

'We are going in opposite directions in time. I'll remember you for a while, but I will soon be *unlearning* complex ideas. Just as you have always learned new things. Scientists call these meetings a function of *quantum gravity*. Your future is my past, and my past is your future. At some point, all our paths meet, like ships passing in the night. The *doppelgänger*, alter-ego, the evil twin. Simple astrophysics is to blame.'

Shocking how much you are so like me. 'The spit of you,' my dad would say. My voice. The same intonation, insistence. Chattering on, like me. But one difference. Where is my white gold ring on your left hand?

His *other*, sitting at the end of the bench, followed his hand.

'Spotted your wedding ring,' he smiled. 'Mislaid my own somehow.'

'My Laura is your Laura's other,' explained Tim's double, sprawled like him on the same metal bench, warming in the sunshine. In alarm, Tim shook his head, turned to his visitor, and wondered aloud, if this other man was becoming younger every day, what happened at the end?

'Time is reversed, not biology. I'm getting old like you, but I will, in time, forget most things, play like a child, become annoying, selfish and die of old age.'

He went on. 'In your world, the universe expands. In mine the universe will end in a gigantic collision. *Your* sun will dim and die so life on earth will perish. But not for seven billion years, so you'll be alright.'

'Oh thanks,' thinking, seven years would be plenty for him.

'Why now? Why you and me?'

'These accidents are called a *superposition*, where for you, and me, our journey through time crosses. A moment real and rare for both of us. In your case, you move on to build things, learn things, create all sorts of art.'

Not much longer, thought Tim.

'Nothing happens? We just meet like this once?'

'We meet. Most unusual, but in theory, other things can also happen. It's an unpredictable, unstable state. Like riding a bike. Do we ride the bike, or is the bike carrying us forward?'

'See this ring,' said Tim, remembering meeting Laura all those years ago. Tim held out his finger, the bright metal having a blue shimmer from the cloudless sky. 'When you lose our ring, you'll part, never meeting her again. How long have you been together?'

'Two months, but of course, we know *everything* about each other. We are both already forgetting important things.'

Tim fell silent. Two months? His wretched letter suggested the same. This other Tim began life, fully formed, in just two months' time and that must be when I will die. My life ends, when his began. All I have is two months, and he has *all my life* to live.

Out in the estuary, several ships crossed in the deep-water channel. Did the crews wave across the roiling waters? Occasionally, port pilots taking tankers out of one estuary, transferred by orange boats to visiting freighters, bringing them home safe the same day.

The other Tim appeared to be in contemplation too. Reluctant, like him, to leave this turning point in their lives. Except, of course, Tim had faced his future that morning when he opened the envelope. The other had confirmed his death sentence. Nothing to lose. Everything he loved at stake.

'We are both sceptics, right? Prove what you say. Something is happening this coming weekend. What?'

'I had the greatest birthday party. I mean, *you will have* a brilliant party. Laura organised everything behind our backs.'

'You could have guessed. Show me some evidence.'

'I have video,' grinned the *other*. 'I sang a song. *You* will sing that song. Do you want to listen to our racket?' He rummaged through his bag for a phone. Struggled to find it.

Tim grabbed his chance, an instinctive gamble, darted forward and started running with the *other's* bicycle. Swerved. Scrambled on, fumbled for the *sport* button, and hurtled across the grass in the direction he had arrived.

A breeze brushed his face as he pedaled harder towards the trees, the road, gasping, glimpsed clouds sailing and white caps on the sea. In one last glance over his shoulder, saw the *other* with his head in his hands.

As he pushed open the gate, Laura came to greet him.

'Thanks for the bike,' hugging her. 'Best present ever.'

'You took the red bow off.'

'Lost in the bushes. Sorry.'

'No accidents?'

'Of sorts. Nothing painful. I worked things out.'

He needed a shower and as Tim pulled on his clothes again, he found the letter from his oncologist. The first paragraph began, 'I am glad to inform you…'

He collapsed on the bed, flooded with relief but also despair. His *other*, a kind man. Himself, born months in the future, was now busy dying. With one strange and unique moment behind him, he would have to live with what he had done.

Buckling his belt, he went down to meet their friends. At the foot of the stairs stood Laura. That captivating smile.

'Your ring.'

'Oh,' inspecting his hand. 'I lost that too. Sorry. Not been myself.'

'Looking good though.'

'I'm good,' said Tim. 'Feeling younger every day.'

About Writers of Whitstable

by Joanne Bartley

Writers of Whitstable was founded in 2013. I was looking for a particular kind of writing group; one where people would read my words and give me feedback. I'd written a few stories and when I read them through, I decided there were good bits but also bad bits. I noticed paragraphs that could be deleted, and sentences that might change. There were characters that needed tweaking, plus some settings that needed work. I'd work on a new draft and think my words were entirely bad, occasionally I'd read the stories through and decide they were actually pretty good. Sometimes I'd think they were terrible, and then brilliant, and then terrible again, all within the space of one day.

I wondered whether meeting other writers might help me through this confusion. So, Writers of Whitstable, or WoW as it's affectionately known, was born. We get together every month in the cosy Marine Hotel with our chosen tipple. We listen to honest thoughts from fellow writers and take notes for the next draft. Of course, everyone who sends in a story hopes the readers will say, 'this is perfect' but there will inevitably be suggestions for things to rework. Some writers will attempt to tackle every point of criticism, while others will be confident enough to only work on the points that hit home. It's certainly the case that tastes in stories vary wildly, and I usually tell writers to take particular note if two or three readers make the same point. That's usually a signal they need to do some work.

I sometimes wonder what would happen if great writers from the past turned up at WoW. I expect we'd tell Dickens to work on pace, and someone would be bound to suggest Tolkien should find a better name for Orcs. Any writer knows there is no such thing as a perfect story, and that a final draft is only a writer deciding 'that's enough' and calling it done. I think WoW helps with making that call, suggesting which stories might be good enough to seek publication, or which aspects of a novel need chopping or changing before sending to agents or self-publishing.

Writing stories is often seen as a solitary game, but it doesn't have to be that way. I think any writing can be improved through feedback, and WoW is proof that this works. Its members come and go. Some drop into the monthly stories group, while others make a commitment to write a chapter a month for feedback in one of the two novels groups. I'm happy to report that we've celebrated a few successes over the years with several novels out in the world for all to read. We've also had WoW stories on BBC Radio Kent, a play at the Horsebridge, and one writer even has a tale for sale in a short story vending machine!

I'm grateful to all the writers who've helped me with my writing over the years, and I always look forward to reading others' words and helping to shape them. If you write and want to get involved with the group, the link is below. I can't promise we'll tell you your story is perfect, but I do know we'll give friendly guidance to help you make it the best it can be.

Joanne Bartley
Writersofwhitstable.co.uk

About the Authors

Jo Bartley

Jo studied Scriptwriting for Film and TV at university, which inspired her interest in story structure and novel planning. In 2015 she launched StoryPlanner.com, a website to help nerdy writers just like her plan well-structured stories. It has helped her plot several novels, though so far it hasn't helped her finish them, find an agent or secure a six-figure book deal!

In her spare time Jo likes to write and solve treasure hunts. Her website GoldenOwlHunt.com is the only English language website devoted to the Chouette d'Or treasure hunt. Jo and her daughter are currently planning a podcast series about this fabled missing treasure. Jo works for an education campaign group, and when she's not working, writing, or treasure seeking she enjoys baking, hiking, and pointlessly tracking her cats' behaviour in a spreadsheet.

Richard Barton

Richard has had many stories published in magazines for pre-school children and has contributed to the range of Sherlock Holmes pastiches available. He has had a career in business training, HR and consultancy. This work includes writing learning and internal communication materials and so it benefits from some level of creativity. However, writing fiction is a more direct outlet (and more fun).

Richard has four grown-up children and lives in Littlebourne.

Nic Blackshaw

Nic fell in love with words as a small child and a love affair that began with the spoken word soon progressed to the printed form as reading opened up new worlds and the chance to see life through others' eyes. As the relationship deepened the writing of words followed, but life and career intruded and they grew apart. Fortunately the split was not final and, after a long estrangement, Nic returned to writing fiction able to draw on a lifetime's experience. With two short stories included in the previous Writers of Whitstable collection, *A Pinch of Salt*, Nic is very happy that two new stories are included in this anthology. Nic is currently working on a novel.

Guy Deakins

Guy is a literary polymorph. Author, journalist, garden writer, award winning poet, design historian, waterman, tame swimmer, psychology student. He has many strings left on his quinquagenarian bow.

Writing has been part of his life since he first picked up a pen and redesigned the wallpaper – much to his parents chagrin/delight (edit as you will). A love of reading is something that has arrived later in life. He enjoys experimenting, creating the abstract, scratching the darker parts of the mind, playing. However, writing, as all true writers know, doesn't pay the bills half as well as proper jobs, so he tickles people's borders for a living. At some point he will qualify as a neuropsychologist and start to analyse his writing in a much more professional manner.

Phillipa Ferst

Phillipa has been both reading and writing voraciously since she retired. Her reading pattern now is fiction rather than fact and mainly focuses on thrillers like those written by authors such as Adele Parks – dark and dangerous. However, Phillipa also likes reading books that make her laugh, like those by Bill Bryson. As for writing, she has made up many poems and songs. More importantly she has started writing her memoir *Lust For Life*. She has chosen twenty chapter headings but so far she only written eight pages which bring her up to the age of nine! Her aim is to complete it as soon as possible since in January she will become an octogenarian ...

Duarte Figueira

After a lifetime as a grey bureaucrat writing published factual reports with numbing titles like 'Developing Suppliers in Engineering' Duarte Figueira was amazed to discover you could actually make stuff up in your head and write it down. When WoW very kindly actually published one of his stories in their *A Pinch of Salt* (2020) anthology he totally freaked. As a joke, he then self-published his first novel *The Ginger Flic Casebook* (2021) about a Whitstable detective who is a cat. He had to have a lie-down when some people actually bought it. Now fully recovered from the shock, he is living the dream writing a second crime novel, set in Victorian Canterbury, *The Canterbury Suspects*, improbably involving conveniently deceased historical figures. However, he stubbornly hangs onto his non-fiction comfort blanket, contributing articles regularly to the 'Whitstable Whistler' quarterly magazine and other publications, utterly confident the fiction stuff will never work out.

Aliy Fowler

Raised on a farm on the North Devon coast with no television as a distraction, Aliy spent a lot of time reading (when she wasn't making secret hay-bale camps or roller skating in empty silage pits with her brothers and cousins). All this bookishness culminated in a degree in French and German literature before an improbable segue into teaching Computer Science at the University of Kent. She now fluctuates between web design, photography and travel writing and has been working on her first novel for far too long. A reluctant runner, avid sourdough baker and chocoholic, she lives in a wonderful village community with her supportive husband, gregarious son and wilful Norfolk Terrier.

Harry Harrison

Harry passed away on November 25th, 2023. He was diagnosed with leukaemia in August and spent his remaining months at home with his loved ones. Harry dedicated his life to building communities, both through his work as a senior social worker and in his personal life through his hobbies and interests, which included sailing, carpentry, film, and of course his writing. In that respect he was a prime mover in getting this collection of stories out there.

He was two chapters short of finishing his novel The Welfare when his illness struck. However, never one to give up, he put together a team of Writers of Whitstable regulars to complete the book. It is a moving and funny tale of a young social worker in 1970s London, well deserving of publication. You can buy a copy on Kindle or paperback soon.

Harry will be remembered fondly and missed by all at Whitstable Writers and beyond.

Kerry Mayo

Kerry is a writer and photographer who also runs a successful business just outside Whitstable. She has been published with the titles Whitstable Through Time and Whitstable History Tour, both photographic/historic works looking at the development of Whitstable over the last 120 years, has had serials and short stories published in the women's magazine market and online as well as self publishing two novels.

Peter Quince

Peter Quince writes short stories, novels (three published), poetry, essays, magazine articles and even shopping lists when occasion demands. He has recently published a volume of essays on the theme of nature/spirituality. He taught English at St Edmund's School, Canterbury and loved the ambience of the place, especially in the haunting Chapel when the congregation had newly departed.

Apart from creative writing, his interests are eclectic and include gardening, watercolours, philosophy, meditation, tai chi and Zen Buddhism, but not necessarily in that order. He runs a philosophy group with Nietszschean authority and is also a Companion of the Chalice Well in Glastonbury, to which he retreats in order to take time out from modern technology.

He volunteers every Wednesday morning in the wonderful Fleur Bookshop in Faversham, the town where he lives with Jan, his wife, and family, and welcomes bibliophiles to the bookshop to talk literature, philosophy and creative writing.

He might even offer you, gratis, one of the much-sought-after bookmarks of his own design. 'A Living Presence' was written when the inspirational high tide of Whitstable was full upon him.

Gillian Rolfe

Gillian has lived in Whitstable for over twenty years and first met some of the seagulls when they were eggs. She enjoys writing stories, reading stories and discussing stories, especially if it involves cake and tea. Gillian has had several short stories published and is perennially enchanted to see the thoughts in her head become words on a page. She lives with a very lovely fella and two over-opinionated cats.

John Shackell

John has been dabbling with creative writing over many years. More recently he has begun to take it slightly more seriously. He has written several short stories and has a novel at a late-draft stage. A new novel is planned but has yet to really get off the ground. John lives in happy retirement with his wife and has several family members living near by. Until recently he took an active part in helping to run folk music sessions in Swalecliffe.

Oliver Whitefield

Born in France, Oliver spent long years in Switzerland near the shore of the Geneva Lake. From an early age, he had a passion for reading, writing and history.

In 1999, he moved to the UK where he started to write little stories for the pleasure. In 2019, he returned to the UK and moved to Kent. In 2020, with the dramatic arrival of Covid19, he took the opportunity to complete 3 novels: *The Eagle & The Dove*, *The Professor and I* and *What If*, and also started to write short stories. He has a passion for historical and crime novel.

In June 2023, he published his first novel and work on the release of a second book for early 2024.

Eileen Wellings

Eileen has always wanted to be a writer and has written many short stories over the years. She wrote her first full length book in lockdown, which she is now very slowly trying to edit. For the last twenty years she has worked as a hypnotherapist and two years ago decided on semi retirement. Since moving to Herne Bay in 2021 she has become actively involved in the Seaside Museum where she enjoys finding out more about her adopted town. She enjoys walking along the seafront and still finds time to write.

Lin White

Lin is an avid reader, and has been making up stories in her head for as long as she can remember. The Internet brought the realisation that others enjoy that sort of thing as well, and she soon discovered fanfiction.

Writing original fiction was the logical next step. To date there are several novels in various levels of completion, plus a bunch of short stories.

In her real life, she has been involved in publishing and education for many years and currently works as an editor, typesetter and proofreader, helping other writers to polish up their work ready for publication.

She also runs regularly, and enjoys life with her husband, three sons, two cats and a dog.

Richard White

Richard wrote nothing but letters and film scripts until after several professional lives, mainly in the film industry. Returning from two years in the Caribbean he discovered writing, and started two novels, one of which is being developed with Writers of Whitstable.

In 2005, with his partner Rose MacLennan Craig, he wrote, produced and directed a play at the Edinburgh Fringe, resulting a series of others, until in 2015 the last of these, *The Mythmakers*, was produced in venues in Scotland, California, London's West End and New York, and in a radio version which won the audience prize in 2016 at the International Radio Drama Festival in Herne Bay. Other plays were mostly collaborations with the Bonnington Playwrights, a group of London writers.

Over these years Richard has also written short stories, two of which appear in a previous anthology, *A Pinch of Salt*.

David Williamson

David is an original member of the WoW and enjoys writing short-story fiction. He has self-published and is currently writing his next novel *Give it back, that's MY wasp!* David spends his time between Kent, Ireland, Rapa Nui and Tristan da Chuna which are all sources of inspiration for his writing.

Beyond the Beach Huts
features stories set in
Whitstable

A DIFFERENT KIND OF KENT

SHORT STORIES

WRITERS OF WHITSTABLE

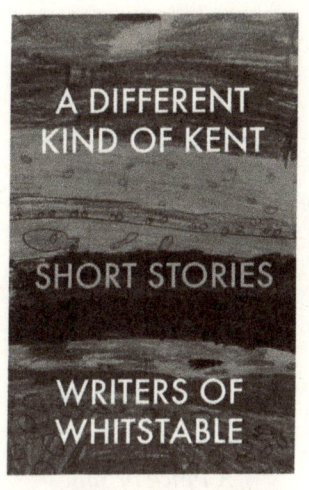

A Different Kind of Kent
travels wider, to cover the
whole of the county

A Pinch of Salt
again features stories set in
Whitstable